DEAD CENTER

Randall Ford Jr.

authorHOUSE®

AuthorHouse™
1663 Liberty Drive, Suite 200
Bloomington, IN 47403
www.authorhouse.com
Phone: 1-800-839-8640

AuthorHouse™ UK Ltd.
500 Avebury Boulevard
Central Milton Keynes, MK9 2BE
www.authorhouse.co.uk
Phone: 08001974150

© 2007 Randall Ford Jr.. All rights reserved.

No part of this book may be reproduced, stored in a retrieval system, or transmitted by any means without the written permission of the author.

First published by AuthorHouse 8/15/2007

ISBN: 978-1-4259-9107-4 (sc)

Printed in the United States of America
Bloomington, Indiana

This book is printed on acid-free paper.

To:

-To my beautiful wife, for the long hours spent typing for me. To enhance these book character's situations on affection, is only a reflection of how much I love you.

-Briana, simply for giving me the privilege of being your father. Love you more!

-All of those who wanted to know how the book was coming along. Thanks for asking.

-Yellow pads and black gel pens.

-Malissa, for believing in me. Your reviews were perfect. You're an awesome person. Only the best is what I wish for you.

-All of those who thought that I was too damn dumb to write a book.

-Everyone who reads this book.

-God...for everything.

www.randallfordjr.com

Preface:

...intense.

Contents

DEAD CENTER

Who Am I? 11
The Right Side 20
The Left Side 27
Tuesday 11th 38
Major 48
Minor 57
Vacillation 65
Dead Center 77
For Jessica 92
Mea Culpa 103
Perder Mi Mente 111
Mens Sano In Corpore Sano 119

THIN BIRD

25 Years Later 137
Thin Bird 147
Who Am I? 156
No, It's Beautiful 164
Freedom In lock 174
Olden Days 183
Dead Center 191
Ayrelia 199

Uncaged 206

One Step Higher..228

I Will Die Loving You.....................................232

The Empirical...239

WHITE CAGE SYNDROME

Don't Blink 259

Don't Hear 266

Don't See 272

Don't Worry 288

Don't Think...293

Don't Feel 299

Don't Breathe..305

Don't Believe 311

Don't Remember...321

Don't Forget..344

Who Am I?..349

The Diagnosis 360

DEAD CENTER

Chapter 1 *Who Am I?*
(Friday 1st)

The officers of the squad patrol shined the spotlight down the long alley, which consisted of two small brick buildings and a driveway.

Braylen, opened his eyes to find himself surrounded by a blinding darkness. His senses were overwhelming as they rushed back into place. His clothes were drenched with blood and the smell of the dumpster engulfed his nostrils with a shocking stench. The ache from his head was that of holding one's breath.

"Who am I?" He thought. He placed the palm of his hand onto his forehead for comfort while slowly sitting upright. Blood engorged the running of his veins.

Where am I? Should I move? Have I been ganged up on and left for dead? Has the memory been knocked completely out of my skull from such impact? What time is it? How did I get here? What's my name? I feel so hungry.

Randall Ford Jr.

Does anyone know I'm here? Is anyone concerned? Is anyone aware of my existence? Am I dead? Is this a dream or maybe this is just a brief thought. Have I been drugged?

Who's life is this? Am I living out a scene of a nightmare after being diagnosed with a coma? Who am I?

Braylen, rubbed his neck muscles to relieve the tension which buried itself into the area. The feeling re-entered his feet as before they were tingled from the lack of circulation.

The edge of light creased the crevice of the plastic lid that derived from the power light of the police car. "How's it look down there, Sergeant?"

"Pretty clear. Let's roll."

Braylen struggled to lift himself to the top of the dumpster. When the lid opened he began to cough from the acute smell of the unit's containment storage. He fought with his coordination and pulled himself from the metal bin.

He rested his body onto the top of the rusted outlined frame. His hair and eyelashes were soaked with a puss-like fluid. He blinked excitedly from the brightness of the alley lights to adjust his focus.

He forced his weight from the top of the structure to the ground. After landing onto his feet, he fell back against the raw iron guards of the bin. The rain began to fall heavily.

Deep pain from his head caused his equilibrium to swim. The fading balance of fainting desires left him in a mobile state of an intoxicated stagger. "Help!" He leaned his hand against the brick of the wall for security. He walked his way in this manner until he reached the corner of the building at the entrance of the walkway. Dizziness flooded his head and caused his stomach to be overtaken with an anxious nervousness. "Anyone there?!"

The blood puddled onto the ground from his steps due to the rain draining it from the cuffs of his saturated pants. Small flesh-like chunks rolled with the streams of blood that poured from his ears.

He shook his head to obtain a conscious state. The rain pushed the thick solution of his lashes into his eyes leaving his sight temporarily blurred.

Braylen turned the flat of his back to the wall. The lock of his knees released sending him to a sitting position. The daze of the street lights began to strobe about his vision as the stars of the sky spun about. "Wake up! Wake up!" He shut his eyes tight.

Am I drunk? Am I a pedestrian watching myself from a distance. Maybe I am a character in someone else's dream. Could it be that I am on a merry-go-round and can't escape it? Is this the reason for my spinning vision?

Why won't someone respond to my plea for help? This has to be reality, for the throbbing pain in my skull is radiant. Am I caught up in imaginations? Am I daydreaming? Is this a simple fantasy?

Am I good or bad? Am I an angel in search of my life or has death claimed it and sealed my time. Did I die or is my life killing me? Am I trying to find me as I lay? Has my body severed from my thoughts? Am I a wounded conscience or a dead imagination? Invisible I am as the whole world is blind.

Will I wake up? Hang on tightly someone has to see me. Get up and walk away. Wake up damn it! Is this blood mine that runs dry about my cheek? Have I murdered a life? Has someone took mine and thought to have ended me? My heart is with great capacity but my mind is empty.

Should I keep screaming for someone to recognize my presence? Who am I? This cold rain that drops on my skin is though it was for the first time. I feel as though I am falling through the sky and have not hit the ground yet. Am I the reader or the writer? Maybe I should attempt to get back up. "Help!"

Finally, the harsh pain hurled him into a blank state as he heard two car doors slamming.

Who am I? Who am I?

(Four hours later)

Eric and Melinda ran the emergency floor of the hospital hallways. They met the charge nurse by the front counter. He grasped for air then asked, "Which room is Braylen Adger in?"

She checked the pad and scanned her index finger abroad its page. "One zero eight. Down the hall over."

They continued to run and came to a group of doctors standing by the room. "Just a minute folks. Who are you?"

"I'm Melinda, Braylen's girlfriend."

"Eric, his best friend."

"Can we see him, is he okay?"

"I need to discuss a few things with you first, " the doctor stated. "Braylen claims he can't remember anything or anyone. Our skillful EMS found him laying on the sidewalk downtown. Although soaked in blood, we found no trace of injury anywhere on his body. My guess is he must have been walking home and gotten mugged.

Evidently it was a clear swift blow to the head blacking him out. There was no money or license in his wallet, just your card Eric. I think perhaps this knock to the head rendered Braylen with a temporary case of amnesia."

"What about the blood?"

"Well, ma'am I have not a clue. There were no reports of any crimes in the area, heard or seen."

"You aren't insinuating that he committed any trouble to wind him up here are you?" Eric asked.

"Seeing as though no one submitted anything of any crimes, he's not going to be held for any suspect detainment. Ma'am, you may enter the room briefly. I can only allow one at a time."

After she went inside, the doctor pulled Eric away from the closed door. "Listen, we can't find anything wrong with this guy. I am going to order up a CAT scan for him in about one hour."

"Great, but can't we speed this up a bit? This is my best friend on the line here."

"After the scan, I will indeed need to follow through with some additional old-fashioned x-rays. Now the reason why I conference you about such things is that Braylen has no insurance on file. Therefore, I will need a co-signer for his bill and medical records."

"Did you say x-rays? Why not just a simple brain probe?"

"Sir, I do apologize, but you cannot pay for just one part of the procedure."

"He's a great guy. I'll flick the bill for my friend." Melinda came from the room and wept sorrowful. "It's okay," Eric said calmly.

"I didn't want to wake him from his sleep."

"Doctor, if I may go in now?"

"Yes, but of course, Eric. Mrs. Walters real quick, has Braylen dealt in drugs that you are aware of?"

"Not at all."

"We found heavy doses of anabolic steroids in his system. The conclusion is that the overdosing could have possibly thrown him into a quick phase of a subconscious reality and make-believe."

"Doctor, I had no idea of such abuse."

"These specific drugs were injected so immensely that his blood resembled cooking oil. Very expensive also. This certain anabolic is at least thirty dollars a shot and that's on the street market.

I must warn you, Melinda, that it's in your grave interest to rid your house or his home of these items. They are very illegal. I suggest you clean your car out thoroughly."

"We don't live together, but I will search for them."

DEAD CENTER

Eric walked slowly up to the hospital issued bed from which Braylen lay. "Braylen, can you hear me?" He whispered. Eric looked at his face and slightly moved his hand over the crown of his head. "Can you hear me?"

Eric raised to a full standing position. He became suddenly startled as Braylen reached out and grabbed him by the collar of his dress shirt. He pulled him close to his face with great force.

Braylen opened his eyes and angled his face to Eric's and asked, "Why did you do that?"

"Do what?"

"Why did you wand your hand over my head? I felt the angled tips of your fingers pass my skull."

"I didn't touch you, I promise!"

"I didn't suggest that you did, I simply request an explanation as to why you grazed your hand above my head."

"Seriously all I did was rest my hand onto the pillow underneath you."

Braylen sat up from the bed and kept his latch secured. Eric backed away as far as Braylen's reach would allow. "Who are you?"

"It's me, Eric, your best friend."

"What happened to me?"

"I don't know. They discovered you on the sidewalk knocked out. They called me in. I brought Melinda with me."

He depressed his grip and let his arm fall to the side. "I'm leaving."

"You can't leave yet. They need to do a scan first, just to assure you're able to leave."

"Fuck that, get me out."

Eric drove while Melinda sat in the back seat with Braylen. The rain slighted to a drizzle. "This is weird for you isn't it?" she asked. "I mean not being able to remember anything?"

"I remember one thing."

Eric shifted his rearview mirror. "What might that be?"

"Pulling myself from the metal dumpster covered in blood."

"Blood, from what? Melinda asked. "There's not a scratch on you."

"No telling. Could have been some useless fat, bones or such scrap from the restaurant down the block," Eric stated. "Or maybe someone hit a dog or a dear and threw it in there with you. Whoever cares, the main thing is why would someone do this to you."

They pulled up to the house and Melinda opened the door with her key. "This is where you live Braylen."

"Okay, look, I got to go, but I'll check on you later," Eric said.

"I'm not leaving you alone tonight," Melinda stated.

"Go. I'll be fine," Braylen requested. She turned and walked out with Eric.

Braylen stared at each photo that hung on the wall. Stills of Melinda and him as well as Eric. He opened the top wooden cabinet of the kitchen and found neatly stacked rows of cereal boxes that were each thirty days out of date.

He looked inside of the refrigerator and discovered an unopened spoiled container of milk. He then made his way to the bed and laid unto it roughly, as his body was weary.

Chapter 2 *The Right Side*
(Saturday 8th)

Braylen lie onto his bed and fell into a deep sleep. He was sprawled over several puffed trash bags that were spread about the inside of the dumpster. They were soaked in blood that leaked from the plastic. The screeching cry of a hundred babies bellowed the confinement. Cries of helpless abandonment that were not their faults.

As I lay, the screams became more defining and irritable. The rage of their broken silence deserved them the right to be heard. Such fragile beings of innocence and humanity. For their course of nature was ended prematurely, without the hope of future persistence. Only the conscience of those who committed such treachery upon them should have been in place before them.

The noise grew and my eardrums shook from the vibrations of oncoming disaster. Suddenly a quick silence halted the invisible cries.

DEAD CENTER

I could not move when a wide stainless steel sword pierced the side of the metal wall. The long blade hoovered above me, missing me by inches.

Braylen awoke and placed his hands over his head. The loud yell for help scratched the pain, which insanely dulled his mind. He stood and clumsily bumped into the wall as to make his way outside, to seek the defendant.

He ran to the door and squeezed his skull snugly with both forearms overlapping his ears. He looked in all directions. The rich heat that inflicted throughout his brain was unbearable.

He quickly turned his head while a woman was being shoved to the ground by her boyfriend. She moaned loudly from the degree of pain. The deep agitation of Braylen's head bent him over and then forced him to lean his weight against the wooden deck railing. The man pulled her to her feet and latched onto the back of her hair.

Braylen began to act upon the situation. The pain began to leave his head. He walked up to the man and stood in front of him. He let the woman loose and looked Braylen over. He slyly snickered and then turned the beer can up to drink. Braylen drew back and launched the blow of his fist to the bottom of the aluminum.

The can crushed flat causing the top rim to flush the bridge of the man's nose. He dropped the beverage and held his nose in agony. Braylen looked at the woman and made his way from their yard and back into the house. He laid onto his bed, closing his eyes in wait for the headache to reappear from nowhere.

Randall Ford Jr.

After a disappointing session of tossing and turning, Braylen sluggishly threw himself together. He called for a cab to escort him to the nearest gym. He tipped the driver and rushed inside of the establishment. Several hours later, the sun had risen as it was well pass noon. He continued to supply his body with prolonged exercise achievements.

The shift consultant made his way to the area from which Braylen stood. "Hi, I'm Jack Pace."

Braylen strenuously curled the dumbbells. "Nice to meet you."

"You know, I'm not one to price regulations on the people here at the gym, but I must tell you the importance of a timed workout." Braylen pulled the large weights in tightly with extreme pump.

"I've been watching you workout and you've been lifting for almost five hours," Jack mentioned. Braylen reddened from strain and began to speed his rhythm. "Anyway. A solid round of training should not consist of more than ninety minutes."

Braylen slung the iron plated bars into motion. The veins of his shoulders spiraled from the surge of pressure. "So maybe you should simply modify your routine a bit and slack the time span."

Braylen's skin bulged while he stopped. He handed the barbells over to Jack and said, "You're right. Got to go." Jack dropped the pounds for they were of substantial weight.

Braylen jogged home and slowed to catch his balance. He spotted Melinda sitting on the top step of his porch. She wore a brown fitted shirt that wrapped her sides. Her jeans were light denim and flared at the cuffs. She

DEAD CENTER

sported a side hugging suede belt that waved high on the hip.

"Melinda. This is very difficult for me to endure as this life is not my own. You would only be further confusing it if I persuaded both sides of my emotions into one."

"Well, when you change your mind and need a loose place to put it, don't hesitate to call. Don't put me off for too long, Braylen. I can only keep it hot for you for so long."

Later that afternoon, Eric pulled up to the front of Braylen's house. He left the car running and walked up to his door wrapping it with a cluster of cartoonish knocks. Braylen allowed entrance and laughed aloud.

"What a way to greet a friend, laugh at his new locks," Eric stated.

"No man, it's not your hair. Check this out."

Braylen flopped down onto the sofa and held the remote control up to adjust the volume. "I'm not sure what this show is called, but the bald guy is hilarious."

"Braylen, how long have you been watching this?"

"A couple of hours. This is great stuff here. What a concept of entertainment."

Eric sat beside him and said, "Look don't let it bother you about that ordeal with Melinda and all. She called and explained it all to me. Just between you and I, she wasn't good enough for you anyway. That's why I'm here. Tonight we celebrate. By the way, don't tell her all of that I said, after all she is our team leader."

"Team leader?"

Randall Ford Jr.

"Yes, at work which is reason number two as to why I'm here. See man, I nor did Melinda mention anything to anyone about the incident. We just lapsed you in for an emergency unscheduled vacation time. One week to be on the mark. Now I know this is going to be hard seeing as you can't remember anything, but with a little help and some expert advice from your colleague here, will prove you a worthy employee of Zear & Ginn Inc."

"Where are we venturing to tonight Eric?"

He stood and walked into the kitchen. "To the strip club down off the square baby," he replied with an eager attitude.

Eric extended his hand to the chrome handle of the refrigerator door. "Stop! Don't touch it."

"Why not? Is there a bomb planted somewhere in it?" Eric asked sarcastically.

"Actually I just cleaned it with a special solution mixture and it's not dry yet," he lied. "When was the last time you went through my fridge?"

"Dude. I raid your fridge everyday. Well, before the incident that is. Alright then, off to see the titties," he chanted.

"I think I'm going to sit this one out."

"Nope. Get your big ass up and out of the damn door. I can take you Braylen. I'll slap you around like that guy on the television there."

Braylen smiled. "Fine, let's go."

"Yeah, that's right. You don't want no part of me. I can lift forty pounds of weight and that's not counting my sausage."

DEAD CENTER

They arrived at the low profile club and was carded by the bouncer. The cigarette smoke circulated the room as scenery. The women were curvaceous and voluptuously figured. They skillfully surrounded the shiny pole that was bolted to the floor and connected with the ceiling. They engulfed the metal stem with their lower body's and dangled their visual existence, flashing their areas widely to reveal the close smoothness that was separated by the border of their panties.

Braylen sat at the table alone and drank bottled water while Eric stood in the corner and made a special arrangement with a female star attraction. He slipped her a large sum of bills and made his way back to Braylen. Alcohol took charge of his condition.

"Hey man, do me a favor." He slapped his hand over Braylen's trapezium muscle. "I need for you to go into that far room behind the stage and get my coat and then drive me home."

Braylen waltzed into the back and searched the room over for the garment. He saw a stripper sitting. "Excuse me, I did not realize anyone was occupying this room." The environment was dim and the atmosphere was cool.

"What's your name?"

"Braylen."

"I'm Violet, but my friends call me, The Boss."

"The Boss? Why's that?"

"Because, I get the job done. Your friend paid me a full price for a lap of luxury that is to be performed for you." She guided him to the red plush fur style loveseat and backed him to sit. She spread her legs over him and put her arms around his neck. "Your friend also said that this dance was in celebration of you hitting the rebound of a single status again.

Do you want to know what makes me so different from all of the other girls here when it comes to giving lap dances?" She unsnapped the front flap of the purple panties and secured an even line of bare skin to him. "Are you ready for a good ride?"

The heat from her made him erect and weak. She spread her knees apart and buried them into the cushion. This allowed her to sink lower into him.

"This untamed aggression that flows through my blood burns with the excitement for you to drive me into the loss of my senses. However, Violet, so does the ongoing events of searching for my life."

"Don't resist me." She playfully held his hands down against the sofa. "You don't need to know who you are because, once I'm through with you, you'll forget your own name." She began to glide back and forth.

Her movements shocked him as never felt before. She buried her waist deep and continued to rotate her pelvis. His eyes remained closed. At such precise timing, Braylen began to see sharp flashes of light. The slight familiar pain of his previous headache began to surface. He immediately refrained from her grip and broke her physical clutch and stood.

"You're not finished yet, I didn't feel it contract," she said.

"Sorry, I have to go." He walked away from the room and grabbed Eric by the upper back of his dress shirt. "Time to go."

Chapter 3 *The Left Side*

(Sunday 9ᵗʰ)

Eric pushed himself from the floor and shook his head from the hangover of the night before. He sat up against the base of the couch and rubbed his temples. His eyes lit from the cup of coffee that was handed to him. He took the cup by the handle and sipped the contents. "So, um, Braylen. Did you nail that strip teaser?"

Braylen sat by the computer desk and researched the online results. "No."

"You should have."

"I would have took you home, but I didn't remember where you live."

Eric attempted to stand normal. "What on earth are you doing?"

"Nothing."

Eric squinted at the screen and read, "Sudden migraines. What's that all about?"

Randall Ford Jr.

"I don't know. I've been undergoing some severe attacks on my head as of late."

"Well, dude, maybe you just have a badass hangover like me."

"No, this is different. My head pounds with such intensity at such odd times."

"You should request Mr. Barrett."

"Who's Barrett?"

"He's the company shrink, or counselor, I should say. He is completely confidential and a great stress management consultant. I have to go and work this hangover off."

"Eric, wait. How come I don't drive regularly?"

"Braylen, I've told you twenty-four times already. Your car was stolen. That's why you were walking home that night of the incident. The cops haven't confiscated it yet."

"Okay, I need to borrow yours today."

"My car? Braylen, what for?"

"Just for a few hours. What do you say?"

"Alright. Here." Eric took the brass ring from his pocket. "Just take me home first."

Braylen dropped Eric off and proceeded to the local mall. He passed stores that carried a large assortment of makeup items, but only in the women's sectional departments. He walked by a dark store and then returned to the front glass of the retail business. It contained a huge line of skater apparel and goth-like clothing. He awkwardly made his way to the counter and began to look through the plastic shield of accessories.

"Can I help?" the lady behind the counter asked.

"Just looking. Well. Actually, ma'am. I was looking to purchase the F-2 row there."

"Ah, great choice. The submarine black eyeshadow. Will that be all for you today?"

"Yes, ma'am, thank you."

"Actually, my name is Ava."

"Ava. That's very alluring. And so are you."

She looked surprised. "Thanks."

"I mean you're very pretty." Her hair was the shine of silk and the color of jet black, complimented by quarter inch streaks of red. Her lips glossed black and her eye shadow was a dull matching grade as well. She had a round end of a silver stud projecting from just under her bottom lip. A loop was placed through the top right eyebrow. Her tongue also carried a stainless steel stud in the tip of it.

The choker she wore was spandex black with a diamond in the center. Her shirt was fashionably ripped about the front and designed with a purple undershirt sown beneath the material. The sleeves were black, long and resembled ladies stockings. The skirt was plaid at the knee and her platform boots laced to the top mid-way of her calf.

"I'm sorry. I offended you?"

"No. It's been a long time since I heard someone say that to me."

Randall Ford Jr.

He smiled and took the bag from her hand. "Braylen, by the way."

"Cool name."

"Not as cool as yours."

Later that day Braylen emptied the compacts onto the counter of the sink. He opened each container and flipped them upside down. He used the hard plastic handle of a screw driver and tapped the chalk-like powder out from each metal tray. He put every square block of makeup inside of a porcelain cup. Next, he used the small end of a wooden spoon to pound the chunks repeatedly, until the powder turned into a fine dust.

He took the can of hairspray and held it a distance from the handle of the refrigerator. He misted the spray briefly and took the eyeshadow brush and mixed it with the dust. He quickly spread the black powder about the chrome and waited. The spray molded several fingerprints that stuck to the handle of he door.

Braylen carefully engraved the prints by pressing the tips of his finger onto the dusted area. The prints were the exact match of his own . He spread it onto the faucet and every knob of every door. He sprinkled the powder to cover the television screen and onto either side of each c.d., including the cases.

After some time had passed, Braylen stood in the middle of the living room. All of the prints matched his and no others were found. "Great. Another clue to the mystery of not knowing anymore than I do."

He dialed Melinda's number and anticipated her answer. She picked up. "I knew you'd be calling soon."

"How'd you know it was me?"

"Caller Id., women's intuition and the fact that you can't resist me."

"You didn't seem to take our breakup too hard?"

"You were right in a sense, Braylen. There wasn't much love involved. Just fuck buddies."

"When was the last time we were together in that way? Tell me about it. Detail the whole event in my imagination."

"Dirty talk? That's a start. Well. Try to fit this frame of lust into your dirty mind. That particular night, you tied me to your headboard, as I enjoyed the submissive position mind you." Braylen held the remote phone between his shoulder and his ear. He took the black dust into the bedroom.

"Which post?" He asked.

"you secured both of my cupping palms around the right one."

He dusted the finish of the wooden post. "Continue."

"Are you enjoying this, because I can hear your movements clash with your breathing?"

"Yes. Give me more. Please."

"After you blindfolded me and slid ear plugs into my ear canals. This way I could not hear nor see where you were going to put what. I must tell you that it's very spoiling to woman to be straddled and suddenly have you come down on her surprisingly."

Braylen awaited the alcohol of the spray to dry and shrink the dust to form the ridges of the prints.

Randall Ford Jr.

"Then I recall you jamming your knees into the mattress, just below my armpits. This allowed you to enter my mouth. Then you took my tied ankles and crawled in-between them. Needless to say, you touched the back of me forcing me to orgasm as you penetrated the skin. Later you withdrew from me and onto my breast and stomach. That was by my request."

"Damn!" He whispered. No prints shown through.

"What was that?"

"Nothing."

"A short time later, I left and apparently so did you. So. Ready for me to come over?"

"That's it?"

"Hello? Braylen? Are you ready for me?"

"Oh. I'm sorry, I already came," he lied. "Thanks, bye." He hung up and made his way back to the mall.

He walked into the goth store and became disappointed at the sight of a different cashier stationed at the counter. He walked to the back and retrieved another can of spray that hung from a hook. He began to head for the checkout and collided with an employee exiting the stock room area. "Ava, hi. I'm very sorry, are you okay?"

"Other than a mild heart attack, I think I'll be fine." He bent down to pick up the boxes and returned them to her arms. Her skin was fair and her smile was regretful if missed. Her nails were black and was as an illusion of wetness that highlighted her skin tone.

"So, um. How did the submarine black work out for you?"

He chuckled. "I don't wear the stuff. I was only working on an experiment."

He paid for the product at the register and started to leave. He then turned back to walk toward Ava. She knelt down and priced the items of the bottom shelf. He closed in on her and said, "This time I was just going to push you over and then against the wall."

She laughed and stood to face him with an enlightened interest. "Listen. I was wondering if sometime, when it's suitable for you, if you'd like to get together? If not, I understand. Damn, you're hot! I'm going to go now because, I don't think your heart attack could override my death of embarrassment."

"I'd love to. I'm off on Tuesdays. So whenever you set a time, here's my number." She handed him her manager's card.

He glanced over and asked, "Is eight o'clock okay?"

"Perfect."

(Monday 10th)

The next morning, Eric drove, as Braylen occupied the passenger space. "Eric. You ever feel out of place in the world, but hang on to that flare of hopefulness?"

"You mean like, how are you going to get through this work day without anyone recognizing your lack of memory.?"

"No. I feel as though I don't know anyone or my ownself still. Like yesterday. I dusted my entire home for prints. Am I crazy or just lost?"

Randall Ford Jr.

"Why did you do that?"

"I don't know."

"Where in the world did you get an investigations kit?"

"I didn't. I made my it myself."

"Ah. Using the left side of your brain.

Look Braylen. One's mind and life can be a complicated assortment of problems, love, etc. For instance, take the males brain. Disgusting and perverted is a common lateral. Like women tell us our stuff taste nasty, but we long to do it in their mouths. Or around their mouths. Maybe near the cheek, sort of dripping the chin."

"Okay! Point taken."

"See that's sickening, but it's what we desire amongst everything else freaky. Don't fret it. I called Mr. Barret first thing this morning, before I came to pick you up. I made an appointment for you after work."

"Eric, I don't know about this arrangement."

"Braylen. Therapist are confidential and are pledged to uphold all that share to them."

At the end of the day Braylen reclined into the large chair. The plush cushioning was comfortable and very soothing. Mr. Barret sat with the back of his chair facing Braylen's discretion. "Tell me more about these stressful head pains you've been dealing with?"

"I lost any insight to any fragment of memory that was stored in my head. In times of nervous random mishaps or explicit happenings, I quickly develop a surge of sharp blunt pains flashing in my head. The hurt is so dense with energy, I have to react on such impulses."

"Do you feel the need to be a hero?"

"Hero? No. A mediator to the problem, yes."

"Braylen. Take the two pens and the pad over by my desk. Write your name on either side of the tablet using both hands to work at the same pace. Write your name simultaneous with both pens."

Braylen took the two scribing utensils and pressed them firmly to the paper. He froze. He struggled to move them into a collaborating agreement. Finally the plastic lining of the pens snapped in two.

Braylen's face fevered from the panic after the attempt. "Now. Tell me from the top of your head everything you remember from my physical appearance. Giving you only caught a quick glimpse of my face as we shook hands and I sat away from you. Whenever you're ready, Braylen."

"You're a white male approximately one hundred ninety two pounds. Your hair is black patterned in grey with a receding bald spot above the forehead. Your beard is neatly trimmed with the exception of one miscellaneous hair sprouting the left cheek just above the bone. You've been married for over twenty-five years, gathered from the silver wedding band that decorates your left hand.

Your limp, from which ever ailment that has stricken you, has worn the sole of the heel of your left shoe. I suggest you to be in the early fifties range, perhaps fifty-one. This would mean that you have gotten married at age twenty-six. No children, due to the fact that there are no pictures about the walls or desk area. Don't you think it's weird that you choose a profession that requires you to listen to other people's problems?"

"What defines weird to you, Mr. Adger?"

"Abnormal, as in the span of my senses."

"It's like driving. I know how to and the purpose of the vehicle. However, I can't tell you any past experiences with driving or even how the seat cushion felt. That's my version of weird. No memory of anyone, but everyone knows who you are."

"Tell me more about this dream you had the other night."

"I told you all there is to know about that."

"Perhaps, Mr. Adger, there's more to the nightmare. Perhaps you killed someone and hid in the dumpster that night. That would explain the blood."

"There were babies crying in my dream."

"Well, maybe you hit someone's child and hid the car, along with yourself. Your memory deleted its data of that night as to suffer a paranoid shock of the mind. How did you feel when you awoke in the dumpster?"

"Ashamed. Cold. I hated myself, but don't remember such reasons for being."

"Did you kill that night, Braylen?" Mr. Barret trampled him through interrogations. Braylen began to perspire. "Who did you murder? Was it an innocent by-stander? Were you drunk that night? Could it be that the pains in your head are not migraines, but possibly aches from the thoughts of such helpless tragedies?!"

Braylen locked his elbow tight around Barret's neck and pulled him until the office chair left his side. "I didn't kill anyone!" Braylen grit his teeth.

"How do you know? You have no memory, but surely possess the will to hurt!" Mr. Barret eased his arm away. There are two sides to the brain. The left side produces the thought of aggression and the right acts upon it.

I was judging you by any means of accusing you, Mr. Adger. I was simply bringing out the right side. This is an ability that I have studied throughout the years known as aggressive psychology. Now, tell me Braylen, did you feel the stabbing pains in your head when you were just angered?"

"No."

"There you are. My diagnosis is aging more clearly I see."

"Can you make me better by tomorrow?"

"Why tomorrow?"

"I have an important engagement set for eight o'clock."

"Braylen, I have not fully labeled you with any mental disability yet. Be careful with yourself and around others, especially with whom those you feel closest. I need to see you the rest of the week. Therefore, I'm excusing you from work to come see me the next four days. I am not allowed to carry out more than one hour with a patient at a time."

Chapter 4 *Tuesday 11th*

Braylen slipped into dream as his sleep turned away from his conscious state. I lay in the dumpster in the same position as the dream before. *I lay still and deaf. The only sounds heard were the ones that broke through the barrier of my mind. "Help me! Don't let them get me," were the types of pleas that sought shelter from corrupt devastations.*

"I'm alive. Mommy, it's me. I can't die if I've never been born. Don't destroy me! I will stay out of your life. I will not interfere with your job title. I won't cost too much. I need love. I need to be held. Comfort me from nightmares. If you plan to kill me, then why do you have a name picked out for me? If you take my existence, I will continue to love you. For I am unable to emotion hate yet."

These were all phrases that I heard from different babies that sought a second chance. They went back and forth echoing next to me. "Why won't you help?" one asked. I could not reply to them as I seemed part of them. Tiny voices that longed to touch the ones they loved cried out to me.

The screams stopped. My heart fluttered and would not let go of the frantic boost of adrenaline. "Wake up. Wake up," I thought.

I faintly heard the whisper of a small child saying, "Please, don't leave us." The top two plastic lids flew from the bin! Swords entered the metal walls from every direction. The steel rubbing the metal puncture gave the most eerie sound. Death was nigh.

Braylen opened his eyes. He felt the throb of his heart pumping. He exhaled from the holding of air. He breathed deeply to catch up to the filling of his lungs.

Braylen swallowed the saliva that sat in his throat. His quick breaths were labored. He tried to relax his control while lying the same way on the bed as in the dreams. The explicit pain of his head felt as though cells and nerve endings were bursting together. The phone rung abruptly. He sat up and answered, "Hello?"

"I'm sorry to have called you so early."

"Ava! Hi. No, that's okay."

"I'm aware that it's 5:20 in the a.m., but I have to tell you something. He held the receiver closely to his ear. "Do you remember Sunday when you said that I was hot and you were about to die from embarrassment?"

"I do."

"I just wanted to be embarrassed with you and say, I can't stop thinking of you. See you soon." The dial tone placed.

Randall Ford Jr.

Braylen sat facing Mr. Barret. "What happened next, Mr. Adger?"

"After Ava had said that the pain left my head with great speed."

"Understand Brayen, that this stage of diagnosis is still in development. I will not be influenced to lean on hypothesis without a thorough undertaking of your mental stability.

Instead of telling me your dreams, I want to get inside of your head. This would in fact be done by hypnosis. This procedure will help me better understand you and possibly allow me to draw some memory into light."

"You can bring my memory back?"

"Now, I didn't impress that upon you. I simply hope that I can shake things up a bit in there and see what's going on. Take this form, read over it and sign the consent line that grants me the right to do this. Bring it back tomorrow and we will begin. Also take these about forty minutes before you get here, provided you have a designated driver."

"I do." He took the blue pills. "What are these?"

"Alprozalam. They will help even you out into a physical mellowness."

"Why do I need these, are you not experienced enough?"

"Of course, Mr. Adger, it's for your own benefit that you take them. Likely you will be entwined in another upsetting nightmare. This will calm you a bit.

This brings me to another topic, Braylen. The dreams you keep having. It may be what we therapists like to call sleep apnea. This is achieved when your brain has automatically cut from the supply of oxygen, along with the rest of the body. This disorder causes one to hold his breath in his sleep. The deprived air can cause a release of panic through the nervous system, triggering the dreams.

A steady prescribed dose of the proper medicine will clear those unwanted occurrences. After all, you have shed every square detail unto me without any misconstrued information?"

"Yeah. The babies cried and I awoke instantly," he lied.

"Good. That's very reassuring, Mr. Adger. It's nice to have clients that don''t hold anything back from me." Braylen signed the paper and laid it face down on the desk. "Mr. Adger, this assessment that you have appealed on this document represents the first step toward identifying your true self."

He shook Braylen's hand and said, "Be here at 9:00 sharp Friday morning. Until then, rest awhile."

"What about my job?"

"Your pay will not plummet in any way, as long as, you uphold your appointments with me."

"Thank you, Mr. Barret, for all your help. You're very good in your field. Any assumption otherwise on my behalf in doubt, I do apologize."

The evening set and Braylen sat opposite from Ava at the dinning table. The restaurant was classy but down to earth. Ava's hairstyle was fashioned very diverse from their last contact. The streaks were gone and she had a slight part on the right front crown that bent the bangs. It veiled her face and fell about the right eye. The lights of the room illuminated the deep black strands that glistened.

"I really like your hair that way."

"I only wear it this way on special occasions. Tomorrow it will be primped in the routine trend as before."

"Tell me more about yourself, Ava. What do you do?"

"Other than managing the apparel store, I attend college part time. I have majored in journalism and creative writing. I hope to someday become a publicist. I will give earned breaks to those who are talented and deserve to be discovered."

"So, you're a writer?"

She blushed and shook her head in agreement. She tucked the corner of her lower lip underneath her teeth and then broke into a smile. "I write poems mainly."

"Can I hear one?"

"No. I don't remember any of them," she fidgeted.

"Come on, it's Braylen here. Don't be shy. Recite for me a creation of your very own."

"Do you really want me to do this here?"

"By all means. Besides, no one is sitting close enough to hear."

"Okay I will, but don't laugh."

"Don't worry."

"Actually, I wrote it this morning. Here goes.

Jilted I once was. Protagonist, I now proclaim. Isolate and restrained my emotions celled. Wild and spontaneous I now fly. My anger infused with society that estranged it's weight upon it's shoulder. Dismal gloom filled my path as I carried the torch of hope for to reach the line. For the actions of law are futile and desolate, but the love of the heart is where the conscience of justice lies. The world seems too weak for asperity and cruelty, but too strong for love. Have we no love left in our manners? Is there any nice thing to say? Jilted I once was but not today."

"Ava, I'm at a loss for words. That was amazing. What's it about?"

"It's about being unable to tame society and it's ways."

"What about the last part, "but not today?"

"Like I said, I wrote it this morning, right before I called you." She conveyed eye contact and grazed his hand openly feathering the skin.

"You ever feel like what I wrote in the poem? Like, life is too far out of place and you can't break through to your own world?" He leaned back into his chair and felt very connected with her feelings. "It's like I have this friend who works at an abortion clinic in the city. She knows it's wrong , but refuses to quit. So. What do you think, Braylen?"

"I agree. Maybe you should send her a copy of the poem."

"Why did you talk to me in the store the other day? Why aren't you here with some hot blonde in a summer dress, wearing strapped shoes? You don't look as though you'd be out with me."

"I guess looks can be deceiving. I Certainly don't fit the description of what you may like."

"But, you make me laugh."

"And you stimulated my mind when I first laid eyes on you. You're by far the most incredible array of beauty that I have ever been privileged to see."

She looked at him and said, "Take me home as fast as you can. Rush me home quickly."

He smiled deviously. "Very well."

"Please don't get me wrong. I'm not going to have sex with you, for I do not acquaintance you well enough. So when you drop me off I will be masturbating, as soon as, I hit the bed. Thinking of you of course."

"I said it once and will again. You are very unique, Ava."

"Just remember, when my head touches the pillow, I will be touching myself."

Braylen parked Eric's car inside of the garage and secured the electronic lock of the key pad. He entered his home and sat middle of the couch. He turned the television on and sunk into the layered cushions. His feet propped over each other as they aligned the coffee table. "Now, where is that black and white show I like so much." He laid the remote down and took the handle of the ringing phone. "Hello?"

"I thought this would double my pleasure if I involved you in my private party," Ava stated.

DEAD CENTER

He muted the sound and said, "Oh really?"

"Use your imagination to picture me as I describe myself in vivid form lying here. But create in my mind a lustful performance and make me feel it.

Cut your lights and all accessories off. Concentrate without distraction.

I lay under a blanket. I have divested all of my apparel with the exception of my black go-go boots. I had not the time to dislodge them from my feet due to the fiery desire that willed me to the bed. My breast stand as though pulled. My knees are extended outward opposing each other. The grips of my boots connect as the bottom of my feet touch. This submissive position allows it to feel as though a tight band that stretches. Now, take charge of me and control my fantasy. Tell me what to do. Tell me what you would do to me."

"First, I would take the blanket from your body."

"No. Do it in poetic form."

"Ava, I'm not a writer."

"Just visualize me in front of you and exemplify your imagination."

He closed his eyes and relaxed himself. She lingered and lightly fondled the outline of herself. He pressed the handle closer to his ear and envisioned her lying in such configuration of erotic ostentation.

"The covering that veils your body is one that must be ripped from your physical structure by my hand to match the sight that sculpts my mind of your natural image before me. Your unclad body is of lavish perfection.

The underside of my tongue is the texture of silk sheen, as I flux the tip of your entrance. The fold that bends my tongue forward is rigid and firm to catch every nerve that tantalizes your clitoris."

She moved with her hand. "That's good."

"No talking." The playful authority of his voice made it hard for her to hold back her wailing of sensual outburst. "The vigorous flicker sends you into the embroiled state of a lavish high. From top to bottom I swill your area with the wetness produced by my mouth. As your bareness dilates beyond normal, I round my protruding finger just below my tongue and rotate it inside of you.

Hang your head over the side of your bed and press your feet against the wall. Enable your legs to bend shape with distance apart from one another."

She scooted into place and tossed her hair over the clearance of her neckline. "Finally, at the peak ardent blaze of intense passion, I append with you. While invading you with such pleasurable vim, you release a small amount of built up pressure that is stored at your fingertips, as you lay there.' 'Her breathing was frantic. She craved the ending of his dominate tale of ecstasy.

"I thrust you with power upon insertion, to take your mind and your breath. Nature collides with carnality. I rest my weight to your shoulders increasing the ongoing helpless desire that you have in your head at this moment."

She switched hands to hold the phone from the stiffness of her shoulder. "These touches are mine but long for them to be of the one whose voice I hear," she began. "Enraged with a mind taken loss of control, turned me victim to burn the compilation of our loins. For the imaginable depth that I felt has pushed me in a trance.

The repeated submersion of your hips allow me not to hinder my longing to detonate my secretions inside until they flow onto you. This exertion has been much alluring. Especially to have your service rendered at hand." She dropped the phone by her ear and dug her fingers clutching the sheet.

Braylen heard her climax. She moaned lively and eased her mouth to the lying phone. "The conclusion was as great as the strive to unite in this harmony."

Chapter 5 *Major*
(Friday 14th)

"Now, just relax your body and let your mind drift." Mr. Barret said. Braylen laid onto the brown recliner. Mr. Barret began hypnosis. "Clear your mind from all divert wondering and concentrate.

Send your mind to surround those dreams that shade your fear. Exhume the things that continue to feed and produce such arduous sleepless nights."

Braylen felt floaty and deep in abatement. The entire room became a color extorted in a gray static haze that toned his vision. "Braylen, can you hear me?"

"Yes. I can see you as well."

"Mr. Adger, that is nearly impossible. You're just experiencing slight hallucinations prior to the descending vertigo. Mr. Adger, you are now entering fantasy land, per say. This is called your dream world or the *major* part of the brain. Here's where the imagination can run savage through one's head.

DEAD CENTER

Malice, lust, happiness, depression, fear, aggression. All of these and more emotions run together in a visual synchronic accord called dreams.

Place yourself center of the dreams in which you had. Tell me the requested details of the striking visions."

"I see a field of clear woods brightly lit through the top of the trees. A creek streams the middle edge of the valley. It is covered by dead brown leaves from the season passed. A small boy is standing along the embankment of the water's flow."

"Speak to him, Braylen. Ascertain all information you can from him."

Braylen stood next to the young boy. He tossed pebbles into the stream skipping them in distance. "Hi," Braylen greeted.

"I shouldn't talk to strangers," the boy stated. "But, I know you."

"How?"

"You're the one who survived."

"Survived?"

"What is your name?"

"Braylen."

"That's a weird name."

"What defines weird?"

"Weird, as in I have no name. How old are you?"

"Twenty-eight."

"I'm eight."

"Where are your parents? Why are you here alone?"

"I don't know."

"What did you mean by, I'm the one who survived?"

"From the chase of those who did this to you in the same fashion as us. I'm only a figment of your thought. You will soon discover the secret of this conundrum, when your reality will set into effect. See, the dreams you've been having are not of reality, but they are a reflection of a certain past of memories. Can you give me a name?"

"What memory? I have no recollection of the past."

"You didn't until you ran. I always liked the name Jessie James. Will that be suitable for me?"

"Explain to me exactly what you meant by that and what is going on?"

"Don't be like the others who tune us out."

Braylen acknowledged his sorrow and his own mistreatment. He bent down eye level with the young man. "No. Jessie James is already taken. You are unparallel with any other, for you are special. You look like an Alex to me."

"Alex? Now, what about a last name?"

"Okay. Wise and strong you seem. However, more intelligent than your name, you will be called Napoleon."

He giggled. "Napoleon? What about a middle name?"

"Alright, we got a strong name and a cool name. How about a weird name for fun?"

The boy smiled. "Yes."

"What about, Alex Braylen Napoleon?"

"Alex Braylen Napoleon, huh? I sound like an American bullfighter." They both laughed from their interactions and happy conversation.

"One night, not too long ago, you ran from a group of trackers." Alex continued. "They tagged you and left you for dead. Then they threw you inside of the dumpster, In which of many of my friends lie as well. Would you come with me to meet them?"

They walked the beaten pathway of the dirt that was the core of a flower garden. "You're here to protect us aren't you?"

"Protect who?"

"My friends and I."

"Alex, tell me more of the night that I ran from the men."

"Your memory was stolen from you, Braylen. However, you have three sets of memory. The first was taken away from you three months ago. The second is from the three months until now. They drained that set as well. The final clash of memory is from when you woke up in the dumpster that night."

"I'm terribly lost." The boy took him by the hand and walked up to the brick building. "Where are we, Alex? What is this place?"

"This is where my friends live. Some are older now, but many are still in tears." They walked inside of the complex. The entrance room was pure white and very bright. Several babies lay peaceful inside of their cribs. They stirred not, but was content with tender hearts.

I walked through the center aisle of babies. Each were different in weight, color and ethnicity. By their cribs stood small toddlers and slightly older children. They stood as cherubs in guard for the infants and newborns. Stern were their faces and strict was their soldier-like stance. The floor was polar in hue.

"How come you didn't recognize the outside of the building?" Alex asked.

I was astonished by the quietness of the room. "I can't remember why."

"This is where you died, but not inside."

"You mean the garbage bin by the side of the building right? What is this place?"

"Hope. Hope that will turn our lives into something extraordinary."

"Like what?"

"Like, to be alive. Hope to grow, breathe, swim, play ball, be happy. Things like that."

A blunt thud slowly began to tap the door. The babies all began to cry in one agreement. Their screams drew pitch. The knocks of the barricading structure became heavier and dense. The door was at the far end of the room. It was three inches in thickness and bolted sturdily.

A harsh pound began to hit the door as though a ram in charge. The room darkened. The door shook. The hinges loosened and pried from the molding. The babies yelled. The children picked them up and cradled them.

They ran with them and stood behind me as a shield of protection from the fear that stood at the door. Alex, placed two of the newborns in my arms and then clung to my leg, in fright. Finally, the door flew from it's place.

Smoke followed leaving the doorway dark and mysterious. I felt the small heartbeats of the infants including Alex, while we waited. A sword waved the doorway from top to bottom. The children ran rambunctiously behind the curtain. They stood and hid from the figure. The swordsman wore a thick glove, which was the only part of him that I saw.

I handed the babies over to a nearby little girl and pulled Alex by his shirt to release his hold on me. I stood for the innocent faces that scurried about the room. They looked on behind the edge of the drapes. I shed my jacket to confront the open threat that drew battle for the right of decision to denounce their existence.

Mr. Barret stood and walked directly behind Braylen. He squatted and began to examine the crown of his head. He ran the end of his index finger through the hair. Braylen's head began to increase with sharp spear-like torture.

"No!" Braylen yelled and awoke. He sat up.

"Incredible." Mr. Barret said. "You snapped yourself out of a hypnotic trance by your own sustained mentality."

"I got to go back! Send me back to the room."

"You are still illusional. On the count of three, you will come down to your safe place. One. Two. Three." Barret snapped his fingers.

"What are you doing to me? I saw you stand and then fumble through the rear of my head."

"Nonsense, Mr. Adger. I was merely observing you the whole time from over here," he lied. "What did you witness? What happened?"

"The dumpster by the alley."

Mr. Barret stroked his chin. "Who put you there? Did you see anyone around?"

"I didn't see anyone around."

"You are a very advanced piece."

"What's that mean?"

"Look Braylen. This may shock you, but you clearly have an abnormal disorder called split-personality."

"Because of a few illusive dreams?"

"And the fact that you turned rage upon me the other day. The dreams are nothing of use in the analysis. It's the suppressed rage I'm concerned with, Mr. Adger. Don't fret, there's hope for such a case, as yours hasn't worsened any. I do believe you picked a fight the night of the incident, which left you for dead. By the way, Braylen, this is just an account of your split, uncontrollable side.

The hope is that there is medication for you. This is upsetting for you to hear, I know. But, believe me, you're more normal than you think. By your dream you long to save the day. In reality, you may blow up and think your actions are justifiable.

Fill this prescription and start medications right away. Report to work duty Monday. See me in ten days for medical evaluations. Take this. It will relieve my worry, Mr. Adger."

(Saturday 15th)

Braylen awoke and opened his eyes to the flat of the ceiling. "Damn it!" The hope of dream was not yielded unto his subconscious, for to jolt any hint of memory that impended somewhere in his mind. The phone began to siren. Braylen responded to the call. "Yeah?"

"Dude! I'll be right over." Eric said in a distraught voice.

"What's going on?"

"Dude. I'll be right over with some garlic bread and wooden stakes or something."

"Seriously, what's up man?"

"Man, I just passed by your house and saw some dead chick walking through your yard. Now, I'm on my way to the hardware store to get these things."

Braylen rolled his eyes and opened the door to greet Ava. "Very funny, Eric," he responded while holding the phone.

"Hi," she said.

"Hey. Please come in."

"Say that girl has a nice voice." Eric stated.

"Goodbye, Eric." Braylen hung up. He turned about to face her. She fastened her lips to his with a lengthy assertion of gallantry. "What honor do I owe to the visit of my fair queen?"

"Are you trying to entice me with poetic intrigue?"

"If I said, yes, would that be considered a scheme or a desire?"

"What's the difference?"

"Trick question." They held each other close and found a new livelihood that geared them together while gazing in eye contact.

"How do you feel about me?" she asked.

"If only I could be given the chance to prove as words cannot express."

"I really want to get to know you for the longing to share myself with you."

"Well, I do have two phones in the house you know."

She gently slapped his arm and they laughed. "Words can't express as you claim, but document me the proof that abides in your heart. For this exerting urge to be with you is as to loose control. And for my imprisoned virtue this is what I give to you to claim as yours.

Your touch drives me mindless. Your words bring disorder before my nerves and the unbalanced aggressions that insanely impel such sensuality, is a longing to fuck you.

Until then, record your feelings for me on paper and carry me away to an elevated sweep of affection."

Chapter 6 *Minor*

Braylen wrote diligently the words that crippled his heart for Ava. Without pause he jotted the notebook with meaningful sentences. The door sounded from Eric's knocks. Braylen opened it quickly and let out a ferocious roar. Eric rested his hand over his chest and said, "Damn dude!"

"Did I scare you?"

"Yeah, because I actually see a smile on your face. Happy for once. What's up?"

"I feel great today, Eric."

They drove down the highway to reach their work destination. Braylen scanned the radio and turned the volume up. "So, Braylen, has Mr. Barret finished up with you?"

"Finally."

"What's the verdict to your condition?"

"You know. Some pills are a quick cure."

"Cure for what?"

"Nothing. I didn't take them anyway. Listen, give me the scoop on our company. After all this is my official first day back. Give me some work related knowledge."

"We are the executive decision, the membrane of the company. We, my friend, are the suit and tie extension of the world's largest government / army production facility. We make devices of all sorts for the United States Army. Government approved of course."

"Like what exactly?"

"Computer technology, advanced weaponry and some odd, but effective experiments."

They entered the lobby of the building that was heavily guarded by a force of armed security personnel.

"Excuse me, Mr. Adger," the front receptionist requested. "Mr. Barret wants you to come by his office, first thing." Braylen separated from Eric and found his way to Barret's location.

"Come in, Braylen. Good to see you."

"What's going on, Mr. Barret?"

"Great news Mr. Adger. I've found a way to actually set your head straight from your disorder. I have unlocked a new technique of hypno-theoretic behavior analysis. I can make it where you don't have to dose that medicine ever. All we need to do is re-hypnotize you and find the forte of your mind, Braylen. Once again this may induce the chances that you may remember again."

"Just one more time?"

"That's all I need to do to find out what I need to know."

"That's fine with me. Let me know when." Mr. Barret waved his hand over the couch. "You mean right now?"

"The sooner we achieve this, the better for your well-being." Braylen shifted the knot of his tie and laid onto the chair. "Clear your head, Braylen. Rest your stress in the arms of relaxation as to be cradled in the comfort of security. Slow and deep are the breaths that should be."

Braylen slipped into a lofty hypnotic state. "Braylen, is my voice audible unto your ears?"

"Yes."

"Where are you?"

"Here in the office with you."

"Mr. Barret chuckled. "That's not correct. You are in neverland, Mr.adger."

"I see you distorted, but I can see you."

"I need you to carry me to a place inside your head, Braylen. Tell me what blocks out everything and engulfs your mood"

"Ava."

"Ava. Who is she?"

"My girlfriend."

"Describe her to me."

"Hair black as night. Face neon like the sun. Sex appeal of twenty women and a delicate voice that can excursion the heart with delirious love."

"Love? Did you say love, Mr. Adger? Yes! That's it! Braylen, will you stay here briefly with continued thoughts of Ava? I will return soon."

Mr. Barret ran to the tenth floor of the building. He made his way to Mr. Zear's office. He entered with granted permission. Mr. Zear stood facing the window. The ceiling of the room was outlined in marble and trimmed in gold. The space was approximately fifty-eight feet by thirty-nine. Four thousand eighty psychology and health books were neatly aligned about the shelves that stretched from half of the walls. The silence was of a pin drop. Not for even a phone was in his office.

Mr. Zear's hair was white and full. A short man, but trim from active cardio. Stern without emotion his face sat. Always in a proper stance. He wearily acknowledged Mr. Barret. "Do not infuriate me with useless details."

"Yes sir, Mr. Zear. I have discovered the clue we have been searching for, that Braylen has been using to block us."

"Mr. Barret. You know that we only use last names when in conference. Therefore, obey my regulations."

"Yes, sir. Mr. Adger apparently is in love."

"Love!"

"Yes. It's evident that he's met someone. I hold him hostage in a trance at this present time."

"Expunge her from his mind."

"Should we follow up on this lady?"

"No. She's harmless and knows nothing, just as Mr. Adger is unaware of his own state."

"Yes, sir." Mr. Barret headed for the door.

"Mr. Barret. I trust there will be no room for fallacy in your evaluation upon him. Don't reduce our relations of honesty into the hands of failure. Do this right and don't let him get away twice. Don't fail me. Refrain from bringing such ardor of hate out in me by exploiting my work. If this fails, you will become one of my own experiments.

"Yes, sir." Barret rushed back to Braylen and sat in front of him. "Braylen, I'm back. Can you hear me?"

"Yes."

"Braylen. What if I told you that this girl isn't right for you?"

"Then, I would tell you to fuck off."

Mr. Barret laughed. "Do you love her?"

"Yes."

"Explain to me how you need her, Mr. Adger."

"Actually, I've been in works with a poem to word my love for her. Would you care to listen to an excerpt?"

"By all means, Mr. Adger. Spill me the love of your thoughts."

"For to run with you and walk by you is to catch up with time held without you," Braylen, recited. "These feelings I once beared in a lonely shell. Distraught and vulnerable I grieve from a mindless grave of an effaced memory. Archaic I became in my own world of solitude. For a mind without a trace has little purpose."

"Very crafty, Mr. Adger." Barret prepared a long needle full of a light solution. He squeezed the air from the metal stem by pushing the plastic handle inward.

He bent down behind Braylen and observed the molding of his skull. "Now. Mr. Adger, focus on Ava. Imagine her in front of you. The environment is an extravagant flower garden that stretches for several miles.

You two stand center of the colorful nature painted portrait of vegetation. Picture her before you wrapped in a long white wedding dress and you costumed in a tuxedo, as in a wedding. Tell her your vows. Read the poem to her. Remedy yourselves with love."

Braylen took Ava by the hands and indulged in her eyes. "Ava. I've finished the poem that files my heart for you." She smiled and looked on. Braylen unfolded the paper and began to read.

"Joined together is what I have hoped from your vitality and brisk energy. Your face is a welcoming aurora that draws one's heart. Although energetic, your lack of loquacity led me to think of you to be quite timid.

Intrigued you were. The less complex my head became. For to be with you is as a season's change. Always different, but still in love. Your personality is vivacious as the day. Your voice is shimmering and celestial as the angels. The wings that you soar are navigated by the charm of your appealing personality. The beauty that you display is of a never-ending well. For not to pass you by with a lack of lust, time has born me into a madman of sedulous endearments."

DEAD CENTER

"Very nice, Mr. Adger." He pointed the needle into place over the wreath of Braylen's head. "Now. Say goodbye to her." He slowly began to inject the needle in place while Braylen carried on with his persistent dream.

Braylen moved in closer to Ava and said, "The interment is the old me. Zealot and in love you became me."

"That's the sweetest thing ever," she said. She leaned in to kiss him. Her mouth became saturated and poured blood. Her body grew frigid and limber. The garden faded to darkness as an all to familiar brazen edge interspersed straight through her chest. Braylen jumped back to avoid it's attempt to repel his body.

"Ava!"

"Run now, from the blade that seeks you," I heard as though a small child had cried. "Wake up!" Alex said, as he clung to my leg. "Don't let them get us for we're all that's left in your life. Save her. Now!"

"How?"

The hurricane-like winds tunneled and plowed the now bleak field. "War is waged, but only through small battles will you win." Alex's hair tossed about. "Don't let the blade burn you from it's stroke!"

"But, I must stand even with this prowess of havoc."

"This in no man Braylen. This is a method. A pure sinister plot to denounce us."

"If this sword bearer is no man, then you're not a real boy are you?"

"You must eradicate this hypnosis immediately or Ava will die."

"How?"

"Wake up, Braylen! Now!"

Braylen screamed loudly and raised up.

"Damn it!" Mr. Barret said. He tossed the needle behind the chair as the contents were only half used. "Truly amazing how you can surpass your own subconscious level of a coma."

Braylen breathed roughly and screamed. "What are you doing to me!"

"Mr. Adger, not to worry. You were merely experiencing a reaction to your medication."

Braylen grabbed him by the collar and shoved him to the cushions of the padded couch. "I can feel your feeble heart pound for mercy." He pushed his weight onto Barret's extended arms and restrained his motions. "You know who I am don't you? You know who I used to be don't you!"

"No, Mr. Adger. I do not. Unhand me at once or I'll have your job!"

"For if any reason anyone ever desired harm over Ava's head, I will extract their heart from the vessels that hold it in place. By the way, I quit."

"You're a psychopath, Mr. Adger!"

"Yeah, so I've been diagnosed." Braylen left the room.

Chapter 7 *Vacillation*

(Thursday 20th)

"I knew it would be you." Braylen said, after opening the door for Ava.

"Are my knocks distinctive between any others?"

He pulled her in tight and locked his lips to hers. The soft gentle caress of the pair was of a last request from the hardship of fatality. She sat beside him with her feet slighted inward and her knees apart.

"My lady. I have finished the poem for you." He handed her the envelope. She pushed her skirt between her inner thighs with her hands.

"So, it's going to be a good night."

"I long for it to be. For you're too sexy to look at. It took me a few days to complete it. I wanted to thoroughly enclose my true love for you with perfecting lines of communication."

"Im sorry, for the loss of your job."

"I'm glad of the circumstances that came about. What happened that day reminds me that I do not know what I'd do without you."

She smiled. "Tell me what you want to do to me. Make your words precede and entrap my mind with the thoughts of what you want to do to me tonight."

The doorbell rang as to interrupt them. "Hold that thought." He stood and opened the door only to be made uneasy by the sight of Melinda.

"Hey baby!" She said, while entering. She tried to hug him, but failed from her attempts when he shrugged away from her reach. "Come on, honey. I just came by to visit, hang out, fuck awhile. Oh. I'm sorry. I didn't know you had company. Who's this clown?"

"Melinda, please leave. I told you to never come back here again!"

"No. Actually what you said was, leave for now. Therefore, this is now and I'm ready to push you over the edge." She endeavored to interlock her hands around his neck. He fastened his hands to her wrist.

"Let me see the way out for you."

Ava stood. "No need to. I think I should be leaving."

"Ava, no. I can explain this."

"Yeah, like how I got this gap between my legs. Amongst other places." Melinda ruefully stated. Ava sat the note onto the table and stood in a very languid fashion. "Are you staying to watch or are you leaving?"

"The despondent words that excel from such a vociferous inhumanity, such as yourself, does not influx my self-esteem with your slander."

"My, aren't you the use of proper educate. Well, here's a word you should familiarize yourself with and that is xanthous. Which means blonde, as in what he prefers, honey." She ran the tips of her strands between her fingers. Oh and by the way, is that earth tone colors your wearing?" She asked while referring to her makeup.

"In deed it is." She glanced with disappointment at Braylen. "It's called, six feet under." She stormed the door and made her way to the car.

Braylen backed Melinda out of the house. He slammed the door and then locked it. "The next time you notion to popup here again, I'll phone the police." Melinda began to walk away. Braylen charged Ava's car. He stood in-between her and the door. "Ava, please."

"Please, what? Try and understand that you have a girlfriend already?" She began to cry and looked away from him.

"She is not my girlfriend, Ava."

"Was she ever? Why would she just waltz into your home and attempt to cosset her hungry arms about your neck? Did you have sex with her?"

"No! I mean, I don't know. Far as I know I have not.

"A simple yes or no would have been sufficient. So, you're not quite sure if your penis has entered any *gaping* orifice on her body?" She asked in sarcasm clearing her tears.

"Ava. There are some things that I need to explain, but find it difficult to do. However, she is not one of them. I beg of you to stay. For your presence of love is the calming of my mind."

"Fine then. Ride with me." She sat and took the steering position of the car. He secured her door and entered through the passenger side.

"Where are we headed?"

"I decided to take a copy of the poem in which you have influenced to devote to my friend."

"The one who works at the abortion clinic?"

"Yes. And even though you accompany me with supported solace, I prefer to drive in silence. For my feelings are bruised and my heart now grieves."

They stopped in front of the clinic. She placed her hands middle of the wheel. "My emotions bleed as an enclosed hemorrhage. Although this be my feelings to say, my true feelings for you have not changed. You make me feel as an opened rose instead of some closed up flower that hides from light and is deceased for winter.

Different to the world I look. Different inside you make me feel. Good about myself are the feelings you have placed. This rage is the flutter of my veins that palpitates the stimulation of an aroused heart, when you near. I deserve you the right to pursue your side of the story with brief hesitation. Until then you can either sit here or join me."

Braylen waited inside of the lobby, while Ava was escorted down the hall by a nurse, to her friend's station. Without warning the distress signals of sharp pains broke into sensations of panic in his head. He breathed slowly. The pain magnified.

He stood and paced the floor. The voluminous pull of his head was as a magnet that locked his eyes onto the *in progress* sign that flashed above the far door. Behind the door was the operations and aborting room.

The lady behind the door wore a regulated gown and stood as though bashful. "Please. Won't you have a seat on the edge of the table?" the nurse asked.

The lady sat on the padded vinyl of the table. The nurse guided her ankles into the chrome stirrups. They were cold from the cramping touch to the skin. The nurse tilted her back support down. Her legs were now elevated from the incline.

The doctor, sat on the swivel stool in front of her. He pushed himself forward and was now in placement between her legs. He said nothing, as for the explanation of the devices he adjusted. He checked the force of the vacuum unit and then wiped the sterile cloth from end to end of the long needle-like instrument.

"What is that used for?"

"Miss Meredith. It's probably best if you refrain from such questions."

"Please, Doctor. I must be informed."

"Fine. This rod obelisk aid is used to puncture or jam into the fetus skull. After that, I splay the opened area to enlarge the hole. Finally, I use this vacuum to suck out the contents thereof."

"Is this murder?"

"Well, Mrs. Meredith, it's legal by the state."

"No. Is this the actual taken of one's life?"

"Let me assure you ma'am, that this tiny thing has no heartbeat as of yet. There is no possible living thing

Randall Ford Jr.

inside you. Now. If you don't mind I have four others that await. So, I need to proceed steadfastly."

He slipped the latex glove onto his hand and pinched the webbing to form snugly around his fingers. He positioned the stainless steel device into her and began to open the clamp, separating her inner walls apart. He looked on the screen of the ultra sound image. He began to ease the sphere-like gadget into her birth canal.

The baby shifted it's place away from the sharp rod. "Slippery guy." He held the needle at the base, for it was submerged inside of her. The nurse laid comfort as to distract her with conversation.

Braylen's head screamed with loud impulses of pain that persuaded him to make his move. He kicked the door open and hooked his hand around the under elbow of the doctor. "Wait!," the doctor yelled. He watched the monitor carefully. The baby began to move signifying a loss trial. "Damn it! Who are you? You caused me to miss again!"

Braylen pulled his arm away from her along with the needle. "Release her now!" The nurse feared and hastened not to comply. He twisted the doctor's arm behind his lower back. He then gripped his hand, crushing the bones of his fingers, until fractured. He screamed in agony.

Braylen leaned into the woman and asked, "How did you feel three minutes ago? How did you feel as the approaching time marched, to attempt to death your unborn child?"

She began to weep. "My baby has no heartbeat as of yet."

"So that inserts justification in your mind? Let me tell you something. Your baby went from microscopic to the fetus size it is now. Therefore, nothing is going to grow, except it be alive. Now, get out of here and consume yourself with thoughts of raising a healthy baby."

She left the room. Braylen continued his assault on the doctor. He pulled his arm high above the mid of his back. "Let me go, now!" The nurses fled for safety. The receptionist phoned the local law enforcement agency. Braylen shoved him to the side desk.

"Look at these pictures of your family on the desk here. What would you do if someone like yourself murdered them both?"

"These are not infants or children. They are not living creatures!"

"At conception the egg grows, meaning It's alive. The arms. Legs. The entire cavity of the fetus would not continue to form if dead. If I find out that you have harmed another young being, I'll break your other shoulder."

He loosened the ball from the socket by separating it tightly from the upward pull of the elbow. While inflicting this harsh punishment, his shoulder blade disconnected, as well.

Pariah, I was looked upon as they were the managers of hate. Every eye starred at me in shock from the bitter hate of my emotions to denote me from, "caring" to deranged". From the love of "innocent" to "lunatic of society". "Peace keeper" to "jury of wolves".

For my stability was ragging, but envious to those who declared admirable sanction to clone my intentions.

Braylen fled on foot to avoid any confrontations with the authorities.

Late in the evening, Ava sat with great fatigue. She reversed her thoughts of Melinda and possible secret relations with Braylen. The feelings of being used and deceived were ones of the first. For he was the only whom she considered, to explore her untouched body. How complex the ways of love are. Even with the remnant of her hurt in tact, she loved him still.

She jumped in a startled manner, as Braylen spoke. She looked up from the counter quickly. "Hey," he said, while looking at her. She immediately felt the zesty feelings of compassion to engage with embrace. However, she looked away to express deep insipidity. He laid the letter onto the glass casing of the counter top before her register.

"What happened to you earlier at the clinic?" she asked. "I looked for you, but you were gone."

"Yeah. I decided to jog home."

"To catch up with Melinda, perhaps?"

"I was not. She isn't my girlfriend or even my friend. But, you're my everything." He pushed the letter toward her and turned to walk away. She slid her finger inside the corner of the envelope and tore the seal back. She pulled the note from the paper casing and held it intensely as she read.

The leaves may crumble and the world may dream. Nature could die and the frost of winter could cease. The days could fall and the moon could fade. With that all be the exception of life, I'd still be in peace with my heart that beats my chest. For the blood that surges my body is mixed with the love that is of you.

The dizzy hours of my head are regretful and weary, when compared to you. The daydream you forever

DEAD CENTER

instilled in my sight is the most beautiful of days. The sun against the sky and the birds that quartet the trees all in competition. Every flower for bloom as not to miss the season's mood.

Rara Avis, is defined as "rare bird" by Latin terms. To me there the truth lies in awake of reality. Only your beauty is the clutch of a mesmerizing ploy to make the eyes of men fall to love you. For me as to be the chosen for your swain treaty to become blended as one, is the waive of my heart."

(Friday 21st)

Braylen's sleep was dreamless until the visions of the orphanage door began to vibrate from the loud knocks. This dream was of the previous hypnotic replay at Mr. Barret's office.

"Alex. Run and hide. I'll handle this." Alex hung onto his clinging grip for not to break the security.

The door fell over and the smoke rose from it's path of the hallway. The silver sword swung violently in every direction. Although the door had broken from it's structure, the large pounding increased.

Braylen began to walk toward the sword. "Daddy, no!" Alex screamed in vain.

He bent down to the boy. "I'm not your father. Go now. Run for your escape. Find your parents for they will protect you." Alex walked backwards and then turned to run from the fright.

Braylen awoke from the pounding of his door. "Ava!" He jumped from the head of the bed. He ran to greet her, only to be stunned by the sight of several men that surrounded the yard. They resembled the personal protection for the president. They each were formally designed in black suits.

"Braylen Adger?" the man asked.

"Yes."

The sidekick of the first man drew bead on him with his handgun. "Mr. Adger. To glance at you is, is to kill you. So, unless you hate life, my suggestion would be to do as we say. Now, place your hands behind you." One of the men locked the steel binders about his wrist and patted him down.

The rest of the morning Braylen sat in an air conditioned, squared interrogations room. The man that detained his arrest entered the room and stood beside him. "Mr. Adger. The reason for this confinement is to hold you until the bus is fully capacitated. It will arrive for you shortly."

"What bus?"

"Let me explain." The man lit a cigarette. "You are here until the crazy bus comes to haul you to the psych ward over in the neighboring state. Your rage and unbalanced mind along with your split personality diagnosis has landed you a spot at the residence."

"Mr. Barret." Braylen whispered.

"The doctor's hand you broke had forced us to pick you up and extradite you over to the mental facility. You will have round the clock supervision and counselors at your request. This is best for you, Braylen."

Later that afternoon, the white bus came for the deportation. The two business dressed men led Braylen onto the bus and then to his seat. They placed him center of each other and sat beside him.

The bus was filled with very sinister shady beings that clearly fell victim to the shore of madness. Some trapped in dream and could not live beyond. Silence was the issue as the two men condemned no talking.

The bus set into motion, while leaving the station. The bumps of the road shook in vibrations. The suspension was worn.

Braylen's mind began to drift, as certain pieces of information fell into place. His thoughts of no fingerprints found in his home. *You are a very advanced piece*, he remembered Mr. Barret say. *Stabbing pains,* echoed in his head from their past conversations.

How would he have known about the sword in my dreams if I never told him these things. He knows. He is the instigator behind the will of these explicit happenings.

Braylen sat in a straight jacket vested over his chest and arms. His ankles shackled in leg cuffs. He sparked their senses and slightly slumped over. "Sit back," the man ordered.

Braylen swiftly dropped his back to the seat of the chair. He threw his legs into the air and entangled the ankle chain around the man's neck in a strangle formation. The man to his left began to assault Braylen's head with a series of battering blows. Braylen twisted the chain with his feet, sinking it deeper into the skin until it resembled wilted rubber.

The man pulled at the steel linked connectors. Braylen continued to hold him in such fashion. His arm strength was no match for Braylen's drive. He endured the punches administered by the second man. He felt not the painstaking bruises, but carried well the jarring strikes. The first man fell limp. Braylen spun himself in the frontal direction of the second.

He pulled his legs in and kicked with all of his physical might. The impact slammed the glass causing it to shatter in rigid pieces. One of which took his life as it stuck from the man's chest. The force of the push sent his body down instead of out of the window.

Braylen sat straight. The bus continued to roll. The driver was oblivious to any type of acoustic pitch, while he pilot the wheel. The driver's seat had it's own door at the left front. The hull of this compartment was sealed by a barrier of tinted glass and was a bullet proof shield, similar to an armored car.

One of the patients placed his hand to the buckles of Braylen's restraint coat. Another hand came from a different passenger, which unhooked the clasp. The jacket laid free and loose.

Braylen took the handgun from the first man's blazer and made his way to the front. He fired a single shot into the plexiglass of the driver's area. He drove another round with an accurate eye. Braylen sent each metal dart into the exact target as before. The next bullet chipped the border. The wall crumbled after the emptying of the chamber.

Only the precise measured support of a sharpshooter could break point with such skillful caliber. He aimed the weapon high to the head of the driver. He took his gun and demanded him to stop. He shot the chain which bound his legs and ran from the interior of the bus.

Chapter 8 *Dead Center*

Late that night, Ava unlocked the door to her apartment. She tossed the keys upon the counter and felt about the wall for the light switch. Braylen grabbed her from behind and placed his hand to cover her yell. She pulled away and screamed boisterously.

"Braylen! What are you doing here?" Her heart felt fearful.

"Please. Don't be mad at me."

"Why would you do that to me?"

"Ava, it's 11:49. Your neighbors are all probably asleep. If you just saw me in here, you'd flipped and woke them. I'm sorry."

"Why are you here, Braylen? I came to your house earlier today. I was ready to give myself away to you after reading your poem, but you weren't there. Where were you? Were you with her?"

"Ava. I'm here before you as to look your house over for safety."

"Safe from whom?"

"Look Ava. If I had came to your place of business you'd fought with me and came home alone. I needed to come here and check your place over keenly."

"Who am I to be afraid of, Braylen? What level of fear should I feel threatened?"

"Ava, I don't know who is chasing me, but I can have this all explained."

"Great. Now, what about earlier? Were you with that harlot?"

"No. I wasn't. Ava, please understand."

"If you wanted her so bad, then why are you, like, with me? Am I a joke? Some clownish looking vampire girl? Is this what I am to you!" She struck him with her fist.

Braylen seized her and gently bumped her back to the door. He kissed her tediously and solid. She continued to hit him. She opened her eyes and halted the punches. "Come with me somewhere and I shed all proof unto your judging conscience." He eased from her. She pulled him in closer as to kiss.

"I believe you," she whispered into his ear.

"You'll believe me more boldly with confidence after you come with me."

"I will come with you, but first, I want to experience what it's like for you to come inside of me. I love you."

She drew the skin of his neck between her teeth. He ripped the fishnet stockings from her thigh to her knee. He clumsily pawed at the buttons of her shirt as not to tear the delicate cloth. Her breathing became erratic.

DEAD CENTER

She backed away and pried it apart taking the buttons from stitch.

"If it seems as though I don't know what I'm doing then that's probably the cause," he joked, as his memory of intercourse was not relative to his past.

"Good. That makes the two of us."

He picked her up and sat her onto the counter top. He slid his hands inside of her black skirt and positioned them at the junction of her butt. Every touch of his hands were welcomed. He forced her to the end of the counter. As his hands displaced from her thighs her panties departed her skin as well. The sides of it was thick, but the flange of skin of her opening was thin to the touch.

She straightened her arched back from the fear of balance. The heels of her boots braced into the cabinet doors below. From this position Braylen brought himself pressing her body with his. "I love you too," he replied.

"Tell me how I look," she said. "Tell me how I feel. Describe to me the color of touch that paints the picture in your mind. Explore me with voiced details. For in mind, I relived this moment a hundred times. Appease me of this lewd feat that lies in my favor. Tell me how my skin feels. Spill to my ears the urging moments that propels your savage impatience to lunge inside of me."

She dropped his pants from the release of the buckle and shoved her hand into his briefs. He bruised the crease of her neck by the suction of his lips. "Take me as the ways you please. Validate this liaison affair by breaking the fissure of my chaste. Hold back nothing. For I am mussed with emotions, even through the threshold of discomfort, which I expect to be very apprehensive.

Haste no longer for this teasing outline of you that brushes against my bareness has destroyed my fight. Unleash this tension that has held me hostage from the barren engravement upon my integrity."

Braylen entered her slowly but anxiously. The separating tear of the cervix muscle tissue caused her to push upward. The deep thrust elevated her sensations as to become as one. "Intrigue my frame with poetic love making," she continued. "This gambit of heightened pleasure has magnified euphorically through me."

He lightly pulled the tips oh her hair down causing her neck to be visible and submissive unto his will. She stretched her fingers to dig into his back, while he repeated a steady thrust into her. "Difficult is the least of words such as it is to hold my own from the taut retention that you grip. Your smoothness is the texture of wet ice. However, the embedded heat of your aperture is addictive."

He released the latch of strands. She sat upright and embraced him with a suffocating hug. "I feel so raw," she said, as she began to fleece the purity which smeared his torso. "Hurt me."

"I can't."

"Fulfill my desire for you to bore into me madly. Seek domination over my listless stability." He began to move rapidly into her, as she had persuaded. "Plow your seed and force me to apex!"

The ripping pain was agonizing, but forcibly delightful. The repetitive motions were animalistic. The feel of their bodies were as a tight woven velvet of skin.

The feelings of vaginal orgasm was hard, but relaxing. They kissed with content love and held each other's body entwined.

(Saturday 22nd)

Melinda sat on Eric's sofa. He was stationed beside her in the single chair. She slid her white sandals from her feet by pushing the backs of them to the carpet. She rested the balls of her feet to the edge of the coffee table. She spread her legs wide with her knees bent upward. Her jeans were tight and form fitted.

"I'm bored," she said. "We should celebrate our new promotional status."

"What do you have in mind?"

"Don't even act like you didn't see this print between my legs. I saw you glance with a wondering eye."

He looked down to the floor and smiled. "Say Melinda. What was it like being with one of those empiricals? Was it normal?"

"You mean Braylen? Please. I couldn't even get to first base with him."

"That's good to know," Braylen said. He came out from around the corner with Ava by his side.

"Braylen! This isn't what you think, man." Eric's tone was nervous. "Melinda and I were just about to go visit you. So. How'd you get in here?"

"That's odd. You tell me how I obtain such skillful talent of entering one's home so quietly? Go ahead, Ava."

Randall Ford Jr.

She walked up to Melinda, who sat in a daze of startled fright. Ava made the large roll of duct tape noticeable from her approach. She bent down ear level and said, "I shave my legs, just as you do. I have the same protruding veins that run through my feet that are sexy, just like yours. I primp in the mirror, just as you do. However, I have an advantage over you." She extended her tongue over her bottom set of teeth revealing the barbell piercing.

Ava stretched the tape outward in a line and said, "By the way, since you were only guessing at the fact the other day, I must confirm this; yes he does have a gapping tool that if he really did have sex with you, you'd be much wider than you really are."

Eric stood, while Ava fastened Melinda's hands together. He yelled at Braylen, "Have you lost your mind!"

"Yeah, I have. What did you do with it?"

"I don't know what your talking about!"

Braylen dropped the clip of the gun causing the bullet of the chamber to fall as well. He slid a different type of bullet into the slot and released the lock of the slide. "Hold your hand out."

"What for?"

"The ammo I took out were hollow points. The one bullet I inserted was a full metal. I did not want to blow your hand off of your wrist, but I will make you talk. Now extend your hand or I'll shot whatever it rest by."

Ava secured Melinda's mouth and ankles. She laid her over the cushions of the couch onto her side and

DEAD CENTER

looked on for the confrontation was heated. Braylen's frustration peaked from Eric's defiance.

He grabbed him with his free hand and pulled him to his feet by his shirt. He walked him back to the wall. He pressed his forearm to the paneling and placed the barrel entrance of the weapon to the ball of his hand. He fired the singeing lead and then stepped back. Eric yelled harshly from the hollowed flesh of his hand.

Eric jerked the thin curtain from the nearby window and wrapped his hand to prevent blood loss. Braylen reapplied the former clip into the gun and adjusted the hammer slide. "Now, listen to me Eric! That was only a full metal that I had. These others will literally remove any part of you upon discharge. Tell me everything! Who am I? The pains in my head? Why are they after me?"

"If I revealed to you such things, they'd kill me anyway."

"Die peacefully or piece by piece."

"Okay. I'll tell you." Eric plopped into the chair from which Braylen had previously pulled him. "You are an experiment. Partial property of Zear and Ginn, which by the way, is pronounced *surgeon*.

Mr. Zear, our boss is under development of creating a device that might be used to control one's mind. The government that employs us is not aware of this. Reason why is because, Mr. Zear, was offered billions to build such an instrument from opposing foreign ambassadors of the U.N. You, my friend, are one of these who underwent the *needle*.

See Braylen. These leaders of other countries wanted to have the perfect protection by their sides. This was not to be the job of some electric robot, but the actual usage of a human body under the control of their will.

Now, picture if you will, Braylen, the precision of a marksman. The tracking sense of a bounty hunter. The boldest bodyguard. The intelligence of a navy seal. The will of a terrorist. The nature of an assassin and the brutality of a green berea all rolled into one. And that, my friend, is exactly what you are composed of."

"How can this be possible, Eric?"

"Like I said, you're an experiment. Over the past five months there have been twenty-five including you, as you are the last.

In the early phases of our procedures or the *olden days* as we like to call them, we were not in tune with this. We messed up a lot and spoiled a few lives on top of it. We needed a way to embed a structure into the brain cavity of our patients. The reason for the high pains of your head is due to the fact that you have a very narrow needle-like rod implanted *dead center* of your brain.

In the olden days, we carefully drilled through the skull cap and jammed the needle into place. Then, we simply cut the end off with wire cutters. Now, we have built a robotic arm guided by the graph of a computer to plant the needle into it's proper location.

This rod in your brain allows us to monitor you as an antenna tracking device. It's position allows you to release certain chemicals that bypass normal functions of the brain as needed. It lets you feel no pain, gives you ten times the strength as to release panic and fear. It overrides lethal injections by supporting your brain's

DEAD CENTER

functions as to shut down in avoidance to it's nervous system failure.

The metal content of the needle acts as a ground rod to absorb the pressure of an electric chair voltage output. This also explains your memory loss.

Your memory central is located center of the brain just under the left and right sides. It's a semi-doughnut shaped part that holds memory in storage.

The needle punctured through the *center* limbic portion location. This totally wiped out your memory leaving it *dead*. This was unexpected, but much welcomed as to have no past. No remembrance of family. No nothing.

However, upon the perfecting of memory clearing the needle positioning, there were still many flaws that we had encountered. Also, this is why you felt high after a prolonged workout due to the endorphin that released."

Eric stood and walked over to the bar. He poured a hard drink to ease the pain of his hand. "Tell me about the experiments," Braylen said.

"I'm not so sure that would be a good idea. This chick's ears may not be able to endure such graphic details." He held the whiskey glass and walked up to Ava. "You people always dress like you're morbid and wear makeup as to appear dead. Be that, you have no clue as to the horrific things that go on with these experiments." Ava slapped him as Braylen pulled him away and back to the couch.

Eric's drink spilled over his pants. He exhaled and continued. "The experiments were some very testing times for us engineers. The first thing our trackers did was hunt down some potential prospects to fill such shoes. Some men were the head of families. Others were bums from the street. Out of twenty-five, only four remain alive. The other three live at the Zear & Ginn building.

My first experiment was a mere crash course to sort of desensitize us with the process. Number three for example, was used for the introduction of heavy steroid induced injections. Those were daily, three to six times. The unbalanced charge of fueled aggressions lead to his downfall.

One night we had him arrested. Falsely of course. This was to see if he could make a prison break successfully. Upon his walk to his designated cell, one of the neighboring inmate onlookers sought intimidation on him. He stuck his dick through the bars and yelled, "Fresh for the taking!"

Number three turned about to his direction. "Put me in that cell," he requested. The guards refused and took him by the arm. Number three slayed the officers with lethal blows to their heads. After dropping the two guards, he paced to the cell of the perverted onlooker. Number three grabbed him and squeezed his penis. The veins ruptured and then he dismantled it by force from his body.

The captain of corrections had no choice but to take his life by way of bullet. The chemical which created fear and offence was released, as the needle was offset. The build up of steroid overdose added to this as well.

Experiment number one died by request of Mr. Zear after the needle swayed causing him to become one hundred percent paralyzed. Ordered dead one hour after this discovery.

Experiment number twelve. Although we leveled out the injections of steroid uptake, number twelve died from severe heart swelling. A direct side effect of the potent anabolic.

Experiment number twenty-two. This time a woman. In the pursuit of limited time we decided to expand our options. Five days after we gave her the needle, we found her dead in her apartment.

The part of the brain that released sexual desire was nicked, causing the chemical to spill over. The brain sensed this and began to replenish this chemical at a surpassed rate. Her libido was so strong that the unbalanced chemical made vaginal pain register as pleasure in her mind.

In other words. The bigger the object the better for her. We found her body nude from the waist down with a regulated baseball bat stuck up inside of her. All but three inches of the handle was poking out. When we removed the bat, parts of her canal was dried and stuck to it.

Most of the other experiments, except for the remaining four, died from other irreparable flaws."

"What was my problem?" Braylen asked.

"Too much heart. Your first mission was to see if you were capable of sniping off a small child from afar. You aimed the high powered rifle and captured the target. You held the gun and never took it off of him. A single tear began to descend your cheek. Finally, the boy became out of bounds. We had to pry the rifle from your hands, while you held it steady. You couldn't kill. Therefore, we couldn't use you.

You sensed destruction from the night of your termination. You ran as we gave chase. We shot you with a tranquilizer and then shot your head with an once of fluid that killed your memory over again. From the drive of the needle til the time you awoke."

"Alex was right."

"Word got back to us that you were still alive, after we thought you were dead from the serum. We tossed you into the dumpster next to the abortion clinic. That's right Braylen. The bags you were lying on, were the carcasses of aborted unborn babies.

This now brings me to those dreams you've been having, reported directly from Dr. Barret. Dreaming is what threw us off. None other empiricals had dreams. The dreams released chemicals that made you happy. The dreams were happy. This chemical blocked our tracking device. This convinced threat as not to be able to keep up with you and your locations.

The babies in your nightmares represent your memory. The sword is the needle to take them out of your brain. The black glove is the reflection of the administer of the operations."

"What about Alex?"

"Just a memory symbol. That's all. This led Mr. Barret to do two hypnosis encounters on you. The first was to see if there were any witnesses that night you awoke from the dumpster. The second was to try and find out why we couldn't track you anymore. Apparently, it was because of love. You uncharted our track once more, when Ava fell into your life."

DEAD CENTER

Ava stood close to Braylen and felt very protected. "Why were you still tracking me?"

"Melinda and I were assigned to you that night. We posed as your best friend and lover. We did this to further our experiments on you. Melinda and I worked the right side of the brain, which controlled sexual hunger. Mr. Barret, worked the left by discovering your reasons for being.

This explains the sharp pains and quick reactions to responsive threats that you occurred to fight. The rod interacted and fed from the emotions of your brain signals. Notice when you were angered. It was only apparent when someone was being wronged or tossed into fast troubled situations.

We took advantage of the time when you broke Dr. Morgan's hand, at the clinic. This enabled us the opportunity to ship you off to the crazy house. There you'd died with the time span."

"What time span, Eric?"

"No one could live with a steel rod in their brain, Braylen. The experts estimate that the time of expiration is ninety days. Your days were numbered for termination around day sixty, which left you roughly thirty days from the time you awoke in the dumpster. Considering today is the 22nd, you have about eight days until your brain dies."

Ava took the gun from Braylen's hand and pointed it at Eric. "What options does he have?" she asked. "Tell me, now!"

"You know Ava? You're not a bad looking zombie. In fact, I find it quite impractical to resist my impure thoughts of you."

She pulled the trigger skinning his shoulder. He screamed. "Try to subdue your quirky fantasies and shed unto me the information that I request, or this malaise of death will burden you until I hit your heart."

The sting of torn flesh burned from the fire if the bullet. Eric pushed his back into the couch and covered the wounded area with his palm. The tiny lumps that schooled his throat were clusters of agony that longed to be expelled through tears. Inside and held down, is where he bound those screams of pain, as not to show weakness unto them. He swallowed the air which were preserved moans from the forced removal of muscle tissue from his shoulder. He stomped the floor with the flat of his shoe and looked up to them with the eyes of violence.

"There is only one surgeon qualified to do a removal surgery and that is Mr. Ginn. Mr. Zear implants and Ginn removes. If you want to destroy the entire operation of illicit experiments, you must kill the remaining three empiricals. One being Zear himself. What better way for a scientist to experiment, lest he become the experiment.

He's even working out a way to control the others by a brain wave satellite inserted through the rod. This could destroy the world, Braylen. Controlled soldiers by the thoughts of your mind.

You have eight days, but I don't think your going to make it."

"Ava, run," Braylen said. "Take the keys and flee."

"Very wise, Braylen," Eric stated. "But, very late. I had pressed the distraught button underneath the bar, when

I fixed my drink earlier. You got about eight seconds before they arrive!"

"Ava. Go now!"

"I won't leave without you," she replied.

"Think about me as you venture into exile. For I'll be back for you."

She ran to escape the approaching storm of vigilante. Braylen was apprehended and incarcerated to the local jail.

That night he lay awake in thought. *Eight more days to live. One more week to love. How could I hold her once more as I am imprisoned*?

Ava cried most of the night. *How could I live without love? How could I survive without his embracing arms? In eight days my life will end as well, without the love I once upheld.*

Chapter 9 *For Jessica*

The jail was musky and reeked of urine. The padded mattress was two and a half inches in width and six feet in length. It was snagged and dusted. The cell was a third of cement blocked walls which met from the bar ends of the cold steel. Quiet was the environment. Braylen lie awake with his hands resting behind his head.

The sounds of a muffled voice became pitched as desperation grew tense. The man's mouth was covered which exposed the echo, but under closed the full scream. Braylen lay and witnessed the frightful stress of the cell beside him. He folded the pillow over his head covering both ears. The attempt to stifle the horror next door was not successful.

Braylen rolled onto his side to ignore the man. His head began to jab with a sphere of hurt. He wrestled with consequence. He sat up onto the edge of the metal wall framed bed and faced the neighboring confinement.

Two men from the block over, were forcibly binding a much smaller inmate to the concrete floor. One of the perpetrators laid across the victim and locked both elbows behind his back. The next delivered flush punches across his face evenly. The man was helpless and vulnerable as to accede their abashment.

The man squealed loudly from the inhumane torture. Tears flooded his eyes as both dignity and aggravating pain rendered him rampant inside. Braylen stood and paced the cell back and forth to clear the moments of hope that the wretched terror would soon end. The man continued to breath quickly for splotched relief of pain.

"Please. Help me!" the man cried. Braylen stopped. The guards were not visible for the call of duty. Braylen turned to face the clear side of the cage next to him. The two men that conquered such fiend destruction upon one's life smiled and laughed as though this were a game.

The man's face reddened from anger, while the inmate roughly beat him. Braylen walked to the end of the bars openings and stooped down to one knee. He threw his arm in reach of the space and latched onto the man's shoe that continued to bind him. He pulled the man causing him to slide. His leg now wedging the bars, barricading the sides of his knee. Braylen twisted the man's leg and beamed his knee cap to touch the raw iron.

Braylen pulled his leg opposite of the flexing muscle. The shin bone snapped and punctured through the flesh as the knee cap separated. The man fainted immediately.

Two officers ran to aid from such harsh commotions. They saw the disfigured man abroad the bared wall and unlocked Braylen's cell door. The officer opened the steel entrance as the other held the tazer with a projected beam of the infer laser pointed at him.

"Come on out of there son," the guard said. Braylen marched toward them without fear nor reason to abnegate. The officer fired the tazer causing the two, one inch darts to break through his skin. The metal points were connected by a live wire that was fed by the voltage of the stun handle.

The officer pressed the trigger engaging the electric shock through Braylen's body. The charge phased him not, for the needle in his head surged the power sending the stun device to the ground. The guards stepped back slightly in disbelief of the situation. He struck the officers with skill leaving them blacked out.

Braylen took the keys from the guard's belt and unlocked the cell beside him. The victim ran out. The offender backed himself to the wall, corner of the bed. "Hey man. Don't hurt me. I beg of you!" the man pleaded.

Braylen handed the keys over to the victim and pulled the cell door closed. He turned to the man and walked toward him. He secured his palm tightly around the man's neck and lifted him to his feet in like manner. Braylen looked at him and asked, "If someone twisted your arm to do something, you'd probably do it. However, if someone twisted your brain to respond in the same way, would you do it?"

"Don't hurt me! Please!"

"Wrong answer!" Braylen backed him into the open door of the cell. He pressed and held the man vertical to the bars and extended his arm out into the doorway. "Avenge yourself," he said unto the victim. "Let your physical pain abet your mind. Commit this man to the pedestal of justice."

The man bit his lip and began to slam the heavy steel structure against the man's arm. After the happening, Braylen walked back to his cell. A gang of guards ran to the scene. The man's elbow was completely shattered. His forearm was clean broken in three sections of the bone. His thumb ripped from the ligament.

Braylen was tossed into a cave-like confinement space known as, the darkness. A space reserved for the outcome of corporal punishment. There, he spent the next five days sunk inside of a five by three foot grave.

(Thursday 27th)

Braylen was let out of the dirt hole. His muscles were cramped and walking became difficult. His posture was slumped. His beard was stubbled. They led him to the rec yard of the court.

Braylen sat dazed and lifeless. Another inmate made his way to the bench and flopped down beside him. The man was old with long gray hair and a matching beard. "Want to hear something odd?" the elderly man asked. "This is a prison. Even though the local inmates from the county come here for holding until trial. They do have a population of prisoners that are isolated from us. They all are located on the other side of the building.

Lots of them are not from the county. They are tried and convicted criminals. Some are here for life. What are you in for? I'm here for a short while, until my trial. Know what happened to me? I got hungry." Braylen turned to set stare upon him. "That's right. I had no money. So, I got caught stealing a box of cereal from the supermarket. Damn. It was some generic off brand on top of that. So. What are you here for?"

"Mental problems, I guess."

"Kill someone?"

"Yeah, but that's not why I'm here to begin with." Over the next few minutes, Braylen, conveyed his amazing story over to the inmate.

"Wow, Braymen. That's an incredible story."

"Braylen. Not Braymen."

"You know, if I had such fighting skills and the ability to obtain the adrenaline strength as you could on demand by thought, I sure would not be here sitting around."

"It doesn't matter I'll be expired soon."

"Well, there you go, Braymen. If I were you, given a handful of days to carry out life, I would make damn sure it didn't end here. Especially, if your fair madden is out there wishing on hopeless stars for you to rescue her from the grief of departure.

I mean look at me Braymen. I'm fifty-seven years old and in jail. Over my first offense at that. I will get off with probation, but if I knew my wife was alive and waiting for me at home, I'd be busting out of this joint.

Oh, beautiful sweet Jessica. Only in the act of love would I have given the beat of my life to have saved hers. Only Jessica mattered to me. Only time was short. If I had a restart of life, I would relive each moment. Each moment with my love."

Every part of Braylen numbed from the tasteless fear. Fear of dying without love to be supplied to Ava. He stood and asked, "Where is Jessica at?"

"Her place of interment is at the Tin Wood grave yard."

"Here's your chance."

"My chance?"

"This is your chance to free this place and do a noble upright deed, in the name of love. For Jessica."

"But, she is passed away. There is no more that is noble to me."

"Her remembrance is forever, but your time in life is now, the present."

"What do you suggest we do?"

"Look for a gate to open. Then run. Do it for Jessica."

"You're right Braymen. I could die tomorrow and not have respected her tombstone by recent visitations."

"For you I thank, for the will of hope to live. And for Jessica, the hope to find my lover's hand once more. By the way, what's your name?"

"Barry."

"Larry. It has been nice meeting you."

"No, it's Barry."

"Larry. Stay low as your escape draws the guards high."

"Where are you going?"

"To get my life back."

Braylen made his way to the end of the fence, where three detention officers stood telling jokes. "Look at this motherfucker," one said.

"Yeah. The invisible electric hero," the other stated. "I tell you, if I pulled the trigger it wouldn't have been from some tazer." The man flashed his shotgun and said, "You wouldn't be able to pull a shell from your chest."

Braylen twirled the barrel in hand and pulled it to his grasp. He held it toward the guards abreast. They smiled and threw their cigarettes to the dirt. There are no shells in that empty gun," the officer said.

Braylen cracked a smudging smile and said, "I know." He pulled the stalk in catching the end of the sighted barrel. He quickly turned about and smashed the face of the middle officer. Braylen, then knocked the first out with a hard side punch. He positioned the gun from behind the first officer's neck, clinching his throat. He neared his ear. "For every fowl thing you commit in expression, there is one good thing in your favor. That is that you are not on the end of this barrel."

He broke the chamber connector and cocked the gun into an angle. The inner bend touched the lining of his neck. He straightened the gun to lock the safety clasp in place. He pulled it forward striking the guard's forehead. The officers lay about the ground.

Braylen slid his fingers inside of the chained links of the fence. *The strength of ten men*, he remembered

Eric say. He pulled with power. The metal hooks began to pop loose from the stationed pole. Barry ran to him and seized a portion of the fence and lead his weight back. The metal gave way and became an escape route.

"For Jessica?" Barry asked.

"For love." Braylen replied.

Braylen entered the local mall and then to the store where Ava works. He walked up to the counter and asked to see her. "She took an emergency vacation," the lady said. "However, she left this for you. Are you Braylen?"

"Yes."

She gave him the note that read, "Look to the right." He left the entrance area and stood into the hall of the strip. He glanced to the right. He turned his attention to the left of the hall and then back to the right. Dismayed to his senses he became, as he saw Ava sitting on the fountain bench.

She uncovered her face from the back of the open book and gave a discreet look. She shifted her bag and began to walk. Her hair was blonde as bleach and her piercings were removed. Her skirt was lavender and low cut. The blouse she wore was business casual and formally attired in a white buttoned down top. The nail polish she wore was red and loud which enhanced the glow of her skin tone. The lined straps of her heels creased the bend of her foot complimenting the curves.

Braylen followed from a safe distance and then into the ladies room. He entered and cleared the stalls from passing to check the room over. He saw no one.

Ava threw herself to him and kissed him as though the end of time. She glided her fingers over his new appearance of facial hair. "I knew you would come back for me. I changed my look for safety precautions. Just please tell me you still find me attractive?"

"Ava. Everyday that we near, is the day that I never wanted you more." They repeated the style of love with their lips. Braylen suddenly pulled from her. His eyes enlarged.

"What is it, Braylen? What's wrong?"

"Ava, this squelching pain is more excruciating than before. The rage of their control is approaching. Their in the mall tracking me. I can feel it." Braylen hit the small porcelain wall tiles with a closed fist to display a forced deliberate instability.

"But, you heard Eric. Love blocked the tracking."

"This height of nerve disintegration is the death of me Ava!" The pain caused him to shatter the mirror by hand. "I'm the only one they hold to vitiate. Run Ava!"

Five black suited men paced the halls of the shopping center with a metal device that was built for advanced tracking. Hand held, but similar to a high powered metal detector. They turned the power knob to it's full search and closed in on Braylen's location.

"This signal in my brain has caused an aberrant vertex of rage to take out my enemies of this mission." He grabbed her shoulder and shoved her against the stall reinforcement wall. "Ava. I cannot hold back this mechanical rod that projects my emotions with this unwanted anger. Please, run away from me. I can't yield my mind to let go of this electronic command to destroy life before me. Remove your shirt from your body and flee, as for my latch onto you is not removable."

The trackers walked forward as Braylen's trail fell with them. Braylen pulled her close and then pushed her to the wall again. "Ava, go now!"

"No. Kiss me!"

"Ava. This rancorous control is the pressure of my mind to fill the end of you through the loss of my mind, for their benefit." She leaned in to kiss him. He jerked away and wrapped his hand over her neck.

"Your finesse of love is the making of happiness. Kill me if you must, but make love to me one more time." he looked toward the floor to distract his mind. "Make not your heart an abater for human life, but keep love for you own life."

He removed his hand from the threatening hold. He threw his passion of kiss to her and said, "I'm sorry."

"Don't speak."

He ran his hand through the back of her hair. He glided her palms to the stretch of the top of the stall's horizon. He lifted her legs to engulf his mid section. She hung for weight.

"We lost him, sir," the tracker mentioned.

"What!"

"The radar shows no active needle in form, sir."

"He must have left. Search all areas of the parking lot immediately. If we can't find him, we'll send the empiricals."

"I missed you," Ava said. He slid her skirt to grip tight to her waist and exposed himself for the primal agreement of their body's turmoil to connect. "Tell me how you missed me." He buried deep into her creating a cramp to overcome her body with climaxing pleasure.

"For never to depart would be the satisfaction of my worry."

She clamped down onto his neck and held her appetite for hardcore stimulation between her teeth. "Elude not the aggressive wounds that you have expressed unto me", she said. "Use your exigency of physicality against me. Only the exception though you love me is to fill my lust for you to savage me."

He propelled into her and rammed her hands lightly to the wall. "Submit unto my violation of strength to turn you feeble. For exquisite sentiment lies underneath my skin, but to turn love into a blend with the splendor of a ravish desire is for my virile duty to apply to your fantasy. Only the exception though you love me is to quench your need to feel dominated, be that of love."

Chapter 10 *Mea Culpa*

That night Braylen lay on the medical bed. He infused reality with suppressed sleep into the state of dream. He sat in a hard wooden chair blindfolded with an even black cloth wrapped around his eyes. His hands confined and tied to the flat of the armrest. His ankles bound with ropes to the pegs of the seat. The restraints matched those that rounded his neck and looped securely to the headboard of the chair.

"You let me down," he heard, as the voice cornered the room. He lifted his head toward the direction of the sound.

"Alex? Alex. Is that you? Free me quickly, Alex! I need your help."

"Just as I needed you to help me."

"What do you mean?"

"I told you to flee, but you stood to fight. You could have ran with me and kept me a shield from the swordsman."

"Who are you, Alex?"

"Don't you know?"

"You're just a representation of my memory."

"That I am, but I was real once. I am the reason you're here alive. Not that you could return the same comment.

You unbalanced the trackers from the heightened dream that you were having that night before the incident. No other empirical had dreamed before. It was a happy time in your former life. The dream involved me as well. Their search devices were scrambled and interrupted as you dwell on the mirage of your sleep. Somehow, this dream memory was the only that survived the needle. The dream you had was of me Daddy."

"Alex. You're just an invention inside of my head."

"No. I'm your son."

"Help me Alex, to recall the dream."

"No. I will not."

"Alex. If you're my son, then help your father to remember." Alex walked behind him and removed the cloth that blocked his sight. He kept himself hid, while he stood.

"I am the only memory that endures tucked away in your mind. Your dream was simple, but complete. That night you dreamed of a past day of sun that fed the earth with the hot season. The verdant field of grass that laid like carpet was fresh and dark. The sky was cloudless. The vamp of the bees unto the flowers was the nature of seduction.

We sat about the veranda as to shelter from the heat. You, mom and myself. All was great with no exceptions.

Perfect and grand was the time spent. Every moment cherished as it would be splendid gratification of companionship. This was your dream."

"I fail to recollect the times."

"The end of the day became the wane of a perfect cluster of life together. This was your dream. However, the ungenial followup to that was the end of this perfect world.

You kissed mom for the well sake of the night. I stayed awake against the will of my bedtime and played video games. I cut the television off and looked on from the window of my room. A group of men, four to be exact, left the car's interior and spread out about the house."

Braylen awoke and found himself to be the only occupant of the bed as he continued to dream. "Clary?" He looked about the bedroom. He left the room and walked into the hallway of the upstairs wraparound balcony. "Clary?" he called from the top. He placed his hands onto the cherry wood sculptured safety railing.

Braylen blinked his eyes with a distorted surprise to what he saw. Clary's head rested onto the shoulders of another man downstairs. They sat on the couch. She appeared cuddled against him with her face. The man wore a black leather jacket. His hair was full and slicked back and appeared wet. Braylen rushed the steps and stood into the floor.

"Clary!" The man lit his cigar while embracing her with his arm. "What are you doing, Clary? And who the fuck are you?"

The man looked forward and said, "This is a shame to do somebody like this. It's not by my choice though.

Randall Ford Jr.

You see, our experiments are normal people as yourself. In your case, a family man. We do look for healthy, in shape people like you. Too bad you had a family though.

The army takes everyday simple men and tear them down. They rebuild their lives to better suit the government. We find good prospects and capture them against their will to rebuild them our way. Kind of similar except there is no sign up, draft, or monthly benefits to be claimed here. So. Wether you are married, single, black or white, we need live experiments. It's our job to go and get them."

The man turned his head to face Braylen. "We also need for your first stage to be in mind shock." He pulled Clary by the hair. Braylen died with heartbreak. Blood oozed from the round wound that dug into her forehead. The man stood and held the silencer barrel to his face. Two other men crept up from the other room and held sights of firearms as well. "Now. Listen to me carefully, tough guy. Tell me where the boy is. Now!"

"What boy?" Braylen attempted to disguise his knowledge of his son's whereabouts.

One man butted his temple. The other punched his chest with the gun's stalk. "Tell me where he is hiding. I won't harm him. I just have to be sure that there are no witnesses to this crime. But, if you fail to comply, I will kill him in like manner as your wife. Choice is yours."

"Like I can trust you."

"Fine. We'll burn the house down with him stashed away somewhere inside, or you confess to me his location for a mere questioning. Either way it is up to you."

DEAD CENTER

"What will happen to him after your interrogation process?"

"Simple. We drop him off at grandma's house."

"Alex. Come out." Alex cracked the pantry door by the den and then opened it fully. He ran to Braylen's side and hugged him. "These men have something to ask you about mommy and then you're going to stay with grandma and grandpa for awhile." One of the men grabbed Alex and the other two secured Braylen's arms. "You lied to me!"

The first man drove a needle of sedation into Braylen's abdomen and said, "Don't worry. In a day or so after the surgery you will not remember any of this."

"Let him go!" The men drug Alex off.

"And that's the story." Alex stated.

"Alex. What happened to you?"

"I do not know this. For once I was real. Now, I am only a memory to you. That, I have no way of knowing for you do not know. All I do know is that this is all your fault."

"Alex, I'm sorry. For my intentions were not to have you caught up in their angry path's."

"Mea Culpa. Do you know what that means dad? It's Latin for, *I am to blame*. You and mommy used this phrase when I was around for secretly conversing of financial problems or having slight argument mishaps. This was done to keep worry from entering my life. Keeping me clear from any such existing thing. You are to blame for that night, dad! It's your fault that they got me."

Randall Ford Jr.

"Alex. Cut these ropes that bind my hands so that I can hug you once again."

"I'd rather die than for you to show love through embrace."

"Alex. Please, understand. They were going to burn the house down with you inside, regardless. I sought attempt to free you."

"Very well, dad. Since you tried to help me I must tell you something that you need to know before you die. Eric told you that in thirty days your expiration of life would commit. However, I wonder just how long you were inside of the dumpster before you awoke?

Was it one day or two? Maybe it was only a couple of hours. You did wake very hungry that night. How many days do you actually have left on count? Is it minus what you thought was set? Maybe this is why your laying here on the medical bed."

Braylen awoke sharply. He sat up and looked about. The doctor entered the room. Braylen pressed him roughly to the wall and asked, "Where is Ava?"

"She's in the waiting room."

Braylen tossed him over the bed and onto the floor. He then tilted it's frame over the doctor. He pulled him from the bed by his foot and used his back for a shield. He crashed him through the heavy medical equipment. Braylen took a long syringe and held it to his head. "Where is my son?"

"Sir. You came with a lady only. No others accompanied you."

"Who do you work for?"

"The state, sir."

Braylen dropped the needle, unclinched his fist and ran from the room. He stepped into the emergency waiting area and took Ava by the hand. He pulled her from her seat and they ran from the hospital. They entered the car in a get away styled heist. "What happened?" Braylen asked.

"You blacked out and wouldn't wake up. I was scared and didn't know what else to do, other than bring you here."

"No matter what, Ava. Don't bring the State into our flee. They will search computers and locate us through hospital admittance records and then track us. If I die right now, leave my body where I lay. Don't risk your safety over to danger. Besides, I think my date of course is shorter than I had expected. Instead of four days, I could go at any time." She leaned into him. He secured his arm around her for closeness.

"Ava. It's not safe for you to be in my company at this point."

"Nonsense."

"I cannot divulge you to the venomous predators that evoke from nowhere."

"To lose you, I must not. Proscribed we are, as now to verve the ace of malignant profusion. Together we need to be, instead of apart, my heart cannot take. For to became my world seared would be your crime of charge."

"Ava, if I be the cause of any harm that comes to you, my valor to conquer this vile plot would be in vain."

"Please. Do not cut the barren love that connects you to me. It is best to fall together from the menicity of the grave than for loneliness apart to perish my volition to survive. Distraught I'd be under a vast nadir of pain. Only for you is my reasons to run with life, as the hope of tomorrow."

"If we are to end this, we need to foul proof our plan of attack. You're all I need, Ava. You're all I have. All the courage that gives me the means to fight the war at this time is the tides of love that fills the voids. I will not lose you unto their hands. Even as my mind disintegrates and leaves me in a full blank state. I long to dream of you and live with your love in my mind."

Braylen drove to a nearby hotel and ordered a room for the night. They walked to the door. He held the silver key between his fingers and wiped the beads of sweat from his forehead with the back of his hand. "Are you okay?" Ava asked.

"Yeah. I'm fine. I just feel sort of tired."

"As soon as you unlock the door, you should rest."

"You're right, Ava. Just for an hour or so."

He starred at the key in a stupor. "Braylen, let me help you" She took the key from his hand and slid it through the slot of the knob.

"I'm losing my mind aren't I ?"

"You're just weak from the run of your life."

"I cannot bond the proper thoughts of unlocking a door with a key. What's next? Will I not remember how to tie my own shoes?"

"Braylen. Rest for now." She laid him onto the bed.

Chapter 11 *Perder Mi Mente*

Mr. Barret walked into the large office. He stood with his hands folded in front of him. Mr. Zear turned to look at him. "You failed me once more."

"Mr. Zear. I can explain."

"Oh. You can fathom the reason why empirical number twenty-five was able to dream?" Mr. Barret tightened his lips together and looked to the tile of the floor. "Nevertheless, Mr. Barret, the reason you're here is to tell me how Mr. Adger escaped our authority control. How did this one man override our technical devices? Tell me, Mr. Barret. How could you have not prevented this mishap occurrence?"

"Sir. Please. This is a very delicate and thoughtful practice."

"You were the best and most skillful therapist that I have ever had the privileged of adopting into my organization."

"What do you mean by were? Am I fired?"

Randall Ford Jr.

"Fired as a therapist, yes. Fired as property of Zear and Ginn, no."

"This is a joke. Right?"

"Sit down Mr. Barret."

"I prefer to stand."

Two large men closed in on him from the side of the office. "Be seated or be hurt." Mr. Barret took heed, for the overpowering figures of his protection drew a menacing creation of fear that surrounded him. He sat into the brown leather chair and became a swell of intimidation. The two men shackled his wrist to either arm rest of the chair with belt-like retainers. His feet were also restricted.

"Mr. Barret. Six moths ago I became wealthy with millions by my side. In exchange of course for my extraordinary offer of protection of safe guarding one's life. I pondered for days and days of how I could provide a human weapon that could be controlled by the use of a remote satellite. Of course, the first experiment failed, as I was dumb to the idea."

Mr. Zear, pulled a three inch pocket knife and protracted it's blade. Mr. Barret eyed the stainless edge. Mr. Zear held it to the side of his leg.

"Many times I failed. The olden days were as the art of empiricalism. Everyone here publically knows that there are four empiricals left. The two that live here on the ninth floor, Braylen and myself. Secretly no one else is aware that I obtain one other experiment. One whom I've kept in hiding from Mr. Ginn himself. I did the surgery on this one person whom no one but me knows about."

"Who?"

DEAD CENTER

"You wouldn't remember if I told you."

"I don't understand, sir."

Mr. Zear neared him and gripped the handle of the bladed instrument firmly. "What I mean, Mr. Barret, is that I have one in storage, but for me to reveal to you who he is would be a waste of time for both of us. Especially when I'm about to delete your memory."

Mr. Barret began to chuckle. "Come on, Mr. Zear. Let me go. This practical joking is over."

"Do you think I am funny, Mr barret? Is this a set up to make you laugh aloud?" Mr. Zear blunted the sharp end of the knife to the top of Barret's skull. The strike broke the skin and caused a throb of nerves to lower in a flare of discomfort.

"Damn it! Have you lost your mind!"

"As a matter of fact, I have and so will you."

"Please, Mr. Zear. I have a wife of twelve years. Please. Don't transfer me into a mechanical fiend."

"Mr. Barret. We like for our prospect's first stage of shock to be aligned before they undergo the needle. You're not married anymore." He reached into his shirt pocket. He threw the finger of Barret's wife which was still connected with the silver wedding band into his lap.

"No!"

The two men held his neck steady. Mr. Zear sat behind him. "Not to worry, Mr. Barret. You will not remember this."

Braylen lie in a daze. The strife of death against the will of life, became the pull of mindful stress. "Ava. Remember what I told you. If I die, run and don't expose yourself to their reach. Leave my body for decay and shed not any information to the authorities."

Ava patted his forehead from the sweat as to relieve the heat of fever. She cried as he slipped into an insensible conscious sleep. She anticipated the worse and held his hand with hers.

Braylen lay in dream. His environment became a black covering that veiled his own world. The air was light and blindness was the only color of shade.

"Look at you," he heard Alex say. "You Failed me. Now, you're failing the person who loves you more than life. You might as well turn yourself in to Zear and let them claim defeat with their personal victory. I cannot uphold the thoughts of you ever being my father."

"Alex. This misfortune I cannot control. Please, spare me the lack of love that excuses your reason for being."

"Why did you say that?"

"Why shouldn't I?"

"You lie there as though helpless and confined. I understand that we as a family, were caught up in the middle of this terrible bloodshed, but fail to see the reasoning that you have acknowledged to carry through this way."

"Alex, son, my body is becoming calloused and frigid. My mind is losing touch with reality. These things are not my fault."

"Son? The role of father now encourages you to scream for my forgiveness. I need you dad, to protect me and safe my way. Then, you literally handed me over to the blackguards of destruction departing you from me. Separating your heart from mine. Now I am only to be of memory to you.

You see, my father was a strong willed man, dedicated to the love of his family. Always doing the right thing. I must tell you that I said these things to you in hopes that your mind would be stiffened with chivalry, for to break through to fearlessness. I am only a memory, but I love you, father."

Ava felt the pulse of Braylen's hand lessen and become pliable. His touch was now cold. She pulled a letter from her purse and unfolded it. "Braylen. I don't know if you're able to hear me, but I need to share something with you. I was enchanted by the poem that you wrote for me. The mood, the emotions and the thrill of the words that I declare mine. I wrote you a poem as well to express my love." She looked over the paper. Her eyes blurred.

> "Forever engaged, I will be as not to have a marriage completed by vows. The loss of you would suspend my love and carry me not over the seas of the ocean. My facade of murk obscurity did not raze your feelings of me, but instead created a fastidious evince of affection towards me. Unlike those before, you quickly tore down the impervious ramparts that bricked my heart as a cage of holding, as to be freed. As such you claim that my name is defined as "bird" with Latin initiative of "rara avis," which means rare bird. Free from the metal skeleton that entraps, but never apart from your grips.

The versification of words that you drew with pen engraved the very sculpture of my heart. My nerves raged as to become salacious with you. I donated the very proof that held me for safe keeping. The purity rendered over to my lover with chances of uniting the very courtship with a sealed harmony. For such elegance of physical touches was a mix of confusion and content emotions. Brash you were, timorous I felt as to be touched for the first of times. The natural embrace of your arms placed me to the zenith of comfort.

From the first of your showing to my eyes there was no ambivalence to be found amongst my feelings. My heart in love and my feelings dispensed from the overwhelming exhibit of love from your face to look at mine. Never the same will I be if not to be the Queen of the one who treats me with such admirable honor. The clearest skies are seen through the eyes of those in love.

At the thought of you, my skin swelters from a burning incandescence. Low flames that blaze with resilient pleasure. My longing to be with you is as a contagion that soon turns into a plague.

How dare you steal the very thing that I kept for I? The blood from my life, you took to make your own. Now, I rely on you, for I cannot live without you. Overrun I was to be, overtaken I became, when I first met you.

Even as I fought to uncover any improper factor of you, I could not. I nearly hoped to find

DEAD CENTER

some fight against my emotions that would have provoked us as an union. For this was only due to the reasons that now I need you for all that love provides. I cannot function the way's of another life knowing of the one that I have now with you.

Only the present is where we live, but the future is to become us. Wishing is buried along with fantasy as my truest of love has granted me the dream to be freed. Real and undying is the fantasy. Unchanging and breath taken is my reality.

Your life has now become a match to mine. To breathe your air through kiss. To touch your body to mine from hugs. To holding your fingers over mine. Pressing our lips together. Thinking your thoughts. Reading you eyes.

For to breathe easy is to be fake, but to die inside without anyone noticing becomes them the hypocrites of sensuality. Only you could see through me and only you I love."

She folded the note and placed it onto his shoulder. She added to the poem spontaneously while looking at his face.

"Now the conditions of time worry me. For I have been scorched by your love. Addicted to the poison from which you have supplied, killed all lonely times in my times in my life.

My world was once a clandestine state, but now I am of flagrant esteem. For your love has brightened me and the weeks spent have delighted my well-being at the thought of you."

"Use the last of your resources and energy to gather strength," Alex said, as Braylen continued in darkness. "For me dad, do this. For the times we failed, but now is your chance to conquer over all misconception of the past with the plausible juncture of the present. Wake up and remember that the only life I remember, is with you as the only force of memory you have is of me"

Braylen opened his eyes. He raised up and grabbed Ava by both arms. Surprised, but glad she smiled. He pulled her in close and kissed her. "I thought I lost you."

"I don't have much time, but I still have a lot of heart left for you."

Chapter 12 *Mens Sano In Corpore Sano*

Ava wiped the cold beads from Braylen's forehead. "I have a plan," he said. "As I recall there is a masquerade party on the twenty-third, which is today. It is being held at the Zear and Ginn building. Parking is on the seventh floor. Therefore, the crowd will migrate to the eighth floor conference wing for convenience."

"What are you suggesting? That we walk in there unannounced without invitation."

He swayed the blanket over his legs and asked, "What are you going as?"

She briefly jotted her eyes to the ceiling and removed the blonde wig. "How about a pissed off gothic chick with a tired attitude?"

He stood. "With this jumpsuit, we'll be quite the pair. A hot goth and a wanted convict."

"My how the outside world perceives us, but worse the way their heart deceives them. For if my heart not be in a good spot, I would have neglected love. So many see the outside only. However, often those who think that way are the ones that suffocates opportunity to know a friend. Only to give the shirt from my back to the one in need of it is to bring satisfying happiness to my vesture. Unlike the silk of tie and polyester slacks that turn their noses from the less fortunate."

They arrived at the rear of the building at nightfall, three hours before the beginning of he morning. Braylen swiped the card over the computer lock of the door. It buzzed and read the entrance for the I.d. holder. "They're expecting us. Stay close to me, Ava. Be a trap to fool myself this may be, but the chance to take will cause them to be at risk."

They entered the elevator and began to ascend. "Where are we to meet our journey?"

"To the tenth floor. There we should find Mr. Zear, then will we be able to find Ginn to do the surgery on my head. Time is of the shortest hand. Give me your cell phone."

She took the silver gadget from her pocket and handed it over to him. The elevator stopped on the third floor. The sudden halt of the unit bounced from the impact. The stainless fashioned doors parted. An employee entered. He was arrayed in costume attire similar to a knight in full armor.

Braylen dialed the reception lobby and placed his head a slight from the vision of the stranger. He asked the exact location of the party and then flipped the phone to close. He began to overhand the phone to her. The knight retracted a law enforcement issued baton

DEAD CENTER

off to his side. He then jousted the center of the phone. He held it to the paneling of the wall.

Ava ducked with keen reflex. Braylen turned his head quickly for confrontation. With perfect rage from threat, Braylen's will to protect her was that of a lion and it's siblings.

Braylen reached over his shoulder and clamped the striking end of the bar. He engaged his inner elbow to wrap the handle of the stick. He twirled the steel rod from his hand and spun it until it caught the man's knee. The outer shell of his uniform kept him safe from the fracturing blows.

Braylen swatted the nightstick repeatedly with the hands of adrenaline. He landed the full length of the weapon into the chest plates of the proofed metal. He slung the baton to the floor and began to dent the suit with hard fist.

Braylen backed him into the corner of the elevator against the plastic railing. The face helmet fell off from the jarring hits to the head exposing his bare face. Braylen gave swift punches to his cheeks and bent down to secure the metal knee caps. He pulled them causing the man to gravitate into a sitting position.

He braced his neck with the inlay of his foot. Braylen looked toward Ava which stood to hold the elevator door open. She shook her head as to change his set of destructive death toward his opponent. The man laid unaware and temporarily knocked out.

They rushed from the doors and into the lobby hall of the floor. Braylen slightly edged her back to the wall in a flat manner with his arm to become invisible from the balls that held security cameras inside of the tinted revolving glass.

"What's wrong, Braylen?"

"There are cameras hidden inside of those rotating shield. Take this." He gave her the baton. "Smash every one that you come in contact with. Stay to the wall. Do not be voyered. Attack the cameras at an angle. From this floor down, do this method. All of the halls should be clear. When you reach the front entrance head for the car and wait for me." He pulled her into his face and sealed her departure with a kiss.

Braylen charged the industrial styled stairwells until he reached the seventh floor lot area. He jogged the line of parked cars in search of the most dense vehicle. He spied three males securing a large dooley truck. They made their way to the side door that led into the floor party.

"Hey!" Braylen yelled from the distance of where they left their vehicle.

"What do you want?"

"I need to borrow your truck here."

They began to explode into laughter and one said, "I don't think so!"

Braylen ripped the side extension mirror from the connecting aluminum plate. The crinkle of screeching tears ceased the men and called for their attention. "Hey fool!" the man yelled.

They ran for him for to match their punishment of him for the compared damage to the truck. Braylen ducked from the attempted tackle from the first and rammed himself to the man behind him landing on top of his body. He caught the opposing arm of the third victim and twisted it from socket. The lead of the group retreated with a flare of fear and threw the keys to the pavement.

Braylen started the truck and reversed it from the far end of the car lot. He revved the motor in full throttle, dropping the shifter lever into gear. The heavy tires squealed and burned with smoke. After reaching peak velocity, he jumped from the cab.

Several employees were commuting about the ballroom. A loud rumble breached the air. Suddenly the truck crushed the wall of the gathering. The people dodged the screaming vehicle's path, all unscathed. The truck crumbled the large office window and shot into the air upon its exit of the seventh floor of the complex.

Mike fled the camera surveillance area. He ran to Mr. Zear's personal office. He entered the room and said, "Their here, Mr. Zear! The lady was recorded destroying the third floor cameras, sir."

Mr. Zear closed his eyes to concentrate. He remotely activated the empiricals through the satellite wave of his brain. The two empiricals stood in their rooms from the controlled sensor. They walked into the ninth floor hall and stood as soldiers in fight and wait.

Ava rounded the corner of the hall, only to be surrounded by a group of men dressed in black business suits.

Braylen burst through the stairway door and stood enemy of the two empiricals. In order to reach Zear, his mission would be to face the two men. They stretched their arms and loosened any stress before the fight.

Braylen walked in a semi-circle abroad to size them for battle. "Where are your hearts?" Braylen asked, for to spark some conscience within them. "What right of life laws, allow you to free your brutal instincts upon this world?

For the end of the line to behead anger, is soon to be the front. To change comes from within. Who do think you are? Who do you realize you once were? Do you wonder of the type of human that you used to be?

Love blocked the control of abuse of my mind. Is there no love to familiarize yourselves with? The hour of the daylight you know not. Nor the past of minutes that lead to the introduction of a new dawn. Only you can set the limits of your mind. No one can make you think their way by this manual force."

The men kept silent with no convert body language. They rushed Braylen to gain power to out number. His back met the sheet rock of the wall from their tackle sending debris of crushed chalk to the tile.

Ava was restrained by one of the employees that guarded around her. The head man walked from pace of left to right. "Please, Ava, don't make me hurt your flesh upon which my anger is rare at this point. But, by my impatience will I mark your face with the bruises of my temper." He stretched his fingers apart and pulled the leather glove tight against his wrist. He clasped his hand to vice his palm underneath her chin. He positioned his face, eye level to hers. "Where is the guinea pig, whom you refer to as Braylen?"

DEAD CENTER

The empiricals whelped the core of Braylen's skull sending spots of black throughout the center of his vision. The flighty nausea unbalanced his legs and crumbled his body to rest flat onto the floor. They stomped at his chest and kicked his head. Blood began to draw from his nose while veins burst around the pupils.

Ava fell to her knees after being struck by the man. Her arms extended behind her in continuation of being held. He grabbed a great deal of her hair and shifted her face to be visible from his hovered stance. A small trickle of deep colored blood ran from her lip and touched her neck. "So. The dead can bleed," he commented.

"Fuck you!" she replied. The blood between her lips splashed his waist from the force of speech.

"One last time. Where is Braylen?" She looked down and breathed with a fast rhythm. He ordered her to her feet by the commanding nod of his head. The man lifted her roughly and then jolted her with a severe blow across the temple.

Braylen's eyes enlightened from the fierce driven spike. A sense of dishonor was inflicted upon his love. The killing of men upon guillotines was the bitter taste in his mouth, as to feel next in line for a beheading. Endless were his fingertips. His heart was that of the tiger before the chase of it's prey.

He pushed his shoulder up by the will of his might and staggered to his knees. He ran and threw himself into the fatal punch, disfiguring the right side of the empirical's face, shattering the bone structure. He caught the next around the head, locking his arm around his neck. They fell to the ground. Braylen pressed the last of life from him.

Braylen ran the floor halls beneath, in search for Ava. The pound of his head worsened from her approaching presence. He turned the wall by where she laid. The men were instantly slammed to the opposite wall from the impact of Braylen's charge. He delivered single critical hits to them leaving each man to lie about the floor unconscious.

Braylen gently picked her from the cold ceramic floor and laid her onto the lobby's sofa. "Ava, wake up," he whispered. He fastened his palms to either side of her face. Her eyes opened slowly with alertness. "Your tears are those days spent from time before the present when I had not you."

Her smile cracked in slight. "How I choose those days to remain in a far away past. Smile once for *happy* is not a choice, but a freedom."

"I never meant for your well-being to fade out from my error. For I be the very cause of your aches of the moment."

"The physical pain will lessen and soon give out. Only for you to be taken from me, that, I would die from. Which we not forget that our work is not done here. Time is wild and actions are sane." She used his arm as a crutch to level her weight.

Destined to reach the top floor casing they took the stairs to avoid trouble. Braylen latched onto the railing handle and shook his head. His state was weakened heavily. "Stay with me Braylen. We're almost there and soon this will be over." They continued to flee with their steps losing behind them.

They entered the door to Mr. Zear's office. He stood in wait for their arrival. He faced away from them by staring from the large window structure. "At last. The flow of the present dilemma has came to a halt." Zear stated. "I can feel the body heat of your anger from where I stand."

"I will kill you for this!" Braylen yelled.

"No, you won't. You couldn't. For I hold the key and lock of your entangled mind." He turned around and aimed the handgun at Ava. "The lock or the key that turns your heart. Which shall it be?"

"Are you that..."

"Scared, that I need the use of this weapon? Let Ava go and I'll do as you wish. You see, Braylen. I can already read your thoughts. Betrayal and hatred for me is the urge to charge me through this glass. This is what engulfs your brain's circuit. Am I right, Braylen?"

"You and I are the last of the empiricals according to Eric. So, what are your plans here, Zear?"

"At the time, that was true, Mr. Adger. Only there be one exception left. The key you hold by your side, that bitch in which you refer to as *love*. She was the blockade of my plans of personal devastation. However, there be another." Braylen locked a harsh look of leniency onto him. "The lock or the key?" He pointed to the neighboring door compartment. It opened slowly with hydraulics revealing Alex, which stood blankly.

"Alex?"

"That is correct, Mr. Adger. After we took you that night, we took your son as well. Simply to become a protege of my impetuous experiments. One of us now, Braylen. So choose. Ava or your very son? Which shall die for all of this that you have brought to your own self?"

"Is that the plan, Zear? To deny my request to offer myself for their escape."

"Aw, Braylen, you read the very thoughts that wave my mind. Very wise and much too dangerous you've become. To track me, now has become of your own human senses. Even more desirable the aggravation of in-depth knowledge to subdue you for challenge have you become to my intrigue.

How correct you are, Mr. Adger, about your last thought in question. You could shutdown your entire central nervous station and ram me before I emptied this gun into you pain free. So could Alex, as you attempt to find him through your own mind signals. Only one small problem. Your sweetness here has not the acquired tools that equip her mind as we have.

Make your move, but remember, life will be taken before your arm can surface my neck."

"Look into my eyes before your life is disappeared from this world." Mr. Zear smirked with disconcern. "Through this wonderful plan to gain control over me and lay these innocent lives in the way of harm, you failed to control your very thoughts."

"Oh. How is that, Mr. Adger?"

"Brilliant you are to have entrapped us here without route to hide. However, you stopped not to consider the possibilities of your own mind. Perfect this plan was as we were to die by your hands. Foolish you were to believe that to happen. For I have control of another that you thought nothing of."

"I recognized your persuasion of Alex's mind."

"I'm not regarding Alex." Mr. Barret entered the door and speared the path that tread to Mr. Zear. He opened fire sending bullets throughout his body. Zear turned to run, but was unavailing to the stout wrap of Mr. Barret's elbow bearing his throat.

Mr. Zear panted. "Listen to me, Barret. I created you. I command you to unhand me at once!"

"Command this." Barret released him and shoved Mr. Zear through the window pane. He turned and lapsed his arms around Alex.

Braylen stepped forward. "Mr. Barret, no."

"This is the only way, Braylen."

"What about your wife? Think of her."

"She's no more. Besides, never would she have loved me like this. I would have only let her down. Never the same could my life be. I am a freak now." He held Alex and plummeted out of the broken window.

"No!" Braylen ran and slid to the edge of the glass. "This is all the fault of my own." Ava locked her fingers around his stomach and tugged him from the window. "Ava. Death of a man is not of my ways, but death of a child is not for me to live."

"The only death to be brought before you is that of yourself as not to remove this artificial wire from which was the committed reason for us being here. Braylen, move with me, please."

"What life could I face knowing the thing that just happened? I should be dead in place of my son. The only place I recognize is now a heartless depression."

"These things were not of your sin to claim for failure. Your hands could not beset the wheels of time. Nor could your thoughts have changed one's ways. But, you can change your own mind. Please. Time is of haste and the future is pleasant, I promise. A suitor of people you are. Lovely is your heart. Delightful is your mind."

Braylen took the gun that Mr. Zear once obtained and led Ava through the next raise of the building. He kicked the door open to Mr. Ginn's surgical room. Mr. Ginn pushed his glasses by the frame back onto the bridge of his nose.

"Mr. Ginn?" Braylen asked.

"I surrender. I quit this game. Just run me in."

"You're not under arrest. Put your hands down."

"What are you here for?"

"I'm here for you to perform a high risk surgery, Mr. Ginn."

"Enough! I'm fed up with destroying lives. No more will I invent such heartless creatures by transforming them into mind controlled human bots."

"Mr. Ginn, please. This is my last hope. All I've come to is this reach in time. Please. You must remove this antenna from my brain."

Mr. Ginn looked up to greet his face. "Braylen? I've forgotten you. At one time you were my patient in surgery, number twenty-five. How could it be that you lived past your end date?"

"Mr. Ginn, now is the time of change for you. Switch me back to normal and stand for the good of things."

"I can't, Braylen. You would only die or remember nothing. This is due to the fact that once the metal is removed, the space has to be filled with an artificial supplement. One that has no feeling or memory. You'd be a roaming body with no past. Your functions would keep tact, but your feelings of love and people could vanish.

When we first took out your memory cortex from the center of your brain it was supposed to have just left your memory dead. *Dead center* so to say."

Ava looked softly at Braylen and squeezed his hand. "I deserve to spend my life in a cell." Mr. Ginn said. "Every second of my time should be welded onto the thoughts of the families and friends of those experiments we used."

Braylen handed her the gun and laid himself onto the operating table. "Mr. Ginn. I should have burst in here and pedaled you through the reflector glass that mirror your office walls. However, the lady that stands at the end of the room who fights tears, is the vision of pure love to me. To die for this love to abide, I would. The chance that I undergo, you must. I fought to get here and long to be in her surrounding of love once more. This is your chance to justify your losses and help save our reason to live. Please, Mr. Ginn. Please."

"I will," he agreed and began to guide the surgical latex gloves over his fingers. Ava walked over to Braylen and placed her head to his.

"Hold him at firing range. Shoot him if he turns Ava. Assemble the authorities once this is successful. If I die, I will die with you on my mind. All that you are and every piece of life you bring into my lonely world."

Mr. Ginn began to rub the bend of the bicep with an antiseptic swab. "If I pass on, carry me about in thought. Forget me not. Through meals, walks and even through the day. Time is never long, especially when love is the heart of two."

Mr. Ginn injected the serum causing Braylen's eyes to relax and struggle. "Ava. I do and will love you for all my worth. Through pain and discomfort, I will always have room in my mind for you and your love." His eyelids closed and Ava cried.

(Two weeks later)

Braylen sat beside Kenny, at the local pub. The bartender sat the mug onto the glass surface. "Bar keep, my good man. This tab is on me tonight. In celebration of course, for the recovery of my best friend, Braylen."

"Kenny. Thank you. Even though I hurt from this amnesia, I feel as though you're a true friend."

"Well, Braylen, no one heard from you in about twelve weeks. Then some lady called and informed your friends and family that you were healing from a three month knock to the head. Anyway, my man, I got to go and mingle with some of this fine ass up in here. Are you joining me?"

"No. I'm cool here to run up your bill."

"Suit yourself bro, but here comes that awesome redhead that's been eyeing you all night. I got to split."

The woman sat onto the stool that Kenny had previously occupied. "Do I know you?" Braylen asked. "Please tell me that you are my wife and I just can't remember." Her hair was pulled short and knotted into two shorter twist that edged both sides of her head. Her makeup was slightly dark, but in main with the natural tone of her skin. Her lips were the color of her hair, dark auburn. "I'm sorry, that was stupid."

"I thought it was kind."

"I take it that you're not my wife. I don't see a ring on any of those elegant fingers. But, I have to start somewhere." He put his hand out sideways. "I'm Braylen."

She smiled. "Nice to meet you. I'm Ava."

"Why do I feel as though I know you?"

She blinked loosely and asked, "How does your heart feel?"

"At one time, dying to find this feeling that I feel in the sudden of my lifetime. Happy, healthy and crazy enough, in love."

She glanced and said, "leave not these feelings to lie around." She placed her hand over his. "Claim what you mean to me as your desire. For time is never long, especially when love is the heart of two."

THIN BIRD

(The Sequel to Dead Center)

Chapter 1 *25 Years Later*

"It's been two days past since you been here Jimmy," Martin said. "You haven't ate anything. Don't be depressed. I'm your new father now."

Jimmy sat quietly without any physical expressions. The chair he sat in was wooden with a basket type straw weave for the cushioning.

"I'm sorry I frightened you in the mall parking lot the other day, Jimmy. I didn't mean to scare your mother with such vicious threats. You're here to live with me now. This tenth floor of the high rise apartment complex is complete with a view of the city. After the sun has set, there is a beautiful overcast of the street lights. Looks like Christmas season all year round."

Martin dusted his elbow onto the glass surface of the dining table. "Look, everything is going to be okay, Jimmy. You and I are going to have a blast together. The son I've always wanted. Privileged I am, to have you under that title."

Jimmy looked away and exhaled. "What's wrong? Why won't you speak one word to me, Jimmy?"

The small boy looked up to him and frowned. "Because my father told me never to talk to strangers." Jimmy kicked his feet repeatedly into motion as though he were running while he sat. He entwined his fingers to lock his palms together and looked away.

Martin stood and began to pace. "Jimmy. I am going tomorrow, to buy you a new puppy to replace the one of your old home. And with time I will replace all of the old toys you had there as well."

"Can you replace yourself with my real dad?"

Martin's steps bellowed from the heated temper of his walk. "Jimmy listen. This isn't kidnaping, alright? This is just my way of helping you. Giving you room to grow. At your old house, you were under strict rules. Here, you can do as you please. I am your new guardian, like it or not.

It's gonna be great. We can practice passing the old football around in the park. On rainy days, we can compete against each other in the latest video game. World's greatest dad you'll soon be calling me."

"You're not my daddy."

Martin's breath fluctuated under his nerves. He smiled falsely and rushed the table at which Jimmy was stationed. He kicked it over causing it to give way from the brass frame. He then latched onto Jimmy's shoulders. "I am your father you little shit!"

A short echoed pitch, bounced it's way from the open window. Wild were Martin's eyes as rage collided with the quick wonder. The sound of his voice lessened from the noise.

DEAD CENTER

"Just uh, go stand in the corner for a while", Martin demanded, in a pleasant tone. Jimmy made his way to the far end of the living room.

Martin stood straight and glanced toward the window pane that was centered by the dark of the night. He began to force his steps toward the raised window. The criminal that lives within his conscience brought a sudden tension throughout his body. The empty window space was now in front of him within his reach.

Martin tweaked the edge linen of the curtain by the twitch of his thumb and index finger. He turned to glance at Jimmy who shaded himself between the meet of the walls. The bottom flap of the rolled blinds swayed from the wind draft that tunneled through the opening.

He eased his head outside into the open air. Downward he grazed his eyes to sun the street below. He brought his neck up to rotate his face over the left of his shoulder. With thorough precision, he twisted his body to the opposite direction. He sighed with a lifted intensity as he returned his sights to the right of the ledge.

With all the vastness of the sky, only the clearness of the fresh stars perked the night. He gripped the cement frame on the window and chuckled softly. He pressed upward to prepare his way back into the room. With the hold of time and the stop of the heart, a large figure dashed from the invisible line of nowhere.

Martin screamed! The unknown man creased the glare of the building's flood lights to bend as an illusion. He scooped Martin by his side pulling him out from the window. The mysterious man struggled to keep the tight grip of the nylon cable from which he swung.

Martin's weight slipped from his clutch causing his body to drift. Martin raked his fingers over the pants of his leg, clinging for the very panic that kept him alive. The mystery man secured the heel of his treaded boot into the bar linked at the end of the cable. The stunt rope was similar to the trapeze swing.

Martin's fingers bent from the prying strain. The man held the cable with one hand and reached out for Martin's support. He grabbed around his wrist and pulled him until he was eye level.

Martin cried aloud and violently held onto him, as though drowning in a pool. The man put closed fist about the collar of his shirt and rammed him against the neighbor's glass window.

"Where is the boy?"

"What! What boy? I know no boy!"

The man wrapped his hand to squeeze around his neck, holding him by the strength of his hand, in like position. He swivelled a hand gun from within the seam of his pants. He connected the barrel to his forehead with his free hand.

"The only thing that's going to save you right now is that boy! Dare me not to ask twice for you're about to die times three. First, the bullet that will burry inside of your head. As you near death from the wound, your heart attacks you as you fall. Finally, your body hits the pavement below. Now. Where is he!"

"In the corner!"

The man aimed the gun beside Martin's profile and shot out the window. He kicked Martin inside with vigor. He pushed off of the bar and jumped through the

DEAD CENTER

broken structure. The residents of the room burst into verbal uproars.

The man approached Martin's lying body until the head family member of the apartment leaped toward him in a tackle formation, suspecting them to be intruders. The man ducked, while Martin charged him blinding his view. Martin took the small child's folding chair and knocked the gun from the man's hand.

Martin expelled his feet from stance, landing himself onto the side of the man. They smashed the wall. The decorations that hung fell to the carpet extracting the matted photos from the frames.

The squared end-table jabbed the inner bends of the man's knees. He fought to level his balance. Martin engulfed his arms around his, with attempts to subdue his strength.

The man unraveled the hold by the elevated rotations of his spinning forearms. He slapped the palm of his hand across the back of Martin's neck. He took him by the shoulder and slung him with a weighted pivot. The man hoped on top of him binding his knees into his core.

The present draw of breath left Martin, leaving him to retract a dead pull of air. The man revealed a set of hand cuffs from the leg pocket of his black cargo attire.

"Don't move!" the owner of the home said, while holding the man's fallen gun to his own head. "Now. I don't know who you two are, but you appear to be the bad one here. Dressed all in black with that long ass overcoat on. some sort of burglar no doubt. Swinging through my window of shattered pieces like some bird from nowhere. I'm going to phone the authorities."

The man stood with his back to the owner. With the speed of surprise, he turned about and punched his hand sending the gun into motion. The man caught it with his other hand. He then backed the tenant to the chipped wall from which they damaged previously. He grappled his neck and beaded the barrel between his eyes. The cold of the steel was piercing as it flushed the top bridge of his nose.

Martin began to rise to one knee while they fought. The man noticed him and yelled, "Stay down." Martin acknowledged not his demands.

The man faced the owner. "Now listen to me closely. I am not a burglar nor a pending criminal with desire. This man here is wanted by the local police agencies for kidnaping. I will replace your window and wall that we tore into."

He caught the reflection from the sterling silver vase that was center of the end table of Martin standing behind him. He turned and pulled the trigger. The scorching scream of the bullet splayed into Martin's thigh. He yelled in anger from the hurt.

The man refaced the owner and said, "Any other items of value will be reimbursed to you as well."

"Daddy?" the little girl asked from the turning of the corner. The man immediately brought the gun down to his abdomen so she could not see the weapon.

"Daddy, are you brawling with a bad guy?" Her hair was braided and attached with shell-like ornaments on the frays.

"I don't know who you are," the owner whispered. "But, that's my six years old daughter, Shakeen. She thinks the world of her father. These things can be replaced, but not her pride for me."

The fabric of Martin's jeans began to soak through with blood.

The man looked once more at the little girl and then away. "Damn it!" he said softly. "What's your name?"

"Darren".

"Okay, Darren. Knock the gun from hand and then hit me." A stunned fix, structured Darren's face.

"How can I trust you?"

The man pulled the gun to his face and shouted, "Shakeen! Your daddy's mine! Say goodbye!" Darren's blood separated from his heart. The fluttering pump forced his body to react. Shakeen's face mimicked his from the threat.

Darren blocked the man's under bicep with a clumsy, inexperienced maneuver. The man allowed the gun to drop from his finger tips. Without resistence he welcomed Darren's blows to the head and chest.

"You win! Darren, you got me." He pretended to slump and catch his breath. He grabbed Martin's ankle and pulled him through the front doorway. Darren scooped up his daughter and kicked the gun. It hydroplaned and met wedging between the closing door and the frame.

"Daddy, I knew you could do it!"

The man pried the hand gun from it's barricade and helped Martin up to his feet by the chain of the cuffs.

Jimmy ran from the corner and looked around. His breath was exciting. He ran to the door and unlocked it. He made exit into the hall and fled for freedom.

The man led Martin to his room. "Always leave your door open?"

Martin bumped the heavy door closed and yelled, "Run, Jimmy, they're trying to take you away from me!"

The man dug into Martin's pockets and recovered a large set of keys looped together by a brass ring. He glared at his watch and asked, "Which key is it, Martin?"

Tears rolled Martin's cheek as a cry of a celled man. Imprisoned inside and soon to be held from within. This sympathy evinced from the madness of one who murdered the knit of a family by the separation of their stride. A thief of happiness. The slaying of choices. The taking away of harmony by the stealing of a child.

"The tears be a mercy plea. Hope for a sign. But, if you do not tell me which key fits the slot, the judge of you I will become." He viced Martin's leg to press roughly against the door.

"That one with the faded coating," Martin said, while pointing. The man unlocked it and battered Martin's crown to the door rendering it open. He threw him at the foot of the sofa and then walked through the rooms of the apartment.

"Jimmy? Jimmy! Where are you?" the man questioned. He made his way back to Martin and knelt down. "Where is he? Where do you have him!"

DEAD CENTER

Martin's mouth drooled. The splayed opening of his leg throbbed bluntly. "I want my lawyer." He pressed his palm against his leg and panted heavily.

The man stood and walked to the kitchen. He opened each cabinet two at a time. He took a porcelain plate from the tall stack and found his way back to Martin. He took the dish with both hands over his head. He then brought it to plummet over the top of Martin's skull. He pulled his limp body and asked, "Where's the boy?" He lapsed his thumb over the bottom of his eyelid and lifted it. "Damn it!"

He let Martin go, as he was knocked from his senses. He hurried to the open window and looked down. He spotted Jimmy running against the flow of traffic. "Jimmy!" The man planted his boot into the surface of the window and stretched outward for the collapsible fire escape ladder. He used might to budge the rusted unit.

He lifted Martin over his shoulder and laid him harshly outside the window onto the steps of the ladder. He pulled the long belly cuff chain from his waist. The chain was approximately twenty-two inches in reach.

The man hooked the chain over the cuffs that were over Martin's wrist. Next, he spiraled the opposite end tightly over the railing. Martin's eyes became alert. His blood tingled from the sight below. The man thrust the ladder downward. Martin feared his life from the ground which ascended from his fall.

The man ran the steps as it unfolded. The wind blistered from the cutting speed of the cold air that gathered. Martin's body jerked from the hard stop. Still attached to the ladder, Martin opened his eyes wide to discover his face, one foot from the concrete sidewalk.

Randall Ford Jr.

The man jumped onto the ground and fell back against a looking-glass of a clothing shop located in the square of the city.

Jimmy awaited the electric hand signal to appear in the box to gain permission to cross the street. The man ran into the lamp post and looked at him. "Jimmy, my name is Branden. You've got to come with me now."

"My father said never to talk to strangers."

"Good. Very good, Jimmy. I'm here to take you back to your parents. Here is a picture of your mother. They sent me." Jimmy ran to him. Branden checked the streets over for caution. "It's okay, Jimmy. You're safe now. It's okay."

Chapter 2 *Thin Bird*

Branden opened his eyes from sleep approximately one second from the alarm of the clock. He tapped the silence button and pushed the blanket from his body. He sat up from the mattress and stood solid. He twirled the long plastic tube of the blinds filling the bedroom with the fury of the sun.

Several gray pigeons were gathered outside onto the cement molding base that wrapped around his floor of the high-rise apartment. They all sat scattered in a broken line feathering their wings. Comfortable they appeared. Threatened they seemed not, as they stood in front of the glass.

Branden turned his head sharply toward the still phone, the split of a second before it rang. He picked the receiver from the dial mount and placed it to his ear. A dark, calm voice began to relay a message unto him. "I have one available. Meet me in the park by the bench in fifteen minutes."

Branden recapped the phone onto the hook and grabbed the black pants that laid onto the hardwood floor beside the bed. He slipped them on and secured the buttons. He took a cigar from the top drawer of his dresser. He secured it in his palm and then squeezed it slightly before putting it into his leg pocket.

Branden sat on the wood bench, by the man's request, awaiting further instructions. The hood of his sweat shirt draped his eyebrows. His blood froze with the lack of nerves. Stone his face was carved. Delicate his heart from the approaching event.

A dark character walked by mingled into the group of commuters. He tossed a long two inch thick black strip of velvet over his lap as he passed. Branden dropped the hood and stretched the cloth piece abroad. He looked over each shoulder and carefully veiled his eyes tying the ends at the rear of his head.

He instantly felt someone near him from behind. He felt fingertips by his hair. His reflexive sense caused him to jerk while the man roughly knotted the fabric. He then placed Branden's hood over his head. He glided the varnished surface of an oak walking cane about the back of his hand.

The stranger tugged his shirt signaling Branden to stand. He tilted his head down to shadow the blindfold from the pedestrians that paced by them. "Use the cane." The man led him by the arm pretending that Branden was blind. They blended into the crowd without the attention of any suspicious onlookers.

After a brief walk, the man halted. The echo of the doors were loud and heavy. "Step up and throw yourself in." Branden braced his foot and was shoved inside

DEAD CENTER

of the van. He tumbled onto his back. Rude laughter poured from his environment.

The van was old and the axles screeched from rust that built around the bearings. The driver made the curves with speed. Spare tires and tools were rolling over Branden's body. The men's laughter grew louder. Sadistic the pitch of their voices were.

The surroundings darkened. The sun which shone through the rear glass disappeared from the towering trees of the woods from which they entered. The vehicle ceased and the engine shut off. Branden was pulled by his boots and held by his elbows by two of the men. They walked him in like manner.

They entered a building and led him through the labyrinth of rooms. Branden was positioned middle floor of the loud quarters. The walls of the room were mirrored similar to an interview room for suspects. The cloth covering was removed from his eyes. One man patted him down throughly.

"Please excuse the procedure of getting you here, Mr. Hayes."

"Where am I?"

"Well if you must know. This is or was an old farm. Deserted land that we have bought to run our company. We're thrilled to have you as our very first client.

"We have one female caucasian girl, seven year old Brittany. You answered all of our questions on our website correctly. Were proud to say that our skilled team of nap experts, as we like to refer to them as, has found you a new daughter."

"Where is she?"

"Not so quick, Mr. Hayes. Now you know that kidnaping is federal penitentiary material for the assailant. I had to warn you of that. By the way, there are exactly eleven men, co-workers of mine, that are standing behind those semi-walled mirrors. Incase you decide to challenge any of our rules.

Anyway. This is a small amateur business. Taking precious ones from their parent's and placing them up for sale to customers just as evil as we in nature. You're the first of this long to live company, Branden. We appreciate your transaction. Oh and we took an extra two thousand from your credit card. That's a total of thirty-two thousand five hundred dollars for little Brittany.

Now don't concern yourself with bad thoughts. She's totally fine . No harm was brought to her in any fashion. We're 'nappers, not pedophiles. So don't consume us over to the label of predator.

We did however, have some hilarity involvement with the situation. You see she's kept right outside, inside of the red barn, fifty feet from here. The twelve foot high ceilings are completely filled with gravel rock until about ten feet. She's buried in pebbles up to the line of her back.

The fun came, when we, often over the last twenty four hours of her arrival, scared her extremely." The man chuckled.

Branden bit the inner portion of his cheek to hold his anger in restraint.

"We took turns at spontaneous times and put on Halloween mask. We frightened her so, she urinated on herself each time. She's standing in piss and hasn't eaten anything in about eighteen hours.

Please, keep in mind, Mr. Hayes, if even the slight of breath of this place crosses my ears that you ratted us out, we will get you. We'll even kill your family and everyone whom you love. Now that you are familiar with our policies, do you have any questions?"

"In fact, I do." Branden replied. The man smiled with a crooked smirk and stood with his hands in fold. Branden reached into his pocket and retrieved the brown cigar. "Mind if I smoke?"

"Well, frankly I do."

Branden continued to hold the flame of the lighter to the end of the cigar's tip. The man exhaled sarcastically. Branden smeared the air with a cloud of smoke.

"You know they say smoking will kill ya."

Branden let the hood of his shirt down and replied, "You'll find out."

"But, I don't smoke."

"Neither do I. I'm not inhaling."

The man looked away and back again. "Is this a damn joke?"

"No. See I've taken several deadly gas chemicals and soaked the tobacco mid-way in the poisonous solution. When dry it's harmless. When combusted with fire, it's smoke is become venomous.

I researched your company's ad and followed up a a lot of information on your site on the net. Disgusted I burn with a red fever to kill. My rampant veins, overrun with a hateful aggression. But, now, I'm here to stop your "business" before it takes off. I'm not going to try to kill any of you. But, I am going to rescue that girl. And if anyone tries to change that, you've been warned.

Tell me. Feeling woozy? Light headed yet from the after smoke?"

The man smiled. "I feel wonderful. Mr. Hayes".

Branden blinked and starred at him. His face became flush and his body limber as death. Branden caught him and held him in front of him as for a shield. He slid the man's coat tales aside, pulling the dagger from his waist holster. He jetted it through the far window breaking the glass. The men behind the splintered pieces fled for safety.

Branden pulled the man's gun from his belt and kicked his lifeless body. He fired a shot into his chest as he fell. Branden shot each window and ran for the door.

The gang of vigilantes gathered the semi automatics and regrouped to capture him. Branden ran to the described building. He pulled at the lock of the rotten wooden doors. "Brittany!"

He yanked the wilted boards from structure until the space became wide enough for him to fit through. He plowed and dug his way through the gray rock until he surfaced the pile. "Brittany?"

Branden crawled to her over the rocky points. She squirmed from the touch of his hand to cut the rope. She began to holler boisterously. "It's okay Brittany. Your mother and father sent for me." He showed her their family's photo. She took it and looked at it.

"I want to go home."

DEAD CENTER

Her pants and socks were drenched. He leveled the rocks around her and pushed her to the flat surface. "I had an accident," She said.

A large thud collided with the top of the tin above them. "What was that?" She asked.

"I don't know."

"It's probably another monster."

"That was only a mask."

"Rip the roof's layer!" They heard one man yell. The thin metal parting was the shrinking of one's flesh.

"Jump on my back and wrap your arms around my neck. Don't let go." Branden tunneled in a slope until they reached the front entrance. Another crackle of tin was parted from the beams. "Don't worry they won't shoot in here. The hard sediments may cause a ricochet."

He left her aloft the mountain of gravel and slid down to the door. He looked up from every crevice of the hole he made. One of the men was heading full speed toward the barn.

He pushed Brittany into the corner of the ceiling. The dirt mover hit, loosening the nails from the frame. He threw his arms up and caught the two by four which was crumbling overhead. Brittany sat just under the fallen wood, as Branden's strength blocked it from harm.

The dozer reversed taking the weight of the board from off his shoulders. He jumped onto the scoop digger and hid behind the flap of tin that was attached to it. He bent it displaying his face to the driver. He cat walked the welded steel arc that served as a safety rail bar. He kicked the driver in the temple.

The man fell from the rolling tractor. Branden pulled his gun and killed the mad men that were on the roof. He sent shots into each member of the private company, separating them from the heart of their lives.

He stomped the pedal and ejected the scoop in an angle. The forks drove into the driver that fell. Branden lifted the hydraulic shovel dumping it into the top of the building.

He left the dozer as Brittany ran to him. He held the gun in every direction. All of the incriminating, with pending aggravations, were justified. She held the picture close to her side while gripping his fingers with intense emotion.

(Forty-five minutes later)

"Thank you Mr. and Mrs. O'Connell for coming. Please, won't you both have a seat. I'm Eric Grant owner of the Ace Agency. I've brought some good news to share with you.

First let me thank you for choosing the Ace Bounty Hunters Agency Association. We have some talented professionals here, but none can match the one who found your daughter, Brittany. Some hunters specialize in chasing bad lawyers, judges, escaped convicts and so on.

However, Mr. Hayes is not only the best in his field, he's the only one to count on. A weird character. Thin Bird, they call him. Anything, but thin, he is a healthy figure of mass. They refer to him as this because, thin is the escape, free the child is, like a bird.

Strange guy though. He can somehow tell when someone's cell phone is about to ring. He can sense an alarm clock right before it goes off. Wild huh?

Well. Anyway. Your daughter will be in your arms in about four minutes. They are entering the parking lot as we speak." The woman wept while the man fought to contain the tears.

Chapter 3 *"Who Am I?"*

Brittany ran from Branden's side and was cradled by her huddled parents. He strolled past them and to the receptionist window. Tammy opened the sliding plexiglass of the cubical type desk. "Mission accomplished?"

He made no reply to her comment and continued to sign the legal files which she handed him in a chain formation. "Wow, two children in twelve hours. That's wonderful Branden. You don't say much do you?"

He completed the inscribing of his name upon the documents and neatly shuffled them together. "Great. Now Branden, you know the routine. Go see Tera, in resources or if you like, you can see me sometimes."

Branden faced away from her in wait to be buzzed in through the lobby. Tammy lifted her cheek and rolled her eyes. "Oh, incase you were wondering, I was talking to that wall over there and not you."

Branden chewed the gum steadily. "Tell Tommy I said hello."

"Tommy Billards? You know he's in Australia, working on the Judge Frack hunt."

The hydraulic door opened. He walked through it as the phone began to ring. "Hello and thank you for calling the Ace Bounty Hunters," she greeted.

"Hey, it's me Tommy. I'm going to need a wire right away. Okay? Hello? Tammy?" Her eyes slanted in amazement.

Branden stepped up to the accounting resource office. The capacity of the room was half the size of an average library. He approached Tera anxiously. His heart set to see spots from the shortness of breath. Erratic, his blood flowed from the sight of her.

She sat with her head down in concentration of her paperwork. Her legs crossed and her palm rested flat under her chin. The reading glasses she wore were silver which enhanced her medium ebony skin tone. *Her eyes were the dazzle of my day dreams*. Her hair was brown with a light tint blended with blond highlights. It was spiraled and protruded from every direction of her scalp.

Graceful were her thin fingers that brushed her face. Her nails were trimmed in white at the tips and clear coated overall.

The fray of her beige pants, cuffed mid-way of the shin. Her tennis shoes topped just under the ankles as she wore no socks. *Only to ponder of how such beauty could murder a man of his free will. My stomach swims in a sea of nausea. Unclear my mind becomes when I near her. Dead I become. Alive, my anxiety to speak. Numb the real world is. Vast fantasy I reside, as to be secretly in love with her.*

Randall Ford Jr.

I beg of my mind not to think of her. The torment of her eyes that glimpse at mine, torches my world for to love this person that sits with my inner thoughts. What has committed me to this punishment? Hidden my heart is from her. These feelings for her will not relax in a grave of forgotten hope. No matter what I do, her image bears my mind. For to love this woman, I will always. Only if she knew my true error, which is my weakness of her sensual allure.

She broke her train of reading and looked up. Her eyes lightened. "Branden, hi. I've been expecting you. Have a seat."

He sat in the small table-like desk across from her. "Great job on the Jimmy Nelson case last night. I have your check in full right here." She stretched her body over to one side and stuck her hand into the filing cabinet by the printer.

She slid the envelope over the surface of the table. He took it as her hand brushed his. The saliva of his mouth was heated from the unstable excitement. "Anything else for you today, Branden?"

"Yeah. I love you. Will you marry me?" He smiled.

She giggled and replied, "That's what they all say when they get their checks."

He stood as though embarrassed. "You know something Tera? You're the only one who makes me smile."

Her attention was set on his grasp of affectionate words. She put her glasses over her eyes. "I know." She arced her head while opening the notebook from her previous read.

DEAD CENTER

That night Branden lie in an intense dream. The thump of a hollow echo thundered from the heartbeat of his mother from the womb. Darkness was his tiny world of the time. Cushioned by a soft watery cradle. *Pleasant abundance of peace was my connection to her. Safe in this spot. No one could threat.*

Sudden horror was near. I felt the over flooding of suppressing fear. I could hear her pulse beat louder. Something is not right. I panicked from my mother's scream! The black glove that I witnessed with these underdeveloped eyes found it's way to me through her. His fingers served as a clamp to open her. The end of his sphere was destined to find me.

Branden yelled and awoke. The sheet was saturated with sweat. Dehydrated he felt. He walked into the bathroom to splash his face with water.

The telephone alarmed. Unaware of it before it took place in his mind he was shocked. *How could I have not known it would have sounded?* He nonchalantly responded to the call, "Branden."

"Mr. Hayes. At last I hear your voice."

"Who is this?"

"You survived yesterday. My group of men failed me. How does it feel to be a hero?"

"Who are you?"

"You'll find that out soon enough. At which, by such times you'll be faced with a number of obstacles, but only one you can save. Reply to me, damn it! How does it feel to be the super guy of the group?"

"I'm hanging up. If you can't answer my question, then I can't respond to your's."

"Well, that's fair enough. Why don't you just ask your mother who I am." The dial tone squelched.

The floor of the room seemed to give way. A faint vertigo made his head delirious with wonder. The walls melted with a dizzy vision. A sweltering heat imbedded itself into his head. He fell to his hands and knees. His body laid out onto the cold tile to ease his temperature.

My mother? My father? Whom the two I've never saw before. The pain of his head was great.

Who am I? Twenty-five years old and no trace of any relatives. No family history. No memories. No background. Who am I? Who were they? Was I abandoned?

Early after the next day had began, Branden, sat inside of Mr. Grant's office.

"Ten men! You killed ten men. You killed a dime of people yesterday, Branden!"

"Sir, it was out of self defense. I thought it was eleven."

"You could of ran, Branden!"

"Mr. Grant, I was not going to leave Brittany behind for them to relocate and lose her for good."

"We're not police officers. We are simple bounty hunters, Branden! I should fire you! Court will be in about three months for this. The eleventh man survived the intoxicating smoke you drew on him. Not to mention the fucking bullet to the chest! Why are you carrying a firearm anyway?"

"I wasn't. They patted me. I took his for use. I was cornered sir. No other choice."

"Look. I'm not implying that those scum suckers didn't get what they deserved. You should of just handled things with a bit less tasteless means. Now. Out! Get out of my face! Get out of my office! Get out! You're suspended for the next two days. Go cool down. Want my gun so you can pop off a few co-workers here? Let off a little steam? Do you even care that my ass is under attack by the damn law committee for this?"

"Sir, I thought you wanted me to go."

"Smart ass! Get out of my damn space." Branden twisted the door knob clockwise. "Oh wait," Eric said calmly. "Here's your next assignment after your two day grievance period. Now, out!"

Branden left the office and u-turned to head down the hall. He halted at Tammy's window. "Buzz me in."

"Anything for you." She curled her lips at him.

He ignored her seductions and said, "It's your husband." Her phone rang while he disappeared from her sight through the passage of the doorway.

She greeted the caller with a cute voice. "Oh. Hi Honey." She fidgeted with her hair as it tingled from Branden's eerie prediction.

Branden entered Tera's office. She looked just over the top rim of her glasses and raised up. He flopped roughly into the customer's chair. "Say anything. Say whatever. Take me from this worry by the angelic voice that sears me like therapy. Look at me. Stare at me. Glance towards me. Dizzy my balance with such intrigue as only you could."

"Branden, I'm sorry?" she smiled.

"Magnetize me by your stunning aroma." He stood and placed his knuckles onto the surface of her desk. "Do you know what's harder to do, see you from first sight or have to leave from your presence?"

She removed her glasses and sat back into the wooden chair. Branden straightened his posture. "I rescue stolen children. That's what I do. But, the thrill of seeing you afterward is reward enough. You make the fights to complete a mission even more worth it. One touch from you was all I needed to realize that I love you. I'm not crazy. I'm not insane. I'm not mad. Do you realize that I just said the same thing three times?"

She smiled and looked away. "Half the time I don't know what I'm doing. Most of the time I'm missing something. I think it may be you. I need this feeling that I feel. Only I feel it when I'm around you. Grant me only what your heart would permit me for my desire. Please, don't dislike me for this. I can hardly breathe right now. All because you shocked my eyes. I tried rational before, but today I can't hold back any longer." He headed for the door. "I'm going to run away from the moment for now, as I have said too much."

He began to open it. She put her glasses on and began to write. He had jarred it fully and started to walk. "I was wondering when the hell you were going to ask me out."

He stopped. Shut down his body became. She tore the top of the paper with her phone number and stood.

Her chair scooted by the flexing of her calves. "Come here." She folded her arms with the paper between her fingers.

Branden's emotions burned. He moved not. "Come here," she continued. With an eased outlook, he turned and faced her. She tucked the paper into his fingers and closed his palm. "Marriage may be out of the question for now, but we can make it official for a date."

"I'm sorry. I'm just a straight forward guy." She placed the underside of her finger over his lips. She leaned in and gently pecked them.

She pulled away, rubbing her lips together. "See ya later," she said. *This calloused shell, my body, is where I once held all of my emotions bound. But, the ravenous touch of her breath to warm my lips made me forget my existence. A new honor in my vesture she has kindled. A new day to pass.*

Chapter 4 *No. It's Beautiful.*

The chrome needle was a glared blur. Disastrous screams were muffled from the inside walls of the womb. The blackness was light shaded with a blazing redness from the cervix opening by the hand. The point of the steel was irritable. *I tried to move away!* The placenta ruptured only in part with a small drainage of fluid. *My head became implanted with all that was to prepare me to be different from all others.*

Branden awoke in like manner as before. Thick drops of blood ran from the center of his head and down his face. He smeared the streams and looked at his hand. The clock read 2:41 a.m. His eyes darkened under the lids. The phone rang. Clueless to its timing, he picked it up.

"Rara bird," the man said. "I know you will figure this out, but too late it will be."

"Who are you!" The call was ended leaving Branden in confusion.

When the sun appeared in the sky, Branden made a quest to the doctor's office for an examination of his

DEAD CENTER

head. He sat impatiently in the waiting area. Finally, he was called back and led by the nurse.

After another period of drug out time, the doctor entered the room. He visually examined Branden's head with a microscopic light. He ran the short strands of hair back with his index finger. "Do a little fighting?"

"Here and there."

"It seems as though you have a deep black bruise located dead center of your head. Does it hurt any?"

"Lately."

"Well, it's a borderline concussion, but not as major. It almost appears to be bruised from under the surface of the skin. I want to see you in a week to follow up. However, the quick fix is simply not to worry. It's more than likely a cosmetic thing anyway."

Branden rung the doorbell of Tera's home. She scurried to the door from the shower. The towel was wrapped snug over the horizon of her breast and ended just below the thigh. She unlocked the deadbolt switch and opened it wide. "Oh, hi."

He wrestled with the gentleman of his polite nature as not to shift his eyes below hers. "Come in," she replied, with a spunky attitude.

He moved his eyes to the towel and asked, "Are you sure?"

"Yes, of course, Branden. I'm comfortable around you." He handed her a bouquet of yellow flowers and snapped the door closed. His shirt was white with a collar, unbuttoned at the chest revealing the indentations in-between. The short sleeves hugged his arms to make every retraction of his muscles visible. His neck was slightly larger in proportion with the rest of his frame and which was of huge mass.

"Look at you," she said. She slithered her fingers to arouse over the smooth material of his shirt. She clawed the ends of her nails repeatedly over his sides. "All I have left to do is throw some clothes on. Make yourself at home." She shut the bedroom door behind her.

He leaned his back to the door. "Say Tera?"

"Yeah?"

"Any idea what Rara Bird means?"

"Rara, rare, rare bird. Not exactly. Why? Is it some species of a certain bird?"

"I don't know."

She opened the door fully clothed. "I could look it up for you. After all, I am the resource manager. Ready to hit the club?"

"Sort of."

She tilted her head and scrunched her lips. "What?"

"Tera, I can't dance. I don't know technique, coordination, moves, or anything."

"Can you do the robot? I'm just kidding."

"Good. Because, I have no clue."

DEAD CENTER

"Look, it's simple. When we get out on the dance floor. Just pretend you're making love to me standing up. Let your movements show your aggressions. Let the nasty scenes in your head show through your hips. I guess I should have asked are you ready to hit me instead?" She pulled him by the hand. "Now come on lets go."

Her pants were the feel of skin. They tempted lust from the curving of her hips. The hems were loose in form, covering most of her feet. The shoes she canvassed, were soft with velcro platform straps on the side. Her toes were metallic in shine and silver in color. Her eyes were emerald from the contacts.

They arrived at the front line of people. The bouncer carded the members and checked ages from their I.d.s. Tera and Branden came to the velvet rope marker. The bouncer raised his eyebrow towards Branden, as he was the same in stature. He looked at Tera from head to feet and then back to Branden.

He held his fist out for approval. Branden bumped his closed and hard with his to show a mutual respect. The bouncer unhooked the blocker chain. Branden followed directly behind Tera, as they passed by the overhead aluminum awning.

"Just a minute!" the bouncer shouted. The purple light flashed indicating metal was detected from Branden's body. "Arms up. I'm just going to pat you down for security purposes." Tera stood and made silly faces at him and stuck her tongue out. Branden stiffened his jaw with a playful reply.

"Nothing. Walk through again." The light flickered once more. "You don't have any kind of knives or guns on you do you?"

"No."

"Any body piercing?"

"No."

He smiled. "Yeah, I bet that's what it is." He glanced downward and laughed. He patted him on the back. "Go on through my man."

"But, I don't have any at all." The bouncer continued to guard the door.

The atmosphere was alive and the music at full volume. Tera pulled his arm and squeezed between the people that were back to back. The tempo was upbeat and full of energy. The dance space was jammed and nearly immobile to pursue the right of steps.

She pulled him into her arms and said, "Make love to me." She turned about and pressed her backside to him. She rotated her butt in a vertical form and then centered it, bending over resting her hands onto her knees. Her jeans were cut under the waistline and made the thong lining show. The tattoo on the small of her back was a tribal rose that expanded.

The people vanished and the music was no longer audible. Only her in such creative positioning was the thought of me. If never to have made love to her, now was the opportunity to simulate such painful erotic fire.

As she leaned up, he grabbed the seam of belt loops and stuffed his fingers inside the open area of her pants. He pulled her with vim. The thrust caught her unaware. He slid his palm over the front of her thigh. His strong forcing of the pull was satisfaction unto her. He spun her around and neared her lips. She closed her eyes as he pulled her by the hair lightly. He put his lips onto her neck and breathed hot moisture onto the sensitive area. She blinked without to control her heavy eyelids with the massaging of his mouth.

The song stopped. Her mouth remained open. He pulled up. "It's getting hot. Let's order a drink."

He looked past the front button of her denim pants and replied. "I was thinking the same thing."

After several hours had gone by, they sat in a booth arranged at the quiet wing of the party. A lady passed by and said, "Hey, Ayrelia," and then bumped her shoulder.

"Ayrelia?"

"That's my middle name. It was my mother's name. Tell me something, Branden. I hear a lot in the office. What's this about you and phones ringing? Is that just some weird rumor or what?"

"I don't know where to start. As a small boy, I could begin to detect when someone's telephone would ring. A flash of sharp pain flashed through my head just before the ring took place. Through time, it's like my mind coded the call and projected into my thoughts as to read the caller."

"Like caller ID?"

"In a way, I guess."

"What else?"

"The detonation of alarm clocks before they go off."

"So you claim to be a psychic or obtain ESP?"

"No, nothing stupid like that. I can't explain it in full." She looked away and grabbed the handle of her purse. She stood to exit. He chased behind her and pushed the door of the club open.

"Tera wait!"

She turned around and said, "Branden, I think you're very wonderful. You don't have to lie to win me over to you."

"I'm not lying to you. Please, don't go. I'm so lonely."

"That's your own damn fault, Branden. You never talk to anyone at or outside of work. Besides, what other super hero powers do you have? Can you fly with or without a cape? Can you disappear?" She continued to walk.

He closed in on her. "Ayrelia, please."

She stuck the key into the lock of the car's door. "It's, Tera."

"No, it's beautiful."

She cracked the door and faced him. She sighed. "Branden. You are lovely without a doubt in my imagination. But, I don't think I'm what you're looking for."

"Maybe you're right. Most women usually fall for the wrong guys anyway."

"Excuse me? You can't assume anything about me!" She bounced her eyes. "Besides I tried the white guy thing before. I wasn't impressed." She turned and took the square handle of the door panel.

DEAD CENTER

He pushed it shut and said, "Maybe you should try again."

She turned about. He held her in place by the pull of his lips to hers. He looked at her and backed away. "Like I said. I wasn't impressed."

As he inched away, she screeched her nails over the enamel finish of her car and crashed into him turning his cheek by her hand. They kissed with passion.

The end of murk and the beginning of a felicitous change transformed my depression into a marvel of tantric desire. He bumped her against the car and yanked at one side of her jeans causing them to separate. The zipper unlinked as well. He slid his hand between the elastic band of her panties. Her breath was heavier than before. Her eyes opened for such pleasure to be dominated by his touch. This was the peak of nature's way.

He ran his fingers apart missing the center, making her sensitive with the drawing of blood. Her breasts shown through her shirt. She moaned as he inserted his middle finger at the bend of the knuckle and tantalized her clit with his thumb, unleashing her wetness. His fourth finger found skin between her area and her butt. She stuck her nails into his back, piercing his veins with pleasure. "Maybe you're right," she stated. "But, not here. Take me to my bed. Lay my body down. Sift your fingers over my feet. Make me explode inside."

They left the bar and made their way to her home. She stripped her jeans while he pulled her shirt from her chest. Her bare breasts scrubbed his shirt. She sat and pulled the pants off, over her feet. She laid onto the bed and worked the panties off by the side straps that were tied. The cotton lining was a damp stain of white secretions.

He took the comforter that was piled onto the floor and waved it to flatten it out. With anticipation she traced her nipples and asked, "What are you doing?" He took the tacks by the mirror and stood onto the mattress and mounted the blanket onto the ceiling. It draped her waist and he became invisible to her.

"I want to be different for you. This way you cannot see what I do or what I touch you with." He split his shirt open and threw it onto the carpet. She moved herself about in front of him for the ache of applying his mouth to her. He widened the outer area and pulled the top flap of skin to expose her. Soft and quick were the ways of his tongue. The semi figurations of his lapping caused her to cramp. "Not yet."

She found the shape of his head through the comforter and rubbed it. Violently her stamina was waning as she tried to relax the muscle, but was overcome by the thick swelling. His lashing strokes deepened. The smooth tip of his tongue pounded at the raw nerves of her ecstasy.

Branden took the natural lubrication of her by finger and placed it beneath her onto her butt. He teased her by twisting his finger inside and bending his tongue on top of her simultaneously. Finally, he entered her with speed thrusting without restraint. The blanket fell and covered her body. He drove into her with reach. She laced her ankles to cross while her legs wrapped around his back. He stiffened and she pulled herself into a sitting position.

"You take my mind."

"Not yet," she demanded. "Thirty more seconds." He forced himself to stay inside from the limber effect of climax. She bit his neck and pushed her feet in an angle. Contractions constricted tightly over him as a vacuum seal. The making of love seeped from her. "Don't let go of me. Stay here. This moment will fade, but to hang onto it, is my fight. Stay the night. Create this again over and over until soreness has settled with me. Afterward rest your skin to mine and indulge in this genuine thing we share."

Chapter 5 *Freedom In lock*

Tera awoke to an empty bed. She leaned to one side. Her face drooped from the crack of consciousness. Her heart skipped as two hands were softly placed under her. Her voice squealed. Branden picked her up. He was fresh and fully attired. He angled her legs and walked her sideways into the bathroom.

He laid her nude body heel first into the tub. It was filled with soothing aroma bubbles. With care he submerged her to her shoulders. "Where are you going?"

"Thanks to you, I know things can happen. I had zero dreams last night. Now it's time to peruse a dream of meeting my parents." She blinked with a slight of sleepiness. "Also I had no extreme, painful headaches either."

"Maybe you should just get another pillow," She joked.

DEAD CENTER

Branden walked with silence through the top pod level of the jail. Gestures and verbal suggestions were in graphic details from the inmates that stood on the balcony above the floor. He shook hands with the guard of the cell. The officer crinkled the twenty dollar bill and unlocked the barred entrance. "Five minutes."

Branden's black overcoat ended with his shin. Wilks looked away from his appearance. Branden sat beside him onto the regulation bed. "Mind if I smoke? I'm just kidding."

"Good one. What type of chemical anthrax cigars have you got this time?"

"Why do some guys spit all the damn time? I walked through to a convenience store lot and some guy spit, but kept walking. Is it some sort of intimidation factor? If you got something to say, say it. Don't come off threatening and then run with a cowardly demeanor."

"Yeah, thanks for the lesson. Now can you leave? I'm already in jail. What do you want from me?"

"Some information. I'm starting a new case on a 'napped victim. Leads tell me a stalker has been spotted with her today." Branden pulled the photo from his coat. "Her name is Kelsey Singer. Five years of age. Last seen, about three weeks ago at the mall. Missing for twenty-four days now. I figure since you're the head of a nap organization, you'd know something about this."

"Well, I don't."

"There is an incentive here."

"Like?"

"Give me what I want to hear about this and I'll persuade the judge to cut your sentence in half."

"How about you break me from this place and I'll tell you more than you ever thought about some particular things."

"Prison break? Realistically, this is out of bounds."

"You and me have something oddly in common."

"What is that?"

"This is you on the outside," he said, while referring to the caged bars. "This was me on the inside." Branden stood and situated the sleeves of his coat. "Find the rare bird."

"What did you say?"

"You heard me and for your info, you will be freeing me from this place."

"What rare bird? Me? I am the bird, genius."

"No. You're the thin bird, not the rare one. Time is of the essence. Find the bird before its too late."

"Who do you work for?"

"That's not important. I don't even work for a nap company. That was a deploy to get you murdered, but fallacy came into the plan. I know who you are and were. I even known of your father, Mr. Adger."

Branden scrunched his collar. "How do you know Braylen? Tell me damn you!"

"Like I said, you will be escaping me from this dreadful place."

DEAD CENTER

"Tell me how you know of him." Branden lifted his pants leg and unsnap the velcro of his ankle. He took the twenty-two caliber from the vinyl holster. He laid over Wilks. "Tell me, damn it!"

"I know more of your father than you do. Go ahead shoot. They'd kill me if I told anyway."

Wilks grabbed the gun. "Let go of the gun."

"Do it. Pull the trigger."

"Let go of the gun."

"I know why your heads been killing you with pain as of late."

"Let go of the gun!"

"Look at me closely. Look into my eyes." Branden's breath was labored. Blood pumped his veins. "You will need me. I'm the key. The only clue you have is what I know." Wilks surrendered his strength. Branden pushed his head to the foam mattress and yanked the gun.

"Times up," the guard announced.

Branden got up and looked back. "Remember, the Rare Bird is the key to your freedom. I am the key to your destiny. For only part of the story can she tell. The rest is within my knowledge. When you come back for me, have a jumbo cup of coffee waiting."

Branden entered his car and drove with dizzy thoughts that blurred the road. He commuted for some time until he pulled up to the large southern styled house and got out.

The grass was perfect in length and shade. The gloss of the paint set the house into a country setting. The shutters and awnings were trimmed in hunter green. He tapped the door by the gold loop.

An older lady opened it and starred at him. Her hair was black with a mixture of grey. Smooth was her face.

"Hi ma'am. My name is, Branden Hayes. I, um, damn," he whispered. "I don't know exactly what to say, but, hi mom?"

"I'm sorry sir. I have no children."

"Of course not. This was a dumb idea. I'm sorry. I'm looking for an Ava and Braylen Adger. Please excuse me."

"Wait. I'm Ava, but I am not your mother. I know who you are. Many years have passed, as I've been expecting you. Come in."

"I apologize, Ms. Adger. If you're not my mother, then I guess Braylen, isn't my father either."

"Braylen was indeed your father. He passed from this life two years ago. You are the splitting image of him. So handsome. So strong." She ran her palm down his cheek.

"How did he die?"

"His death derived from reasons that should not have been. Which is why we need to talk. You have no idea who you are or your abilities to affect lives in ways for the good of the world.

Twenty-five years ago, I met Braylen by sheer coincidence. The axis of time was perfect. Two completely different folks tied by the stem of love. Who cared what

DEAD CENTER

people saw, let alone thought of us. Special he made me feel. Honored I became, with a tender heart.

Braylen loved life and I loved him. Together we spent twenty-five years living in fantasy, not on earth. In love we were. Forever In fantasy I remain, as my hours are lonely.

Nevertheless, you are something else. Remarkable beyond your own knowledge." She took the thin clear folder from the birch wood shelve and handed it to him.

The title was labeled, "Olden Days". "This is all you need, to know the real you. I cannot resolve your state of mind, but I can give you an explanation.

Just remember, you are normal. Don't change who you are Branden. My time is sad. To see you before me is just as Braylen was twenty-eight again. He died from natural causes. Do you have a lady?"

"Yes."

"I can tell. Lately, you've been happy versus sad. That's called love. It will keep you safe. It is the life of you Branden. Notice the rush of time drift away when she gets close to you." He stood as to prepare for departure.

"No one can touch you Branden. Even those who track the hunter." He walked to the door and opened it.

"Thank you, Ava, for your time."

Early in the evening, Branden sat across from Tera at the diner. "I'm dying to know how your day was. Was your mother surprised to see you? What?"

"Turns out she's a loon. She denied me ever having been her son without any reason. She claims that my father died. She seems really sweet and is still hung up in a state of grief of her loss. Anyway, I guess that's that. She also gave me some literature of some sort." He laid the clear folder onto the table. "She said this contains the secrets of my true identity."

A thunderous burst of collision sounded from across the street. The lights of the establishment flickered. Branden placed his hand upon his head. "Are you okay?" The overhead chandeliers shorted from its connection. Branden yelled from the splintering pain in his head. She stood and caressed his back. "Branden, what's wrong?"

The crowd of the restaurant huddled over the large window to observe the car that had hit the power pole from afar. Branden ran from the café and set his determination with the injured driver. The air that tightened in his lungs was the only sound his ears could sense as he ran. His breath was visible from the cold. He ran the loop around the car to determine his plan of escape. The driver's head strained from the concussion.

Tera placed the strap of her pocketbook over her shoulder and picked up the book that Branden obtained from Ava. She crossed both arms around it and walked to the window. Her eyes were filled with the heroic sight of Branden prying the door from the car and dragging the driver to safety. Her veins tingled with desire for him.

She unlocked the front door of her home. Branden followed in behind her. Her eyes seemed burdened with

DEAD CENTER

sleep as if she couldn't keep them open. She dropped the book and put her hands onto him. Branden pressed her closer.

He ran his palms vertical against her sides. She pressed firmly against him. "Touch me somewhere. Put it anywhere. I don't care where. Only let me feel you on some place of my body." She held onto the valance that curtained the top post of the bed. Her left leg was straight and the right was bent with her weight resting.

Her calf muscles were defined by the arching of her foot by the pushing of her toes. "Don't stop to breath," she said. "Enter me fast and finish me quickly. Show me how good I feel. Pour the sweltering heat over my skin. Take complete control of me." She dropped the denim skirt and buried her knees into the mattress, as she exposed herself to him.

She laid the side of her jaw to the blanket. She clawed at the comforter repeatedly. He stepped up even with her. Her shoulders touched the bed and back sloped causing her to appear submissive unto his physical dominance. He pressed her through his pants.

"This teasing is torturous. Murder my nerves to kill this need to erupt onto you," she continued. Branden's belt fell to his ankles along with the pants. Without to feel his way, he pushed himself inside of her. She moved herself in a semi-fashion causing it to sleeve loosely around him. Every part of her was felt and reached.

He did as she encouraged. After a short time Branden's thrust smoothed as he stretched. She moved up to avoid his extended endowment due to orgasm.

Branden remained erect and began to throttle into her once more. She moaned openly and bounced against his torso. He squeezed her waist firmly. She met her feet together and overlapped them to constrict the tension of his pull. Sweat beaded his forehead. He pulled from her while she throbbed. She bit her bottom lip, as she felt the saturation catch the back of her calve and run to her heels.

Chapter 6 *Olden Days*

Early the following morning Branden stood over the city's square on top of the museum's walking bridge. He used the high powered scope binoculars to take in the bus of the day shift. He pulled out the picture of the napper to store another glimpse of him in his memory. "Alright you scum. Where are you?"

Tera pushed away from the computer screen and propped her feet onto the desk of her work cubical. She picked up the "Olden Days" folder and began to read. Astonished she became from the chronicles and diary of a government scientist named Mr. Zear.

I, Dr. Kenneth R. Zear, have hereby concluded perfection upon research of my experimentations. A fifty-three percent mercury based non expandable metal coated with a titanium chrome. This needle acts as a controlled central function for the brain if planted center of the skull at a forty-five degree top angle and driven at an eighty-four degree pivot.

This device is used as an antenna by our trackers. The primary function of this radar-styled rod is to create the best protection humanly possible. If this procedure is induced correctly, the "empirical" or one who has underwent such surgery will become the actual experiment.

With this needle inserted center of the brain, it punctures the limbic portion of matter cells that hold the entire record of memory in the mind. When disrupted in this way, the total loss of memories has taken over.

Empirical # 1 (May 3rd 1998). Raymond Valaskie. Twenty-five years of age. The first of experiments. Ordered to execution after one hour of implant. This was due to the needle placement being off in measures of the drive angle. Mr. Valaskie became instantly paralyzed from the neck down.

Empirical # 2 (May 4th 1998) John Doe. Deceased twenty-two days after operation. Training and observations left incomplete. Cause of death; premature rod deflation of the brain.

Empirical # 3 (July 10th 1998) John Doe 2. Died by gunshot from lead detention officer.

Jan. 14th 2000. A new discovery upon experimentation has been deemed successful at this time. Co-founder, Martin Ginn, has created a newly formatted and lighter rod. This contemporary needle has been expected to expand the life of such future individual empiricals. Almost tripled in days before their expirations. Ninety days is the current limit.

Empirical # 10 Jason Moore. Died of heart expansion. A direct side effect of the anabolics.

Satisfaction of experiments has come a long way for Zear and Ginn. A high tech robotic arm mechanism has been developed with a laser computer. This is to com-

DEAD CENTER

pass the needle's wedge. Empiricals have been stronger and faster in thinking under pressure. Although this be the case, ninety days is still the average line of life.

Empirical # 14. John Doe 3. Suffered slight hearing loss. Unaware of the hypersensitive nervous system, empirical # 14, died from the physical training, which triggered a massive heart attack.

Empirical # 15. Died from brain folding or collapsing from inside out. Early dementia at age twenty-one. Cause of death, Alzheimer's.

June 2000. Empirical # 17, I myself, Dr. Zear. I have examined all of the proper channels to construct a new polyurethane graft rod. One that will flow the heat and pump of blood throughout the brain with normal daily activities.

Empirical # 17 (June 17, 2001) I, Kenneth Zear, have installed a newly developed piece of equipment into my own brain. Using the p-143 laser it burned through the bone. Drugs used, 5300cc hydrocodone and two times four hundred doses of lithium benzoyl fluid to deaden the surface of nerve endings. Fourteen shots of liponovacaine in the neck and spine.

Surgery time, one hour fifty-two seconds. Stitch count, eleven vertical and twenty-four entrance side of wound. Rod adjustment, one inch shorter than normal. This was to escape the midst of my limbic portion, for my work must live.

Empirical #27 and 28. John Doe 4 and Martin Brown. (October 20, 2001). Both lived ninety days with new rod. Both reside in the Zear and Ginn building to serve as personal protection for myself and Mr. Ginn.

Randall Ford Jr.

Empirical #29 A secret have I kept from all others. An experiment of my own to raise. Alex Adger. Eight years old. Taken from his mother and placed in foster care by the state. Alex was later adopted by Braylen and wife, Rene. Returned to his mother and new father, Braylen Adger, January 2001. Alex currently resides on the tenth floor of the building.

Empirical # 30. Kenneth Barret. (March 30, 2001). The last of empiricals to date. Log entry April 12, 2001, End.

Tera read intensely as she flipped the page to discover a new log of scripts by Mr. Ginn, after the end of Zear's.

April 21. I, Jonathan Ginn, has filled the last of focus of my career. I'm onto the ends of such dreadful experimentations. Empirical #27 and 28 murdered by the hands of empirical #25, Braylen Adger.

Empirical #17. Mr. Zear. Sentenced to death by Emperical # 30, Kenneth Barrett. Alex suspected to have met death, but body was never found. No recorded file of death.

Empirical #25 Braylen Adger went under emergency surgery. Complete success from myself. Number 25, thought to have died with time.

Only one Empirical remains. # 26. Subject in study escaped community health states area. Name and social security number assumed to be falsely changed. These records are forms 829-48. Property of government or relative government officials. Thought to have died in time. Legal alias; Branden Adger.

Explanation of empiricals; to better suit the prime authorities of the UN by means of human protection. Skillful

DEAD CENTER

murderers and classified marksman. Tera slammed the book shut and panicked under her breath. "Calm down," she whispered softly. She exhaled quietly. She picked up her cell phone.

Branden reached into his coat and pulled a phone from his inner pocket before it rang. "Hey baby."

She swallowed the heavy saliva that sat in her throat. "Hey, I'm calling to return some information to you. I did some online study for the term Rara bird. The only sensible conclusion was the Spanish term, Rara Avis".

He spotted the 'napper from the corner of the magnifying casing. "What is your real last name, Branden?"

"Adger." She hung up with a startled notion. "Rara Avis," he wondered. "Ava!"

He turned to run, but locked hold onto the hard safety railing. The expert kidnapper was walking nonchalantly throughout the park below. Branden ran the length of the bridge. The man eyed him and fled with speed. Paranoia grew with Branden as he ran with fear above his shoulders.

The man passed through the crowd of people until his path was split. Branden charged the general direction of his sighting, but was too late. He calculated the area briefly in his mind. He ran with the legs of a tiger. He passed the nearest building and leapt onto the parked cars. He dashed onto the hoods and jumped bravely onto the escape ladder. The skeleton of the ladder was enclosed by a thin metal-like structure. He skipped steps and climbed with friction.

Branden looked through the binoculars. He walked every corner of the building's roof. "Damn," he said, as the man was nowhere to be found. Branden returned to the pavement below and picked up air between his feet as he ran. He crossed the wideness of the streets and passed each store. His speed ceased not. His blood was as a flame of his run.

The environment became woods. Branden made his way to the off roads of the city's edge. He came to Ava's home and jerked the screen door open. He beat on the door. "Ava"! He walked around the home to observe any broken windows. After a complete diameter check was made, he battered the front door with his shoulder until it opened. The living room was empty. "Ava!"

The house was not occupied. He bent over resting his palms to his knees panting fiercely. The phone began to ring. Branden answered. "Where is she, Damn it!"

The voice laughed aloud. "Mr. Hayes. I warned you."

"Listen to me you stupid fuck! Who are you! Where is Ava?" Branden struck his fist to the table.

"You're just like your father. Irrational and incapable of thinking things through."

"If you harm her..."

"I know, kill me you bastard. How did I know you were going to say that? What will the outcome be? Which will you save at the time of choosing?" He chuckled with intimidation in his voice. "You are my only adversary, Mr. Hayes."

"Coward!"

"To move you from my way is the only hope I obtain to gain control of the loss of a powerful company that once existed."

"What must I do to get her back? Tell me now!" The dial tone sounded. Branden tossed the phone across the room and left the house.

Branden entered the lobby of the Ace building. All of the bounty hunters were gathered center isle. They turned to face him with hatred between their eyes. Tera hid herself behind them as a shield.

"Well, if it isn't the freak," one said.

"Yeah, tell me who's gonna call me next," another joked.

"I can tell you who your wife's been calling," Branden replied.

One of the men approached him. "It has been brought to our attention that Tera, has asked for our hand in protection from you. Seems as though you concern her with threat."

"Just go," she mouthed quietly.

"Tera. Is this true?"

One of the hunters shoved him and said, "Get out freak. You're no longer a part of this association per, Mr. Grant. He determined you unstable from Tera's complaint of you."

"Tera talk to me." The hunter made attempts to push him over once more. Branden boldly latched onto his wrist and the arm sending him to wall. He wrapped his hand to his neck. The man's mouth dropped and remained open.

Outcast he was labeled while looking at the mob. They all began to gather. He immediately released the pressure of his hold. They drew their batons and other weapons. Branden stepped backwards until he cleared the building.

Chapter 7 *Dead Center*

The prison guard manually opened the cell door. He took the cash from Branden's hand. "Three minutes."

"What happened to five?"

"Ace Inc., called and reported your termination to the county and state. Your bounty license has been suspended. I need the money so three minutes is your limit."

The cage slammed behind him. Branden held the large cup. Wilks smiled and dropped his feet from the toilet. He laid the magazine to the mattress and stood. He walked over to him with a show of confidence. "Well. My word was correct. I told you that you'd be back."

Branden threw the contents of liquid over Wilk's face and grabbed him. He tackled him against the wall. Wilks shook his head and sealed his eyelids tight only to discover that the java was cooled. "Where is Ava?"

Wilks rolled his tongue over his outer cheek to absorb the sugar. He let him loose. Wilks wiped the fluid until it became a sticky film about his face. Branden hit him above the jaw line and held him. "Tell me everything, damn you! Tell me what you know."

"I will, but first you must uphold your end of the deal. First you brought me this nice cup of coffee. Now. You're going to free me. Don't bother with threats of killing me because, that would be in my favor to end this whole thing. You can continue to kick my ass, but if they found out that I have confessed, I'd rather be dead."

"How can I believe you?"

"What choice do you have? In return of my freedom, I help lead you to the man responsible for Ava's disappearance. I know who you are. I know every damn thing about you and your past. Without me you will die wondering who you were. All of this in exchange."

Branden breathed deeply through his nose. He looked darkly into his eyes. He rapped the bars grasping the guards attention. He unlocked the gate as Branden walked out. Wilks began to follow.

"Woah! Wait a minute," the officer yelled. He tried to close the cell. Branden reached out and secured it open.

Another officer ran to aid the situation. The first showed his baton and retracted it for combat. The other held his tazer and targeted the red beam to his chest. Wilks purposely pushed Branden into their direction.

The guard fired the gun. The sharp prongs broke the skin. The voltage was in full power. Branden felt not the electric shock.

With astonishment he looked at both guards. Fear tore into them. Branden was immune to the effects of the charge. He twirled the wires around his hand and

DEAD CENTER

snatched the weapon from them. The fellow officer swung the nightstick low toward his shin.

Branden swiftly stepped onto the club sending it to the floor. The guard screamed as his hand was caught in-between the stick and the floor. He kicked his face and punched the other guard out.

"How did you know that would not hurt me?"

"This way. I'll explain later." They ran to the stairs of the second pod stage. An immense size crowd of detention officers were gathered at the floor below, surrounding the bottom step. Branden picked the tazer from the ground and handed it to Wilks. He checked the silver prongs to ensure they were still intact to his chest. "Keep the trigger pressed in and stay close."

The cables of the stunner reflected yellow and blue sparks. The guards laid hold of him unaware of the electric field that creased through his flesh. The officers went limp and fell to the floor. Branden's body made the conductor flow more intense than the zap.

Branden ran with Wilks. They made way to his car. Branden yanked the studs from his skin. He inserted the ignition key and turned the switch. A blunt distortion echoed from under the hood. The engine was dead. He turned the key repeatedly.

"The battery shorted from the wave of power that built in your body. We have to go, now." They made exit from the vehicle and ran along side of the jail into the woods.

Sometime had passed from their flee. Wilks fell to one knee in exhaustion. "Give me your overcoat." Wilks slipped it on concealing the orange jumpsuit. He slid to the dirt and reclined his back to the boulder.

"Okay, Branden. Here's the story. You might want to sit down." Branden continued to stand without any reply to comment. "Keep in mind the entire reason why I'm relaying this information to you. Its because, I screwed up on my last job assignment. My boss will kill me literally for that. I did not uphold my goals."

"Which is?"

He looked up and said, "To kill you." Branden's face hardened. "Now, I'm on the run as you are. Together we can stop him. I hope.

In 1993, an amateur scientist, by the name of Kenneth Zear, put his education to use and opened his own research business, Zear Technologies Inc. He was basically the manufacturer of weapon attachment parts for the U.S. government. They heat molded barrel stocks, lens platted infer red beams for m-16s and tank night vision assembly. It was a small lab until time changed that.

Some U.N. ambassadors and other foreign leaders had their eye on him for a while. They offered him twenty-five billion to provide for their requested needs. In 1995 they offered Zear the services of a German engineer, Mr. Ginn.

Ginn did whatever Zear directed in the creation of certain experiments. A search for the perfect form of protection to serve as bodyguards for these country leaders was crucial.

Mr. Zear racked his brain constantly, day and night. Some claim that he about lost his mind. Finally, it came alive. The idea that haunted his employees. In order for one to be the best in defense, it had to be human. Superhuman. Skillful, quick and strong.

DEAD CENTER

Only one minor exception weighed against this. See, a human conscience has a heart attached to it. There had to be more to it than just training an assassin, Branden.

Also, there needed to be no fallacy as to reveal his undercover project unto the U.S. and U.N. Mr. Zear secretly hired top notch ex-marines, green berets etc. They became know as trackers.

Mr. Zear invented a needle that was to serve all the purpose of keeping his plans unidentified unto all else.

This is the beginning. This rod was to be planted dead center of the experiments brain, wiping out his memory. Also, he could control the experiments or empiricals, as we referred to them as.

The needle would allow the empirical to release adrenaline speed, fast thinking, super strength and mental awareness as needed by the blocking or unblocking of such chemicals that produce these emotions. In other words, the best protection, at will.

Such victims were bums or even family oriented husbands. We would get them by capture. Then the implant surgery was performed. We could track them by radar from the needle antenna. Most empiricals died from tragic means, except three. Braylen, your father. Yourself and the man you've been getting calls from."

"You were a tracker?"

"Former navy seal for two years and then tracker with Zear and Ginn. Your father, was one I dealt with for many days. Tracking him was difficult amongst all others. You see, the chemical that causes love, spilled over creating a block to our devices. This purposed threat unto us as to be unable to keep up with his whereabouts.

He dreamed. No other empirical had dreams. This meant that the needle did not totally wipe his memory. Apparently he dreamed about his son. Which was not actually of his own flesh and blood to claim. Alex was his name. He was made to think he was his son as to survive the experiment with Braylen. Braylen's mind was fixed and made to believe that Alex was his.

You and your father are different. At the time before the experiments, Braylen had a girlfriend, Linda. She became impregnated by Braylen twenty-five years ago. Later, he was caught and transformed into an empirical.

Zear held her captive after learning of her state. His chance had come to further his dreadful experiments. At eight weeks in the womb, he set an order for Linda to under go the needle. Except not on her. Zear literally opened her up, ran the needle into the fetus and created Empirical # 26, which is you.

Your memory, however, remained due to the new highly advanced rod that Zear made. This new needle would not age nor kill you. He even had the same style rod in his head. He done this himself.

You're very advanced. You can do things no other empirical could do. The past empiricals were induced heavily with steroid injections by four hundred percent to give them the most power any man could obtain. However, you have never lifted a weight and contain the strength of about eight average men combined.

This also explains why the tazer had no affect on you. The needle also acts as a ground rod. This shorted the car battery after you touched the key."

Branden sat and exhaled with discontent. "That's quite a bit to take in. Ava is not my mother?"

"No. Mr. Zear wanted one like himself, but died by the hands of another forced empirical. With Braylen dead, there leaves only two left. You and the one who all thought to have died the same day as Zear. Nevertheless, he did not.

This man wants to restart the Zear and Ginn corporation, but cannot with you in the world to stop him. He hired me and a few other retired trackers to act as 'nappers, which we were not. Our job was to kill or imprison you until he ordered you dead. He claimed that he'd jerk my very brain from the skull lining if I failed to bring you in. Needless to say, you slayed us all except for me and here we are.

Not only does this mysterious man want you dead for such reasons, he's also jealous. He is your step brother. He survived death. He even dug up Mr. Zear's body and removed the rod and replaced his with it, by his own hands.

You are the only two left. You're the hunter. He's the tracker. He can route you by the satellite of his brain to locate you. His name is Alex Adger and he's got Ava.

Branden laughed. "I'm a freak. A damn freak!"

"If our calculations answer true you can remember everything from the womb until the present, right?"

"That is correct. I'll turn myself in."

"Yeah, great idea. Leave Ava and that other bitch to the hands of Alex. That's right. We know there is another in your life Branden. Know why? Because love blocked our tracking."

He walked up to him and snatched his shirt. "Her name is Ayrelia. If you ever refer to her as bitch again, I'll kill you myself."

"Don't forget you need me Branden. I've been tracking empiricals for years. You acquire my help to find Alex. I know this is difficult, but we have to keep rolling. The cops will be on us as well."

Branden looked between the trees and said, "With such hatred in place, that's not the only group that will follow after news gets back to them." In reference to the bounty hunters.

Chapter 8 *Ayrelia*

Tera unlocked the door of her home and entered. She sat the brown paper sack of groceries onto the island counter of the kitchen. She flipped the light switch. The fluorescent bulb lit the entire room.

"Be careful my gun is over there," Branden stated, as he sat in the living room.

She pressed her hand over her heart and jumped. "Branden! Why are you here!" He stood. She walked backwards until she bumped the refrigerator. "Stay away from me Branden!"

"Take the gun."

She took the .40 caliber and beaded it at him. She held it with both hands as they shook. "I'll shoot you Branden. I'm serious!"

"Good. I"d rather be dead, than not have you by my side."

"Please, tell me those things I read were not true. Are you a bred killer?"

Randall Ford Jr.

"I am, but I stand for the good of things Tera." She threw a nearby glass at him.

"That's far enough Damn it!" He remained cold in his tracks. "What are you?"

"I"m a man, Tera. A simple man. Please, don't be scared of me."

"Is someone controlling you right now?"

"No."

"Are you going to kill me?"

"No!"

"Tell me everything about what's running in tune with your mind right now. I need to know Branden. Ease my mood."

He turned and pointed to the digital clock of her CD player. "In approximately twenty-eight seconds, the time by that unit will flash 10:05. Through your satellite I can tell you what's playing on every channel of your television. Except seven and twenty-three, which are not programmed with the directory. Also channel forty-four is off the air at the present time. Be alarmed that the man that lives across from you has a high powered telescope with defining magnifying power. May be a pervert. Your cell phone battery is low. The fourth outlet by your t.v. is burned out. I felt no frenzy tingle in my head as I walked past it versus the others.

Tera, I mean no harm to you in any from. I understand if this sounds premature, but I cannot mask my feelings. This is me. This is who I am. A person with one request. A dyer's eve unto your arms for to be as one. I love you Tera."

He splayed his shirt apart. "Just be accurate to hit me through the heart, because that's where all the pain lies. The pain of depression, longing and aggravation for you to be mine." Her eyes began to glisten and water.

"Sure I'm different, but so are you. For there is not one other creature even more beautiful than you. I fall weak when I near you. My emotions are quick to suicide when we part. Every part of you is all I wish to cherish and love. Trapped inside a hut of anxiety I used to grieve, even as to ask you for a mere date.

If not for my feet to run away from the fear of rejection, I would have asked you sooner. Don't hate me. Don't be frightened. Don't love me if you feel that you can't, but don't push away any feelings that you feel for me."

While Branden continued to speak a couple of thin blood streams flowed the temple and front of his face from the center of his head. "I'm dying Tera. Dying without you."

"Read my mind." She requested.

"I can't do that."

"You bastard. How dare you keep this from me this whole time?"

"Tera, I..."

"Don't ever call me Tera again," she cried. "Do you hear me!" He shifted his eyes to the floor. "It's Ayrelia to you." He enclosed his body to hers. She clung her arms around his neck still holding the weapon. She climbed his shoulders and engulfed her legs around his waist.

"No. It's beautiful."

Later that night, Mr. Grant, awaited a late night arrival of a new client from his office. He was startled by the slight knocks. "Come in." The man entered and sat in front of the metal desk.

"Eric Grant, I presume."

"At your service."

"Thank you for taking me in so late."

"My pleasure. What can I do for you?"

"I understand that your hunt team is the best in the state."

Eric laughed. "State? Sir, let me assure you that my specialist are the best in the world."

The man smiled politely. "Please. Call me Alex. I chose your company to bring a criminal into custody. You might have heard of him. Branden Hayes."

"As a matter of fact."

"I have reason to believe that he's holding my wife hostage," he lied. " P.I. sources convince me that he's been to our home while I'm at my work place. Here's a picture of him hugging her goodbye from the yard. I want him found and my wife brought to safety."

"Seems as though Branden was not the person whom I thought him to be. Between you and me, he's wanted for some jail break involvement earlier today. The law are out for him. If you would like for us to take the job, there will be a ten thousand dollar bond post requirement deposit from you Alex. Just take this form and fill it out in entirety."

Alex balled the paper and tossed it onto the floor. He propped the briefcase onto the desk surface and unlocked it. Eric blinked wildly at the sight of the bundled bills. "I want every hunter you have to work for me on this case. Two million dollars is all yours if he is nabbed."

Eric swallowed loudly. "Yes."

"Good then. You understand what I mean when I say, dead or alive."

Eric hoovered over the money. "No problem, Mr. Adger. I just need some information from you. Do you have any clue where your wife may be held captive?"

"I think it possible she's located inside of the abandoned Fleece Warehouse building two states over. I think he will try and ransom her out to me or the Feds."

"And the name of your wife?"

Alex's eyes assembled a slyness. "Her name is, Ava."

Branden tugged at Tera's shoulder. She awoke and stretched broad with her arms. "What time is it?"

"It's 3:59 a.m. We have to go. The hunters will be here soon to check on your status. It won't be safe to stay. We'll take your car."

They drove the back roads to avoid any authority figures. "Where are we going?"

"To the Fleece Warehouse building, just over the next boarder."

"What happened to the man you helped escape from the county? It's swarming all over the media."

"I need his help as well as he needs me.

Look Tera. I'm going to park you about a half mile from the warehouse for your safety until this thing blows over. Stay in the car. There are two guns in the dash and one under the seat. I won't be long, but use them if you must. Their loaded."

"This is starting to scare me a bit Branden. What's going down?"

"Wilks called about four minutes before I woke you. He regrouped what few trackers were left, which were ex-employees of Zear and Ginn. They agreed to help him for fear of their lives as well. They gathered some of their old tracking equipment devices and now they got a lead on Alex.

According to the track machines, his radar is reading "stationed" at the warehouse. Wilks believes that this may be where he plans to restart the company."

"You trust him?"

"I have no choice. Besides, he knows that I'm the only one that can stop Alex. Without me Alex would find him and destroy his existence. If Wilks ran from our agreement he knows he would be vulnerable to Alex's threat."

"What plan do you have?"

"I'm going to confront him, find Ava's whereabouts and cuff him. I have to work with Wilks. Ava is at stake. I have no choice."

They pulled into the crowded lot of the convenient store. "Branden?"

"Yeah?"

"What if Wilks is setting you up?"

"Either way I'm going to walk in and walk out with Ava." She pulled his shirt while he opened the car door.

"Don't leave me."

"Tera, I have to do this."

"No. I mean don't leave me. Come back to me alive."

He kissed her and rubbed her face with his palm. A black van with tinted windows arrived into the lot. "If they come back without me, cause a scene and get away."

"Branden. I love you." She said. Her fingertips glided over his.

Chapter 9 *Uncaged*

Branden ran for the side entrance of the van. He looked into her direction and then secured the door behind him. "Branden, this is Mike, Lee, Richard, Johnston, Lauren and Cameron," Wilks said while he drove. "It appears that Alex must be sleeping according to our wave linked monitors."

"Why's that?"

"Due to the slowed blood flow and his position hasn't changed since I called you."

"Do you think Ava is with him?"

"You know we're only trackers. That's all. Who knows?" They pulled into the wooded area behind the building. "Here's the deal. We split with our monitor trackers. When either of our signals off the chart, we channel by radio for Branden.

With all due respect, Branden, Alex is sinister and fearless. This is very dangerous for us. We do not acquire your talents."

The men fastened their ear pieces and turned the radios on. They crept to the side of the metal building. Some doors were without knobs and had nylon straps ran through the open space. The door creaked from the rusted hinges. Each man entered and parted. Branden stayed with Wilks. The others scattered and faded into the shadows of the dark warehouse.

They walked hunched over around each isle, as they remained camouflaged behind large boxes of materials. The cardboard of the boxes were mildewed and speckled with mold stains. The tin of the roof leaked from the years of inclement weather. Various puddles stood water about the floor.

"Anything?"

Wilks held the scanner close. "Not yet. Several warehouses are linked together."

They moved swiftly throughout the building. The white canvas of the walls were torn and revealed the asbestos behind it. They stepped through a roll up doorway that led to another warehouse sector. "Wait!" Wilks whispered. "He's in this one." The detector flashed with speed. "He's got to be in about middle of the floor just around that pallet of boxes." Wilks looked on. "I'm not going any further."

Branden stooped low and gripped the lining of the box. He looked back at Wilkes and then slowly peeked about the edge. Two thick gauged steel chains were bolted to the ceiling and ended out of sight behind some eight foot shipping crates.

Wilkes removed his headset and became jittery. Branden eased his gun from the seat of his pants. He aimed it to the crate and paced slowly before them. He could taste the heated saliva from the adrenaline of his mouth. He neared the side of the wood. He breathed deeply and turned the surface facing the front of the boxes.

Wilkes watched as Branden stood with his mouth open and his face in a stupor. He dropped his gun to his side. "Damn it. Kill him while you have the opportunity," Wilkes thought.

Ava's wrists were shackled by welded metal cuffs that were connected to the chains. Her arms pulled up and her knees together bent while sitting onto the cold concrete floor. Her head ducked and her eyes closed. Blood dripped slowly from her shirt.

Branden placed his right arm under her knees and inserted his free hand under the top of her back for comfort. He lifted her as he stood. "Ava, no. Wake up," he said softly.

Wilkes witnessed the tragedy and called for an ambulance. A sharp object stuck from her chest which pierced her heart. "Find something to cut these chains," Wilkes ordered his crew. "Now!"

"Ava, I am so sorry for this." The team of trackers pulled at the chains to break them from the wooden beams. "Hold on, Ava, help is coming."

"Oh, Branden, it's too late." Blooded soaked over his clothes. His shoes splashed the puddle where she had laid. "Don't let this time worry you Branden. Happy I am. No longer do I need to dwell in the past. Now I am off to reunite with Braylen."

The chains gave way and bumped the floor. One tracker recovered an out of date emergency kit from the neighboring warehouse. "Always remember Branden.

Time is never long, especially when love is the heart of two." Her eyes glossed open. Blood spouted and poured from her mouth. It ran over his forearms.

Branden's heart fluttered as though it were the end of time. The small hairs of his neck tingled with brief panic that crept from the eerie stillness of her body. "Is this a dream?" he thought. *This cold room is lonely. The presence of death and of life stand apart from one another as though each has conquered a goal.* Her eyes glazed over and the pupils enlarged with dilation.

Wilkes neared and studied over the spear that stuck in her heart. "This is what one of those needles look like." He leaned into her and observed the end of the object. "Number twenty-five. This needle that was used to kill her was the needle that your father once had in his brain."

Wilkes shut the tracker off. They all stood around in silence. Branden held her until the warmth of her flesh cooled. He laid her gently to the ground and combed his fingers through the lazy strands that relaxed over her eyes. He grit his teeth as to kill any fear that surged his veins while rubbing his head. His face fevered from the adrenaline that shocked his eyes. They squinted and his voice darkened with frustration. Aggressive overtones vibrated in his voice. "This taker of this life will be taken by me."

"Don't make this any more difficult," Branden heard a voice yell. He looked towards the caged balcony above. A few bounty hunters stood. "We got the proof before us of you holding the evidence."

The trackers ran for cover. Branden stood and was blind sided by a fourth hunter. He landed heavily onto the floor. The team of hunters ascended by cable onto the floor. They piled their weight on top of him to bind. The trackers became nervous. They pulled his arms behind him tightly.

Branden's head bounced from the cement from their overpowering force. He saw Ava's face. The eerie unnatural look of murk reflected his own state of mind. His temper burned like never before. He began to crawl with the hunters buried onto his back. "Hold him still, damn it!"

Branden fought to one knee, while the others whelped him with their fists. He grabbed the nearest person and pulled his foot chest level, causing him to fall against another. He delivered a hard blow to the next two rendering them unconscious. The last hunter backed away and counter attacked by slinging his baton downward. Branden caught it and buried it across his neck. He then pushed him to the wall in a choke hold. He darted each end to strike his head.

Wilkes looked about the lying men and said, "Good thing we called for an ambulance." They fled to the van and loaded the gear inside. They drove back to the store and let Branden out.

Wilks grabbed the sleeve of Branden's ripped shirt. "We will locate that bastard."

Branden walked up to Tera's car. He opened the door as she was missing. The van drove off. Branden circled the entire perimeter of the lot by foot. "Ayrelia?"

He entered the store calling her by name. Customers looked and began to laugh. He ran back to the car. Both guns were in place and the keys were left in the ignition. He opened the dash to answer the calling cell phone. He pressed the button and put it to his ear.

"Good evening, Mr. Hayes."

"Fuck you! You're going to pay for what you did to Ava. Ayrelia! Where are you?" He looked about the lot.

"Tell me something Branden. When Ava's chin was covered in blood, did she resemble a dead vampire?" Branden kicked the door from anger. "How's it feel to lose someone close to you? Ironic isn't it? Your friends and co-workers are working for me now and my trackers are helping you."

"Be a man, you cowardly son of a bitch! Face me!"

"Oh, your time is coming, Mr. Hayes. First I want to distort your mind and have some fun before I do that."

"Ayrelia?"

"That reminds me. Tera, is right here. Would you like to hear her scream?" Did your foster parents give you that last name?"

"Don't screw around with me you idiot. Ayrelia!" She screamed loudly over the intercom of the phone. Branden felt faint from the hard rush of blood to his ear.

"I know your very thoughts Branden. If I harm her you're gonna kill me. Am I right? See, I can read your very thoughts through the satellite of my brain. What choices will you claim, Branden? Save Tera or the Singer girl. Remember the kidnapper is still at large. Don't forget yourself either.

I can't be tracked with this kind of needle, Branden. Therefore, you have no need for those trackers. So, I took the liberty of discarding them. I was tracking you. I watched you all enter the warehouse. I placed a detonation bomb over the frame of the van. Good luck, Mr. Hayes."

"Don't hang up. Don't hang up!" The phone deadened with a silent echo.

Wilks drove recklessly onto the dirt road. One of the trackers fumbled through the back packs. A red blinking light caught his attention from underneath the equipment. The timer of the bomb was attached to one of the extra duty belts. The digital clock was counting down from fifteen seconds. "Wilks!"

He stomped the brakes. The van spun sideways off of the dusty path. The explosion sounded. Flames filled the stalled van, taking the life of each man inside.

Branden's hope declined as he could not contact Wilks and the others. He ran inside of the store and flashed his bounty hunter license at the clerk. "Sir, I need to review you security recorded surveillance."

The overweight man burped and only starred at him. Branden exhaled and rubbed his brow. "Sir, I have reason to believe that someone has been kidnaped in your parking lot moments ago." The man's face changed not.

Branden smiled and jerked him over the counter and onto the floor. The man rolled to miss the rack of chips. Branden walked toward him. The clerk kicked his feet to slide himself backwards across the linoleum.

The man unlocked the back office door and Branden gained entrance to the control room. He rewound the tape. He witnessed a business casual man walking up to the car. He poked the gun through his trousers and demanded she walk to his vehicle.

DEAD CENTER

Branden ran from the store. His head pounced from the soaring level of emotions. "What to do." He thought. *Where should I go? Confusion is the breath I took. This fault is my own to cause blame.*

Paranoia grew with him. Without hesitation, he entered the car and peeled out. He drove onto the back roads of the small town. Beautiful were the trees that hoovered the boarders of the lanes. He took the cellular phone from the glove compartment and called Mr. Grant.

Mr. Grant sat at his desk and gloated over the printed invoice from Alex upon the future capture. He picked up the screaming phone. "Where is she!"

"Where is who?"

"I saw one of your hunters lure her from her car and into the company SUV. That's kidnaping!"

Mr. Grant covered the receiver and motioned for Alex to come into his office. "It's Branden," he whispered.

"I'm heading straight for you. Now, where is she!"

"I'm sorry Branden. I'm lost. I don't know who you are referring to." He snickered and looked away from Alex.

Alex stood and placed his hand over the phone and asked, "May I. Mr. Hayes. Good evening once again."

"Where is she, damn it!"

Branden decreased his speed and pulled onto the shoulder. The surroundings were as a deserted forest. He looked through every path of wooded plains that edged the road. He stepped into the middle lane and observed no followers. He pulled his handgun and began to shoot blindly into all directions.

The discharges echoed through the trees, until the sharp pinch darted with a dense hit. He fired once more tagging the hidden object behind the trees. He entered the automobile and made a reverse u-turn. He drove the car into the direction of the mystery object.

The bounty hunter dropped the binoculars and jumped inside of the high profile vehicle stationed in the woods. He leaped inside of the passenger window to shield himself from Branden's oncoming vehicle. He fell into the seat and jammed the key into the ignition slot.

The angry roar from Branden's speed caused him to push himself upward. The car met the dirt that bordered the wooded path which was created and used for the local highway patrol units for as an undetected prowl on speeders. Large chunks of red clay was tossed about as a windmill in motion.

Finally the car collided into the side of the hunter's, sliding it against the trees. The impact vibrated the steering wheel. The radiator from Branden's car whistled and steamed. He pulled the plastic-like film coating from the shattered windshield. The crumbled pieces gave away allowing Branden full access through the hollowed glass.

He stepped out onto the hood and then crawled through the side window. The console that connected the dash, sliced into the leg of the hunter. It was completely detracted from the plate. Branden placed his knees over his stomach and wrapped his hands around the front of his throat. He pressed hard strikes to his face splitting his lip open.

"Where is she! Why would you be working for him?" The man's voice weakened. "Answer me now or suffocate under this pain that has driven me into hands of doom."

"He paid Grant a lot of money to commission us to hunt you and track your movements. Alex said you'd kill Ava and the others saw you holding her dead body Branden."

"Where is she Rob? Where is Alex now?"

"He went to the office to visit with Grant."

Branden took the shotgun from under the seat and pulled Rob across the passenger side. "You're coming with me."

"Me? Why?"

"You're tracking me, my cars immobile and you have a lead on me. So Alex thinks."

The car knocked, but turned over with precision. "Call him on the cell phone and make sure Alex is still there."

"Don't insult me to this degree Branden. I know, that you know, that Alex would be able to home in on you sitting right beside me. He said you're a freak. Some sort of brain controlled bot. You plan to kill me don't you?"

"No."

"He said you would try if you could. He was right. You attempted to crush me with your car. He has a plan to stop you. Even though my portion of the blue pint failed, the overall attack will condemn you."

"Shut up."

"The hunters all work for him now, Branden. You're in a maze of trouble. Survival will not let you give up the selfishness to save the world. Give into Alex and salvage even the life of the one you love most."

"Shut up! What does he want from me, damn it!"

"Your head."

Branden stopped the vehicle and shifted it into park as they entered the lot of the Ace building. He slapped the ankle cuff to the right side of Rob's foot and tightened the excess linkage of chain through the steering wheel. Then he connected the open end to his wrist holding him in place. He pumped the shotgun to load the chamber.

Branden ran inside of the building opening each conference room door in search for Alex. Finally, he arrived at Grant's office door and shook the handle. He stepped back and threw his leg into the door breaking it from the molding.

Two large Hunters attacked him from the corners of the room. The gun fell to the floor after the jarring blow. Three more powerful bounty guards seized his arms and legs as a net. The men locked their grip about him. Branden's heart was of madness at the sight of Alex sitting in Mr. Grant's desk chair before him. He wore a full grey suit with all in the place of formality.

"Well. The infamous Thin Bird. Branden Hayes or should I call you by your real name, Branden Adger?" Branden saw Mr. Grant's dead body lying onto the floor at the desk. "Perhaps, you'd like for me to refer to you as my brother. Even that be the case I don't claim Bray-

DEAD CENTER

len as my father. This is part reason why you're here in front of me, held captive by my directed will."

"Where is she, damn you, Alex! Where is she? What do you want from me you sick bastard!"

"I'll explain that very throughly. You see, contagious this plot has infected me to end this era of time. Our father or your father I'll refer to him as, was considered a great man. One who upheld the law of love. But, what really pissed me off is the fact that he allowed me to be confronted by the threat of death, by falling from a ten story building.

Braylen, under went a removal surgery. This in return left dead any memory of me to him. How great could this man be to Ava or yourself to realize that he could simply live without me in his thoughts. His very own son. However, I see clearly that you are the one he must of loved best."

"I didn't ever meet him!"

"What's worst Branden, your loved ones dying and you forget them or you having no knowledge of such ones whom are alive? I want you to experience what it's like to choose. Which route will you destine yourself with? I want the rod that is presently punctured inside of your head.

I could waste your life at this moment Branden. I choose not to. I will allow you to suffer and understand how I felt from this vendetta toward you for the last twenty-five long years.

My self proclaimed real father, Mr. Zear, had a goal in mind. To stop at nothing. I am the most intelligent empirical of all. I am the strongest to this day. You are my predecessor. You are just like me. How does it feel to be one step away from being evil, Branden?

Mr. Zear implanted in you the same titanium needle as himself and I. Braylen and all the rest were just some cheap knock off experiment. I might have turned out like you if it had not been for Braylen deleting me from his mind.

You're so special. Like a clone of Braylen. I'm just like my father. You try to save the world. I try to rule it.

Look around at these ex-friends of yours. Look into their mindless eyes Branden. After you're dead, I will create a new line of empiricals. These hunters be the beginning of that army.

I see you've found my location. Therefore. you must have captured Rob. My guess is he's tied down in his automobile. Weak he will always be. Too much distraction in his mind keeps his primary job at bay. When I walk out of the doors to this place I'm going to end him.

Before I do so, I bet you're still wondering where that precious one you love is. The ever so beautiful Tera. Listen to me with all that you bare your conscience to hold. She is also chained down in the back of my car. How ironic that we think so much alike isn't it." Alex swung openly clinging his knuckles to Branden's cheek bone.

"Your father caused the death of mine. So I took your thought to be mother. You stole my trackers so I've taken your hunters. You fuck with me and I'll fuck Tera."

Branden forced the group of men to shift their weight from his angry mode. The men grappled him firmly

DEAD CENTER

and held him in position. "That's it Branden. Surge the energy of emotions that control you.

You and I have a flaw Branden. All of the empiricals did including Mr. Zear. Whether it was love like Braylen or some other particular flaw. Everyone who had been instilled with a rod had been nicked in a certain area of the brain that overflows a certain chemical of the brain. Whatever that chemical be, love, hate, rage the urge to fuck constantly or in your case, depression.

I've been watching you and studying you for years. Branden. I know that you have never failed in a mission to carry out. Your life levels are fueled by bringing these criminals to their justice. Without to rescue the child and save the small innocent beings your brain would pace a state of depression so fast, you'd grieve yourself into a black grave.

The Singer case that's been assigned to you was also of my very plan. I paid the 'naper twelve hundred dollars to render her into my hands. She's safe for now, but will be executed, as well as Tera, in approximately twenty-four hours from the time I leave this room.

I leave you this challenge to save them in such hours. I know if you have fallacy through the ways of greed by your anger you will not succeed in this task. If you were to lose both their lives, your brain would shut your body down until you're dead. This is the mind shock stage I hope you enter.

If you do complete this course and save them, you will be honorable to dual with me. The only thing I want is the rod and your life. First, I want you to undergo what intensity really is. Make it easy for me and fail the challenge or face me for the end of your time Branden.

Randall Ford Jr.

Listen to me carefully. Go to the airport and tell them you have a prepaid ticket. You will have a five a.m. flight. It will be of my best interest to remove you from this town that you are so aware of your surroundings.

A stranger you will be. From the time you enter the airport and exit, you will be watched. Also the security from the airline will scan you for any weapons. If I get a report from my hunters that you were discovered with a weapon, I will slit her throat.

In the city, you will enter the taped off area. This is due to the quarter mile row of old buildings that is set up for demolition tomorrow. Will you be able to find which building she is located in before it gets crushed? The explosions go off at approximately 8:40 a.m. She will be located top floor of one of them.

Will you rescue her before she ignites?" Alex walked to the door and looked at him. "I have the number to your cell phone. Good luck.

Check into the Farside Hotel. You'll be securely eyed and tracked. Just go to the front desk and register your valid key. Stay in the room. Do not leave. Your phone will be on tap and your cell will be disengaged through the track devices.

Here is a clue in the riddle from where she will be. When you step off of the plane, walk straight until you exit the airport corridors. Walk out into the city. Go until your path becomes too hot to travel. Fork your path between the empty buildings. There you will turn to the feelings of abandonment. Go right. There she will be aloft twelve stories above."

Alex made departure from the room. The gang of men began to beat him heavily. Branden pulled away and intercepted the oncoming blows by twisting his body to the side. He pushed away by the kicking of his feet. Alex left the building while the hunters continued to attack Branden fiercely. They shuffled him around the room bullying their plot of meanness into him. They held his arms while another drop kicked his body through the front door.

Branden stumbled over the cement steps onto the dirt of the ground below. After the brutality, they tossed a set of keys to his cheek. They each took a stabbing kick to his ribs as they passed. One of the hunters stuck his head inside of the drivers window of Rob's SUV. He ensured his death by observation that Alex had fired six rounds into him. They all parted leaving Branden to cope.

Branden brought himself to his knees. With difficulty, he removed his coat. Deep bruises surfaced about his neck and shoulders. He staggered as he stood. He made his way to the designated vehicle and entered. He drove to the hotel as directed.

Branden held his side and walked up to the front desk. The clerk handed him the card key. He escorted him to the room and took his bag. "This is for examination. You will get it back when you check out."

Branden looked about the room. He sat heavily onto the bed. He took his shirt off painfully from the swelling of his abdomen. The hotel was luxurious, but costumed to fit by the prearranged demands of Alex. No phone, television or computer was present.

Branden threw himself over the mattress. His energy left him from the exhausting beating. His eyes closed and his mind drifted in dream on days passed. Tera held his hand close while strolling through her yard. "Life is grand," she said while smiling. "I'm getting hooked on you making me laugh so hard. Stop it! No more jokes. My side can't take it." She dropped her house keys into to miry mud. She looked at him with affection. Her eyes shifted towards the ground and back to his. She tilted her face downward in a playful manner. She moved in on him and began to breath onto the raw nerves of his neck. "Could you please?"

He rolled his sleeve and buried his hand into the wet clay. She giggled as he freed his hand with her key set. They walked to the door of his house and he unlocked the deadbolt. He held the door ajar for her. She flipped the lights and he followed in behind her. She turned facing him and took his coat from his arm and ran her free hand down across his imprinted chest.

"I'll get you a towel," she said. She walked in front of him. He took her by the arm and pulled her forcefully to his body. The jacket fell from her hand as he kissed her open neck. She raised her right hand to the back of his head under his hair. He spun her around to lock hold of her eyes.

She brought her leg up to the side of his thigh. He ran his palm from her calf to her hip, smearing the mud. She turned around to position him against her backside. She loosely began to move her butt onto him. She then stepped forward and planted her knees onto the couch. She kept her legs straight and tilted the entire top half of her body forward over the seat cushions of the sofa.

Her face was flush against the padding. "Fuck me dirty," she said. He untucked his shirt and started his hands on her ankles. He slowly savored the touch of her seductive skin from her legs to the baseline of her skirt.

He lifted the skirt up tight around her butt up to the top line of her back. She tucked her bottom lip under her teeth while he ran his fingers over the top lace lining of the thong panties. He slid them as far as they would go around her knees.

She was now fully exposed unto him. She began to tease him through his pants by the bareness of her skin, swaying herself left to right. He brought himself through the opening of his zipper and placed it onto her. The pulsating sensation made her become more impatient for him.

He kept still while she continued to make half circles about the front of him. She stopped as she anticipated his move. Finally, he entered her touching areas that have never been reached before. Each push seemed to get more intense than the last.

Tera buried her face deeper into the sewn pillow of the couch to stifle her moans. She wanted to run her nails inside of his chest, breaking the skin, but instead she ripped the leather. The delightful edge of her voice caused him to exceed harder inside of her.

He locked his hands tighter around her firm waist, bringing his body closer into hers. With all of the perfection of repetition, her state of ecstacy became elevated by the pushes.

The final thrust became the hardest. Her shoe dangled from her toes and the other lay on the floor. Her body began to relax from the cramped muscles.

The two way sounded at 4:00 am. Branden's back propped against the wall as he sat awake. He blinked his eyes to focus from the blurred haze. He held it closely and responded to the call.

"In four minutes, leave your room," Alex said. "Exit the lobby and hand your card over to the doorman. Enter your vehicle. Drive no faster than forty two miles per hour. If you are tagged by a highway patrolmen for speeding, she's dead. Drive to the airport. Do not procrastinate leaving your car once parked. Enter through the security scanners. If any weapon of any style is detected, I'll kill her. Go to the ticket line, take the proper pass and board the plane. Don't screw yourself over Branden."

"I want to hear her voice."

Alex walked over to Tera. She moved her face away from his tracing finger. "She's kind of tied up at the moment."

"Alex, I done as you said this far. I beg of you."

He roughly pulled the bandanna from her mouth. "It's your precious hero." He placed the phone to her ear.

"Branden?"

"Ayrelia baby! Hang in there baby."

"Oh, how sweet. Let me describe to you the fragile importance at hand Branden. Your girl is blindfolded and now gaged again. Her hands bound by rope looping the two by fours of the rafters. Fully clothed with the exception of her shoes being of. Similar to Ava's position.

Take heed Branden that her legs are left free. If urgency doesn't sear your mind to force my demands, then only your imagination could allow you to think of what we're capable of doing to her if you mess this up."

"Take me right now Alex! Send your men up here and take me out. Just let her go. She has not one thing to do with us."

"You still don't comprehend do you? Imprisoned I have been for long dreary years. Now it's your turn to suffer. I was tossed out of a fucking window, left to die. You were spoiled all this time. My time is now Branden. I have you, the precious of the two brothers.

Come out fighting. Don't give up. I want you with all of your anger behind you. It's like a child whose been kicked around all of his childhood. Ordered to live to stand in the corner. When that young man grows up, he'll break loose and run his own rampant wild side. Just as you're that child made to do as I say or else.

I know you're wanting to see her and end me. However, you know you must obey my directions. I want you to grow up and come out fighting with me, Branden. Prove yourself. No matter how mad you become you must remain your feelings of control submissive to achieve your goal. Now, go get in the damn car and head for the airport!"

Branden slide the barrel lock of the chamber. He stuffed both .40 calibers into the seam of his pants. His overcoat draped them and made them invisible.

Branden passed the watchman and slipped the card into his white glove. The air was brisk, as the sun had not yet risen. He did a quick scan of the car's interior before entering. His breathing was slow and deep. His heart cringed with excitement.

After some time had passed, Branden, reached the destination. He entered the airport. The security personnel were using pass through booths and single wands for metal detection. To avoid a pat down he quickly made his way to the bathroom. He pushed the door open and turned to check the isles. The lavatory was small with two stall urinals and a sink.

He kicked the side door frame board sending the plank to twirl into the air. He caught it as it propelled furiously. He propped it under the door handle. The opposing end of the plank was tightly fitted against the second leg of the stall which barricaded him from any intruders.

He climbed from the side of the stall and pushed the ceiling square tile up and over. He checked the safety switch controls of the guns and laid them flat inside of the metal duct. After determining his flight position entrance, he slid them through the tunnel as far as he could.

He jumped from the wall and removed the plank that was lodged in place. He went out and pretended to rub his hands together for dramatic effect, as though they were wet. He approached the ticket clerk and said, "Branden Hayes to flight number five."

The lady smiled and gave him an envelope. "Your time to board is now."

He waited in line to wait for the customers to walk through the metal detector. When his time came near, he walked in with a nervous heart. The alarm remained silent. He exhaled with a tense relief. He handed the envelope to the ticket validator and then made his way to the corner of the hallway.

Branden looked over his shoulder and entered into the next compartment level of restrooms just past the security entrance. He planted his foot onto the far wall and threw himself onto the stall's top boarder. He passed the tile and searched for the guns. He reached his upper body halfway into the ceiling and retrieved them. After securing the tile he dropped to his feet.

Upon his exit, the ticket greeter ran to him. "Sir!" He remained calm and grinned. "Sorry sir. You forgot your stub." He flipped the card over as it read, "Do not go to the bathroom again."

Chapter 10 *One step higher*

Branden stepped off of the plane onto the pavement. Several news helicopters were swarming the sky due to the festival of stripping the old town. He walked throughout the stainless steel gate stoppers and out into the strip of the town.

"Old is out, new is the rule," was the banner that stretched the top of the run down building. The town's people gathered around in splotches to witness the demolition by the explosions of the buildings. Several rows of empty shops and businesses lie in the heart of the square. The live surrounding areas consisted of busy restaurants and street vendors. The parade of folks were increasing rapidly.

Branden walked to the end of the line of businesses. The Big Grill, eating place sat on the edge of the shopping center. 'Fork you path when it becomes too hot to travel," he remembered. From there he turned to the "feelings of abandonment," which was the sight of the deserted towers.

He stood in thought at the Pealaze building in front of him. "This couldn't be that easy," he whispered. He ducked underneath the yellow tape and crossed into the vacant lot of near disaster. He entered the bottom floor of the building.

The door crept open as the hinges were rusted. The wooden inlay of the stairs popped as they settled from his weight. The pitch of the choppers were low just above the building's roof.

"Ayrelia?" The echo of his shout carried through the interior. He pedaled his way to the twelfth floor. His breath was fast. The fear of the unknown struck him. His foot met the surface of the fire escape. "Ayrelia?" He looked about the endless office. No breath, but his was found.

"Damn it! Ayrelia?" He stepped over to the side glass and looked down. Alex's car probed the lot below. "Where is she!" He yelled as he answered the call of the radio phone.

"Mr. Hayes, not to worry she's here below with me in the car. I see that you made it to the top. I must apologize for you being anxiously in wait, only to be empty handed. But, I'll give you one last appeal to save her. That is if you're still in one piece.

In about two seconds I'm running her down the interstate. At some point I'm going to pull over and stand her up on the shoulder of the road. Then I'm going to tie her hands together and place a large refrigerator cardboard box over her body. What young college student or wild passer-by wouldn't mind hitting a flimsy target such as that? What goes up must come down true?"

"True," Branden mumbled under his breath.

Branden's hand released the rail as he stepped back and turned to run for the stairwell across the room. As he ran, it seemed as though a pin drop could shatter the sound barrier. The twelfth floor explosion sounded as if thunder was chasing him.

The floor began to shake. Sheetrock crumbled from the walls. Branden made it to the first flight of stairs and sailed down the steps. In like manner he rounded the tenth level as the floor above exploded. The impact threw him against the wall and caused him to tumble while being forced down the stairs. He stood to his feet without a second to spare and began to run down the next set.

The room he made exit from had made a cloud of fire just above the stairwell. The building felt like an earthquake. The next floor opened it's detonation. The invisible force of explosion hit him. He ran the stairs and pushed himself through it's gravity field of multiplied strength.

He held onto the railing of the seventh floor stairway hall. He slid from the rail all the way to the ground. His head throbbed as if an angered boxer had triumphed over him. Debris blew from every direction. Parts of the ceiling above distributed chunks of cement and caved in the middle.

The next office floor went up into flames. Dust and smoke enclosed the stairs above. Branden spotted the news chopper that hoovered about in front of the fifth floor bay window. The news crew was capturing the event.

Branden got up and ran as hard as he could. Seconds lay between the distance of time until the room would engulf in flames. He ran for the window and lifted his coat tails. He pulled the gun from his pants. He began to fire it at the window. He untucked the other gun from the front side and began to bullet them, breaking the glass into large pieces.

He ran to the edge of the window. He placed the bottom of his shoe onto the end of the tile. He secured the first gun and dropped the other. He jumped from the window and landed his arms to the base rail of the helicopter. As he swung from the air carrier, the explosion alarmed from the story which he jumped.

The force caused the air vehicle to slam into the building beside it. Branden was thrown through the window behind the chopper that was separated by the metal barrier. He slid across the waxed floor grabbing at everything to break his speed. The room sucked him through to the opposite side window.

He shifted himself while being dragged over desk chairs and file cabinets. He panicked. He burst through the glass and dangled in mid-air. He held onto several computer cables and industrial phone lines. Weightless in atmosphere, he gripped with might. The modem he latched onto was lodged between a desk that lay horizontal. It clamped it's sides to the frame.

He pulled himself by the chords with caution. He climbed onto the desk and then touched the floor. His back rested onto the glass particles that were collected from the collision. He hopped to his feet. Adrenaline ran with him. The news casters were out of harm and slight in injury.

Branden leaped from the top stairs to the bottom platform of each floor until he reached the lobby. The front door was chained. He tossed a mid-sized chair through the window making his flee successful. He opened the car door and gave chase to find Ayrelia.

Chapter 11 *I Will Die Loving You*

Branden peeled smoke from the tires and fled onto the freeway. He sat upright with the steering wheel and creased the cars of traffic that caught up to the front of him. He swerved recklessly between the lane of cars. He gripped the handle of his gun tight while passing a state trooper that sat to the side of the medium. Blue lights flashed. The cop pulled away from his designation to gain velocity.

After Branden had passed, the trooper mazed his path and fell directly in behind him. Branden stomped the acceleration pedal. The skillful officer was not shaken.

Branden waited for a clear lane to open. He crossed lanes and slammed on brakes allowing the squad unit to blast ahead of him. The patrol vehicle's tires roared and the entire car fish tailed in his attempts to halt. Branden pulled the gun and aimed it at the officer. His face froze in sight of murder. However, Branden only deflated the tires.

DEAD CENTER

Branden regained his speed and continued to push the car as the suspension became unstable. He saw the box up ahead. He searched a way to keep Ayrelia from being crushed by the racing cars abroad.

He jumped speed and evened himself next to a transfer truck which was carrying a trailer rig. He demanded the driver to stop. The man only acknowledged him to be deranged and kept driving.

He aligned the rear of his car even with the truck. While maintaining a steady speed he pushed the tinted sun roof glass out. The glass was picked up by the wind and tossed onto the highway. He bolted his car several car links between them and let off the pedal.

Branden climbed out of the empty space in the top of his car. As it began to lose speed, Branden stood on the roof. The truck slowed not. When reachable, Branden cat walked the back windshield. He leaped from the trunk and dove onto the front of the truck.

The driver feared for his safety. Branden appeared to be a mad man out of control. He latched onto the wiper arm and wrapped his hand to the motor's cover. The force of air collected beneath him and caused his balance to slip as his hand fell from the wiper blade. He fell at the side of the truck directly onto the step plate.

The driver felt overwhelmed and pushed his door open, knocking Branden off of the truck and onto the hard road. Branden spun himself missing the large truck wheels.

He lay on the pavement under the truck and threw his hands up by the trailer's end. He grasp the rear steps of the rails and pushed his body upward. The truck switched lanes. The cars behind them began to move while they witnessed Branden holding onto the trailer.

He stoutly pulled himself to the rear double doors of the rig. He propped his foot onto the lock and leaned forward pushing himself up to the top of the trailer. After recovering his balance he surfed the heavy machine. He made a run for the front and dashed with heavy steps.

He removed his coat from his shoulders and stabilized his foot on the top valance in-between the vertical tail pipes. He wrapped his coat around the chrome exhaust and looped the coat for use as a handle. He kicked the overhead valance repeatedly until the fiberglass piece broke loose. As it began to give way he, braced the flap down with his foot to adjust it in front of the windshield. The covering blinded the driver's view. The road disappeared.

Branden held the long sleeves of the coat while the driver braked. The truck smashed the concrete barrier and then sprinted into the lane again. The tractor overturned and slid into Ayrelia's direction, until it stopped a few yards in front of her. Branden held onto the cab and then hopped over it. He ran to the box and lifted the cardboard cage.

The thundering removal of the box caused her to cringe. Her arms were roped from behind her. "It's me Ayrelia!" He untied the blinder and held her with a squeeze. "I'm sorry I left you alone in the car. I'm sorry for all of this." The trailer served as a safeguard for traffic to detour around the large vehicle.

He began to ease from her to unbind her hands. "Don't!" she said. "Don't let go." She looked downward and up to him with glistened eyes.

"Oh Branden. I'm sorry." She caught her breath quickly.

"Ayrelia, baby?"

"Don't move. Not just yet . At least not until I tell you something. The time of day that we spent together was the opening of other worlds. You rescued me so many times with your presence, to make me happy. Comfortable you elevated my will to burn the past and pledge the future with you. Remarkable you are and all that you do. Risking your very life for others to be happy is your job. If only to walk away from this would be to hurt. Not only for you, but I also. Miss you forever, I will."

"Ayrelia, what's wrong? I'm here. Everything is okay."

"Alex cut me Branden. He surgically installed a small bomb inside of my chest cavity. When you hold me like this, it set the detonator to unlock, like a grenade. If you let me go, it will release. There are no wires outside of me to slice that would seal off the device. It was a set up. If the building's collapse didn't burry you, then I would. You can move away in time and save yourself, Branden."

"I can call for help. A doctor, policeman or somebody."

"Branden, no one would believe you. They'd label you crazy and take you out to free me as your hostage. After all you are wanted publically for Ava's death. You have to let me go Branden."

"No! I'll die with you. What will I amount to if all the life from me is taken?"

She grazed her cheek to caress his chin. "Listen to me Branden. There are so many people who need you. That Singer girl, I heard, is in his custody. He plans on turning her into an empirical. The first of his army creation to be. So much good can derive from your life, Branden."

"I will not. I can't. This isn't meant to be like this, Ayrelia. Please, wake me or something. I will die loving you."

She closed her eyes and exhaled sadly. She smiled and danced her eyes until she made his connect. "Branden, you will never be allowed to forget me. Your heart could not stand for that to happen. You'll still be loving me when I'm gone. Kiss me. Tell me how you feel about me. Make me smile. Make a promise to me. Tell me what you love most about me. Tell me what you hate most about me. Let me feel your tears puddle my hair. Tell me you love me, kiss me once more and then let me go."

"I rather die with you."

"Please," she whispered. "Fill this of the last of my request. Do exactly what I hope for you to. The sirens are nearing. They'll drop you Branden causing both of us to murdered. That little girl needs you. So does the others who are taken from their parents. Bring them home for me. Do this for me. I'd rather be dead knowing that I bare on someone's mind than to be gone without to remember."

He arced his head. Her soft lips glided his for the taken. Overwhelmed with gallantry and honor she was lifted. Tears rolled from him and descended onto her cheek smearing over the flesh. He looked onto her face and said, "Silent lust was the captivation that inclined me to entertain you. You are the insanity behalf my state of mind. Your aroma. Your beauty. Your touch.

Cornered into the world I hid. With a light , you entered that space. What I love most about you is the actual happiness that surfaces your face when you smile. What I hate about you is that you don't smile enough." She giggled from his words.

"I promise you that the one who done this to you will be punished."

She pushed on the balls of her feet and kissed him. "It's time, Branden. Forget me not. Live life. Don't run through it too fast. Terrible it is to see you go. I don't want you to go. I don't want you to let go. But, the last thing I'll see is your lonely face before me."

"Take me with you."

"I will not deny them of a hero. How does your heart feel Branden?"

"I'm the reason for your sentence to death, Ayrelia."

"No! You're the one who has loved me. There's nothing you could do. Nothing more than walk away."

"How could this be that the last time ever I to hold you is for the last time I'd ever hear your voice or see you smile? How can this be the last time that I can tell you that I love you?"

"In a moment I will be no more. Do you promise to love me always?"

"I do."

"I wanted so much more. I desired you as my husband. I longed for kids of my own." He sniffed harshly and embraced her. "Tell me you love me and let me go, as the last of my wishes. Go find that tyrant and stop him. I love you Branden. I love you."

"When we met, you changed me. Different I will be. If I can't see you in my path, back into the darkness I will go."

"No, Branden. You be and remain that bright and happy person that I have created. Go now."

He kissed her forehead. His arms shook. He released his clutch of her. She smiled tiredly, as he walked backwards from her.

The bomb went off. Branden closed his eyes. His breathing sped up to match his heart rate. Blood oozed from his nose. Drips became a pour that fleeced from the center of his crown.

"Hey Buddy? You okay?" The truck driver asked.

Branden's head pounded with an ill death. The inner hull of his ears were saturated in a puddle of angry blood. His eyes squinted. The sweat carried the flow of blood from his mouth. His teeth became stained and coated. *If only I to die or take my own life, this would be the only thing to spare theirs. For my heart is destruction. Greed, my mind has become. Greed to end their pulse that beats under the skin. Thoughts are now threats unto them that are labeled for my onslaught. This vendition will be short.*

Death has claimed Ayrelia, just a few feet from where I stand. Death is shoulder to shoulder with me. Possibly starring into my face with a jealous delight to have yet stalked another victim. Although this be, I will be sending another to greet him. Alex's blood will be mine as I hold his life until he passes through my hands of murder.

Chapter 12 *The Empirical*

Brian, The senior bounty hunter, pulled into the aluminum carport of his home. His hair was sandy and his face clean shaven. His stature was masculine in size and stood very tall.

He twisted his waist and stretched before entering the door. He walked to the end of the hall and spied his wife sitting at the dining room table. She smiled briefly and then her facial expression showed horror. Brian was struck with reality. He reached for his glock, when he saw Branden holding the barrel to her temple.

"Don't even," Branden said. "Elbows on the table." Brian stood less of motion. Branden bent his knee and placed the flat of his shoe to the table's edge. He then kicked it into Brian's stomach. "Sit down!" Brian fluffed the ends of his coat.

"Not bad, Branden," Brian announced with a hardness that enslaved him. "I applaud your ability to subdue me into your own personal chaos."

"How could you do this Brian? How could you work for Alex, knowing that he is a stone hearted murderer?"

"You've lost Branden. Everything of yours that meant anything to you has been discarded. Although there be one exception, the little Singer girl. Turn yourself in, and spare her life."

"Tell me where Alex is!"

"I will tell you everything because I know you won't kill me knowing that my five month old child is asleep in the next room over. We are not bounty hunters. None of us, including you. All of the proclaimed hunters have worked for Alex for four years. The Ace Company is bogus. None of us tracked anyone other than you. Everyone except Tera, Grant and a few other associated employees.

It was all a front since the time you began to work there. We only wanted to test your behavior. In some ways you're still some awkward experiment. All to lead to this one point in time.

You have no special talent or skills. You are not superhuman Branden. Every child reported to you as napped, was indeed stolen by us. Every case was prearranged. When the parents called about the child being missing, that was real. But, every involved criminal was indeed of our very own.

See, my job was to transform you into the empirical you should have been. Alex's very own experimental freak. With that said, all is left is what I must. For you, Branden to be placed into mind shock. This is the quest to begin the first stages of this analysis.

DEAD CENTER

I could care less if you ended that bitch there. Do you know what her future job is? She is preparing to be a spread. You know what a spread is, Branden? A spread is an employee of the Zear network. A female who is paid to run tests on the empiricals. These tests just so happen to be sexual. This was in fact what your biological mother was.

She slept with all of the empiricals, using her seductive lures. Then she charted everything. Everything Branden. The size of the penis. How hard they contracted inside of her when they orgasm. Afterwards, she'd go to the bathroom and squeeze it out into a specimen container to measure the thickness of the fluid and also study their semen count.

She filed their aggressive energy. Which positions they preferred etcetera. Enjoyed her job, she may or may not have. Nothing more than a highly paid prostitute. Money is the drive here, Branden. A hundred thousand dollars a year? No. She got a hundred thousand dollars per session. Nevertheless, a spread is the bottom of the link. Shoot her. Who cares. She thinks I love her. I'm a trained killer, Branden. A tracker in secret."

Janine held her forehead as though nauseated. Branden turned the gun on him.

"She's just like your dear mother Branden. That's right. Linda, Braylen's wife, was one of these whores.

Alex studied our feedback of you closely for the past two years. He came up with the idea that depression would take you if you could be exposed to failure or other dramatic ties. When we found out you and Tera were together, this was our chance. Brilliant you were, to convince Wilkes to shift sides and work for you. However, ignorant you were to have let Tera fall in our court.

Mind shock is my goal for you. Want me to describe what we did to her?"

Branden stood and walked behind Brian and pressed the barrell to the back of his neck. "Stop it. I know you destroyed my life."

"Get the baby, Janine. Now!" She ran to the next room and brought their son into the den. She looked into her baby's eyes while standing before them. Branden's face soured.

"Why is this happening to me Brian?" He rested his forehead onto the back of his head and began to cry. "I'm going to kill you. I promised I would."

"You can't. You're conscience wouldn't have it." Janine left the room with the baby.

"Close your eyes, Brian."

Brian smirked. "No. No matter how much anger besets you, you would not take a father away from his son. Do it Branden. Fall deeper into your lowered state. Slowly this route of depression will cause the killing of your own self."

Branden pushed his head to the table. "Do it! Here, let me give you another reason to. We laid her onto the office sofa. We fucked her Branden. She knew not to fight. We all took turns, stripping her nude as we just pulled our pants down.

We did her hard and didn't care if she wasn't wet. She lay still staring at the corner of the walls. We used her for wipe rags. Not once did she cry or blink. Sure I felt bad, but this was all due to the attempts of shocking your head. Although now that you know, it's a bit too late.

DEAD CENTER

She was good. Very tight. At least when I started on her, being the first it was. Who knows how it ended two hours later. Sad knowing that you're the cause of her mishap. It's your fault. You left her alone. You're to blame for her being taken by the hunters at the convenience store. You're the cause of her bleeding between her legs that day. You're the very being who killed her by letting go of her. What a fool. What a shame.

Go ahead, shoot me Branden. Commit this sin to murder."

"To take you from the world to be judged is a happy honor," Branden replied. "You are not capable to show love. To have partaken in the deadening of my lover's struggle to live without hardship is now the death of you. Your attempts to stun my mind for your benefit has failed. Actually it's too sad for you, to not have conquered everything in life that you wanted."

Branden raised the gun and said, "Scream goodbye to your wife. Do you feel the sting burning in your mouth right now? That's death standing beside you. Coming for your final human breath."

Brian's pupils shrunk with fear as Branden continued. "Death and hell shall be cast into the lake of fire. Now does this mean that since death is an angel, that somehow he will become evil towards the end? If so can't an angel of all beings realize that scriptures are great? If a man knew he'd wind up behind this bullet of my gun, by stealing the physical sensations of my lady, would you still have done it?

Or maybe this means death in general. The act of dying will cease forever. I'm not sure. How could a man not want to see his child grow up and live life with him? Instead, you chase a profession to destroy lives.

I hope that when you fucked her, you did it as hard and as fast as you could. I hope that her inner walls suffocated you until you gave way. I hope you finished inside of her. I hope you took your time. Soft or rough, whatever you liked. For this thing you all have done will be in exchange for your life."

The blood dotted Branden's face after the eruption of the bullet. He held the gun even to Janine as she ran into the room. The baby began to cry loudly. He dropped the gun and fled on foot into the woods.

After some time of running, Branden fell to his knees in the midst of the forest. His temples sorrowed a heavy spear of pain. A slight grind of his teeth was audible from the active pressure of his head. The stark laughter of Alex's voice was surrounding his mind.

"I can control you," he heard Alex say. "By the means of this powerful satellite of my brain to yours. You can hear my voice. Soon you'll be mine."

"No!" Branden shook his head and focused on the situation.

"The desolate imagination of your attempts to block me has failed. Your unstable conscience will not permit you to think properly. Burned into your pathetic heart of love is now the lost path of unwanted treachery. You should have turned your life over to me. Instead you paid the price for watching Tera slip out of this world."

"Coward! Why hide? Dishonest as the wolf that seeks attack. From behind he appears never to be seen."

"I've no need to hide. All is won. Soon the world will be caged and the rulers of the United Nations will be the dictators of life, with empiricals to carry out their deeds of their wills.

You Branden, will not stop me from destroying security amongst the communities of hatred and greed. For this plot against humanity will I forfeit over unto the government. Just as you have become the murderer upon the soil of the land as Brian lies from your brains instructions to your hands.

I removed all love from your wounds. Without love, you are powerless to continue into the next day."

"If you were so strong you would have had my head above your mantel by this point. Insanity will not create or surface within me. You will be the one who will die from your own personal greed and hatred. Hostile you are to the rays of the sun, for they are perfect and shine for the hour. For you to have thought to have dragged her away from my heart is wrong. Never will such fiendish cruelty ever have part in me.

Tera's blood, poured over the very shoulder of which Ava's heart bleed as I held her. Her broken veins that you punctured, erupted. Her life seeped away with her breath, but her love for Braylen remained."

"You, this scene and all the past days have been nothing more than an ongoing experiment," Alex said. "With this to add of your capture to be the final process of my charts. Then will I set a plan proposal unto the UN and other leaders of the nations of the global universe.

Wealth will please me. Your death will satisfy me. The need for my mind controlled soldiers will prove worthy of my dollar wages. All laws are peaked and promised unto the offices of legislation under the rule of their government. Many changes will be brought forth. I invented yet another constructed plan to make my men a necessity.

I will set up meetings with ambassadors from the Soviet Union, China, and the USA. I plan to preserve space on the planet. In such inquiries will be to rid all countries and counties of spread out homes and land. This will bring an order to build high-rise apartment complexes on the acres of land. This will replace the single family residing of the area.

No bodies will be buried. Instead ground can be used for more building. Creamation will be the law. Branden, when I become rich and authoritative, then will I be able to influence such low minded individual rulers of the states. All in order to boost my demand for their protection. After I hold the rod of your brain in my fingers, then will it all begin. To sacrifice the comfort of the world to fill my pocket with the addition of lust and hunger for wealth."

"To save the world, I cannot, but if I prevent your purpose of defying you I will. The hero of invisible destiny."

Alex laughed at the remark. "You are just like your father."

"As you be the mimic of yours."

"Braylen pieced together clues and searched for his own place in life. He uncovered who he was. As for you Branden, you spent twenty five-years caring less about who you are until everyone in your life are dead before you. Your father murdered mine and took my spot as the closest of the two."

"Zear was not your father, Alex. Who was your real father? You have no idea, but yet you catapult my stature of living into the vastness of a false demeanor."

Alex chuckled with gentleness. "At the hand of the minute of one rotation, I can balance one thousand thoughts on the very edge of my mind. Simple psychology will not enslave my freedom to be reversed. You are the thrive for the pending survival of those who need your assistance. I am the one who craves the fall of all that should be under my control.

The world belongs to me Branden. You desire to keep it from me. Rescuing innocent lives while I hope to ruin the crucial flow of nature with the corrupt fist of distraught humanity. Can you save the world in time from my deed? The face of the sun is approaching as the quiet darkness is calm. Soon the morning will freshen the sky. Another day of my wrath is deepened.

I can feel the sadness of your loved ones that has made you ill. Relentless unto your own flesh you've become to have let them under your guard. Soon you will have to force your own heart to beat by the pounding of your hand to your chest. As this climax of lifeless energy depresses you beyond repair, your veins will melt from the blood that rejects your own body.

Guilt of Tera's death will chain itself around your ankles. Anger will bind your wrist with stretching rope. Grief will suspend you over the plain and depression will bury you.

Poor Ava. Only minutes away from saving her. Seconds rested between you and Tera's life. Please Mr. Hayes, don't make me kill this poor little girl. Don't allow another victim to die for your clumsy sake. Ironic how you fall into your father's footsteps and I follow behind mine."

Branden clenched his head and said, "Do you want to hear something a bit more amazing?"

"Please, Mr. Hayes, indulge."

"Even the more ironic as your asperity to be on top and rule the world however, to have bound your fate by my hands to take your life by the things you've done is the real mystery."

"I will sit amongst the countries in the seats higher than the President," Alex stated. "All that I control and create will be the new leaders of the world. I will eventually cause all of my empiricals to kill those in charge and take their place crowning me the official head of all government. All leaders will be of my own experimental creation.

Within time of shortness, will I become mighty. No one will smile without my permission. The Constitution will be burned and all the flags of every nation will not mast, for they belong to me.

Do you think I'm evil Branden? Of course, you do. However, evil is a fallacy amongst men. Intellect is the key. With my army of brainwashed zombies, I will make for the perfect heist of all time. To steal the world from under its axis.

No one could ever pin me out as crooked. To send messages to kill by brainwave is no proof. No man would ever reveal me unto the crimes at hand. No cause, paperwork, blueprint, internet file, no conversations not anything of me can you detect when your mind is the killer."

Alex's voice cleared from his head. Branden blinked and continued to run his way to Alex as he signaled unaware his location.

Two hours later. Branden jogged into the direction of the frenzied signal that burned through his head. The static lead him into a parking lot of a newly remodeled office complex. The lieutenant bounty hunter met him at the backside of the building's break area. "This game is over," Branden said.

They began to circle each other for the future combat. "Are you afraid of me?" Tommy asked. As they stopped moving, Branden's vessels scorched. His breathing beared heavy through his lungs and his strength flexed through his core. His adrenalin was tasted from the anxious approach of Tommy.

Branden ran to him and tackled him against the large dumpster. With brute strength, Tommy wrapped his arms around his back and flipped him over his head. Branden caught his balance on the top edge of the container and cat walked to the end of the welded handle. He threw his weight from there and double kicked Tommy in the chest causing him to slam against the dumpster.

Branden dropped to his feet and unleashed a series of left to right hand combinations on Tommy's stomach. After dazing him, Branden kicked him back to the steel. The angered giant grabbed him and forced him to the ground. Branden struggled and worked his body at an angle as he took hearty kicks to the ribs.

Tommy's face dropped slowly allowing Branden to break the hold as he was held in mid air. He dropped Branden and placed him in a head lock. Branden shifted slightly and tilted Tommy sideways and threw him about four feet. The black gravel pavement was substantially uneasy and rough on the knees.

Branden began to kick him in the side and rolled him after each blow. Tommy attempted to deliver a brutal low kick, but was rendered unsuccessful as Branden caught his foot with both hands. He braced his momentum and released Brian's foot to smash into the raw steel.

Tommy picked him from the ground by the shirt and the seam of his pants. He tossed him into the air. He then returned the tactics on Branden as he released a punch combo onto his midsection. Branden retaliated by gliding himself away from Tommy's fury causing him to skin his knuckles on the abrasive black top.

Branden tossed himself onto Tommy's back and locked his elbow onto his chin for submission from the maneuver. Tommy became panicky as his oxygen thinned. He used Branden's back for a battering ram and slammed into the dumpster backwards.

Branden's hold remained as Tommy set his mark to empower the same destructional move as before. Tommy ran backward while Branden sought the opportunity and pushed off from him. Tommy's head rammed the raw steel of the dumpster. Tommy laid knocked out with blood seeping from his cut. Branden retrieved the handcuffs and bound Tommy's wrist to the metal bar handle.

Several other bounty hunters began to gather around him. "You don't want to do this," Branden announced. He brought his hand from around his back with exuberant speed and connected his fist into the chest of the first man. He pivoted his body around to add force to his backhand across the face of another.

Two more hunters closed in from front to back. Branden planted his foot onto the metal folding chair beside him and pushed himself into the air. He brought his arm down and around the head of the man. He positioned himself and ducked as the second swung a baton near

DEAD CENTER

him. Branden cracked his fist firmly through his forehead and plowed him into the concrete break table.

Branden looked about the falling men, for most were fatalities. The rest of the group charged his direction.

Branden ran to the telephone pole and shimmed up the metal spokes that pronged the sides. He latched hold of the end cable. Sparks flew from the disconnect of the wire. Branden jumped to the ground while holding onto the active electric field. The hunters all piled their weight onto him, sending him to the ground. After each man was in a knit, Branden shoved the bright end into his own chest, leaving the men electrocuted.

He threw the wire to the ground. His body was tired from the fight. His heart was slow in pace. Time was denial. He sluggishly made his way to the entrance of the building and crawled up the flight of stairs. He fell as he opened the door to Alex's office. Blood ran from his skull and onto his neck. Exhaustion deflated his stride. He crawled slowly towards Alex's direction.

"Mr. Hayes, right on scheduled timing. How's the world been treating you?" he joked. "Look at you. A pitiful display of heroism fallen prey to democracy. My democracy. Feeble your right to live has become. All that's left for me to do is collect the rod that sits in your brain." He put his foot on top of Branden's back as to show a victory gesture.

"How rude of me. Let me introduce you to the napper from the Singer case. Which, by the way, does not exist. This man here is one of my new recruits. Paid to act and to lead you around on a fake mission." Branden coughed and blood dripped his nostrils. "Pathetic. You can't even push your weight onto your shoulders." Alex squatted to his level. "The world is mine Branden!"

Randall Ford Jr.

Branden rose swiftly and pushed him down. He charged the new member of his gang. He held him by the shirt and sent him out of the fourteenth floor bay window.

Branden took Alex and spun him around. He ran him to the large jagged piece of glass that was intact from the pane. He rammed his upper body through the glass. "Look at me you son of a bitch. Where's your world at now?" Alex half smiled. His eyes closed as Branden let go of him. The fractured window piece broke. Alex's body plummeted to the pavement below.

(Two weeks later.)

Branden placed the long stem rose onto the fresh sediment of Ava's grave, about where he believed the heart to be. The birds yelled with confidence the song of the morning. The sun was new and trespassed the sky of the earth.

From the marble tombstone he began to walk the dirt path that led into the city's park. He relaxed his hands into his coat pockets.

The rest of Alex's crew was caught or either gave up a couple of days after the fall of their leader.

A new committee of treason surveyors created by the U.N. government was formed and placed into affect. They called themselves the Inner Government. Their job was to keep a close mount on all governing bodies of the world that ever considered such hideous ideas of such empiricalistic ways.

I burned the book of documented information that Ava gave to me, in order to hide my true identity and keep me safe from being targeted by such U.N. affiliates.

A quiet man I am. Only freedom is what I own. I was released and cleared from any holding charges that hostaged me for the consideration of Ava's death.

As for Ayrelia, all of my memory of her will remain in mind, even as the lesson of time was handed to me by her death. The present does not exist. Only the past and the future. For in an instant, all present is become the past so quickly the present never gets a chance to exist. If you love someone cherish them.

Now I continue to do what I've always done. Find the missing and bring them home. No longer will I be called Thin Bird, Branden, Hayes or even Adger. For this life is an everyday change. From here out, I will be called, The Empirical."

WHITE CAGE SYNDROME

(The Prequel to Dead Center)

"How can I free someone from a beautiful cage when all that I see is a rusted metal structure from within?

Who am I anymore? Simple, but difficult I've grown.

Unusual I seem. Backward my steps lead. Behind me I look from the front as any surroundings are deceitful without warning.

Who am I? Who am I?"

R. Ford

Chapter 1 *Don't Blink*

The glass door swung wide from the vim of physical strength. The metal profile which framed the entrance and connected to the handle, made collision against the painted brick of the side wall of the bank.

The first man to ingress edged the corner of the front lobby partition and held the semi-automatic hand gun to the temple of the guard, which sat facing the line of customers. The next two men to follow forked their paths to position themselves diagonal from center floor to the bordering wall.

The fourth mystery entered the establishment at a high pace. Dressed in a full reflection of murk, each man attired themselves in a complete pitch of black. The cloth threaded mask that veiled their faces hid not the desired bane that circulated in their eyes. The last man to enter stopped in direct of the teller line.

He faced the gun to the ceiling engaging the roof with an eerie detonation. The employees dropped to the floor tile as the man bellowed the core of the building by extracting the shell from it's casing. The uniformed officer slumped his lifeless weight exposing the smear of blood that strewed about the paneling.

The customers screamed with a disarrayed fright that quickly settled itself into their minds. The stabbing of emotions bleed the heart from the splitting knife of reality. This was the awakening of time at the present. The scoundrels stood with the bravery of knights and walked with the threat of death at their finger tips.

The lead tyrant charged the counter and leaped onto the surface. He demanded the female clerks to their feet. "Register tray only, no shift or raising of the contents," he stated.

The first lady neared him for overwhelming fear became her main state. She glanced at his face which pushed her into a paralyzing coma of shock. She stood with her hands groping together. The tears were endless as they dispensed from the sockets. No repeat command of warning was ordered for the empty waste of his time. He tightened the trigger, leaving her for dead.

The robber walked across the counter ejecting the fiery discharge into the window of each worker taking them by murder. He halted at the last teller station and held the gun in aim with her face. "Register money only from every window," he said softly.

Her uneasy nerve fell tense with the numbing of her joints. She willed herself as a forced machine to the secured unit. She stacked the bills into a medium size plastic bag. Her eye contact was limited as to cease to provoke. The dark mask which covered his identity was like death that hoovered the counter top, faceless and cruel.

DEAD CENTER

Her hands fully deadened by the cold that stood before her. *For the pump of my heart I could not feel as it was glazed over with adversity. Alive to myself I am aware, only through the throb of pulse. Such calamity arose unaware to bore a load of worry and despair. The fever of my skin was as the cast of irons laid to the ground before the sun, at the eighth hour of the day.*

She despite the fear and continued to empty the cash dispenser's contents. She handed the dense bag over to the man after walking her down the line of registers. She immediately turned to face the wall and descended to her knees. The man *blinked not* through the course in progress, neither did the other thieves urge this need of contracting movements.

The man jumped from the floor and compressed the opening of the sack. They fell in line with one another and left in a single file. Even though the group of men had departed, the invisible spread of dismay lingered with them all.

Simultaneously the men marched to their vehicle. Upon the attempted entrance of the last hit man, the cops stood behind their squad patrols from afar. "Throw your weapons down and exit the vehicle!" the officer shouted while holding the portable loud speaker.

The man backed a slight from the automobile. He turned the gun inside the passenger window. He took the lives away of his own crew by the lead of the forty caliber, shooting them in the head. The officers heeded cover behind their cars.

The man opened the gas door of the locking spout and ignited the rags that were stuffed in place. He let go of the gun sending it to the pavement. He knelt with both knees in agreement and secured his hands

Randall Ford Jr.

behind his head in accord with police regulations and demands.

Some of the tactical troops closed in on him. The low fire of the rags slid down into the cylinder of the gas tank. The body of the car was suddenly separated from it's chassis. The explosion threw debris of metal into the air as a catapult. The SWAT group drew back from the wild heat that raged. The man stood and ran disappearing within the dusted smoke film.

Chief negotiator, Robert Copeland, Seized the timing and gave chase by foot. The other officers rushed their vehicles and sounded the sirens to give caution to the streets.

The disguised aggressor ran through the cross direction of oncoming traffic. The cars swerved and alarmed their horns, as Robert fought to catch the suspect. The man ran with fury in-between the marker lanes, bypassing cars on either side.

The man angled his steps and approached the hood space of a compact vehicle. He climbed the car with lengthy steps and then hopped onto the road. He was met by the fender of a small blue truck. His body was tossed above the cab and rolled over into the flat of the bed. The blunt of impact sent him to break through the tailgate.

The driver stopped and got out. "Get back into the truck!" Robert yelled. He assisted his request while the screened face individual commenced his way. Robert followed his move to the side of the alley of the seventh floor building. The fellow officers drove with vast hysteria to aid Robert's quest to capture.

DEAD CENTER

The man jumped for the brass ladder of the fire escape. Robert was frantic for not to render this victim of hatred to flee his vision as the man rounded the top of the complex. Robert planted his feet firmly into the pebble-like rocks which were loosened under the tar sheet.

He was under quick suppression of anxiety after being faced with the open end of a high powered hand gun from which the man took from his boot. "Tell Mr. Copeland to give up his weapon," the man heard.

"Lay your gun from holster and then to the ground," the man commanded.

Robert gently slid his light green blazer from his arms evincing the brown leather shoulder strap. "Easy now just relax," Robert replied. He unbuckled the silver hook and collapsed the entire holder. The gun touched the ground. He kicked it over to him. "Let's talk. I'm your prisoner now. Work something out with me."

"Tell Robert to keep the peace over his own head," the man heard.

"Stay put in your tracks, Robert. Your psychological laws do not exist to me."

"You know me by name I see. Are you talking to someone? Perhaps a police scanner? I see the ear extension clipped." The man walked to the raised base of the ledge and looked down. Puzzled Robert became from the connection piece attached to the rear of his belt.

"Hey listen man, I can white wash this whole ordeal for you. I can tweak the truth and bend lies to make your story look a bit better in the judges eyes. What do you say? What's your name? I am here to help.

Is the guy on your cell relaying to you what to say? Talk to me man. We're stuck in the sky without the world to hear. I'm a trained professional, but right now I hope to be a trained friend. At least shed your mask and tell me what's it going to take for you to trust me."

The man pressed the ear device close with his fingers together. "Yes sir," he stated. He held the gun on the aligned position of Robert's heart and pulled the trigger back. The gun registered empty as the slide latch caught the end of the handle jamming it outward. He drooped it and backed away. He ripped his shirt apart from the front and unadjusted the tail of his silk tee. Approximately three, seven pound stainless steel caps surrounded his abdomen. Highly explosive bombs were mounted with entwined cables.

"Damn it!" Robert yelled. He pulled his phone from his pocket and flipped the cover. He pressed the security gauge on the side. "Clear the sidewalks. Now!" He snapped the plastic cover together and became dazzled at the man's eyes which blinked.

The man's eyes shifted from side to side. He placed his hand onto his forehead as for comfort. Robert eased his index finger to the operation mode of the opening flap of the phone. He purposely clicked the piece to reattach it to a closed form. The noise quickly drew the man to his previous conscious state.

The man stepped onto the end of the cement and said, "This is a personal message for you from the one you can't see." He brushed his palm to the ear unit of the private ear plug and continued. "Unwise it is to upset me. For the imagination I can control, Mr. Copeland. Your heart will be the death of you. For it will be the cause of you to end by the blade."

The man kicked off from the edge releasing the detonation chord. Robert ducked from the extreme combustion. He ran to look over the top. No harm was on the heads of any pedestrians below. However, *the one who threw himself to his own grave left me with the ache of confusion. Just as painstaking was that I failed as my skills of duty were weak. For the tools of trade that I work with is the description of thought to search certain paths to intercept their ways with a psychological tuning of the mind.*

Chapter 2 *Don't Hear*

Robert sat an inch from sleep. Weary sags draped beneath his eyes. He rubbed his head roughly to stimulate the freshness of the morning before the work day began. Alarmed, he slipped his prescription glasses over his veil and picked up the call of the phone that rested center of the dinning table.

He engaged the phone executing the silence. SWAT Captain, Stan Weber, began to flood direction unto his attentive ear. "We have a hostage situation occurring at 24, end of Johnson st. House # 43. Critical is the moment as two minors are withheld." Weber disconnected the line. Robert took the cup of coffee and hung the blazer jacket over his arm.

Robert arrived on location of the troubled neighborhood. Several people stood in their yards in search of and hope for any brief action to entertain.

He left his vehicle and made contact with Captain Weber. "What's the verdict Stan?"

"Some of the neighbors called after seeing a couple of juveniles entering the side window, burglar style. Commotions echoed as an apparent fight of them and the owner of the home set. When the city police came, the man that lives here waved his 12 gauge double barrel at them retreating the officers to cover. They dispatched our units. Apparently this guy has the two young men under the gun. Want this bullet proof vest?"

"No. That would just mean that I was preparing for error. I plan not to flaw."

Robert walked fearlessly toward the front door. He tapped it slowly with low toned knocks. It was unfastened. He pushed it open and entered. He witnessed the two teenagers sitting in wooden chairs back to back from one another bound in rope. Their eyes blindfolded and their stability surprisingly calm.

"Who are you!" the man yelled. He flashed the threat of the barrel toward him.

"Relax. My name is Robert Copeland, head of negotiations. I bring you no harm and solve no crime with you."

"Put your hands down and don't make any sudden movements!"

"Allow me to remove my coat and reveal my gun. You can take it from the strap underneath my arm pit. I'm your prisoner now."

"Just take it and place it on the carpet in front of the couch. Kick it far underneath it. This way if you attempt to retrieve it, you'd have to take the time to slide the piece of furniture away from the wall."

Robert did as requested and lapped his jacket over across the arm of the sofa. He glanced at the two victims. One was bleeding through the white tunicate bandage that was double wrapped about his head just semi-level with the cloth eye binder.

"What happened here, Mr..?"

"Knowles. Herschel Knowles."

"Can I call you Herschel?" The man answered not, but continued to hold him at gun point. "Tell me how I can help fix this problem. Let me know what's going on Herschel."

"The only problem here is these two punks that broke into my house for the last time. I'm gonna kill the jerks. Both of them! They don't deserve to live. Taking fruits of my labor to fill their expensive addictions."

Robert walked to the wounded person and knelt down to him. "Can you hear me?" he whispered.

"No! He can't."

Robert stood forcefully to his feet. "Why not?"

"Because I cut his ears off." Robert's face became flushed while his mouth opened.

"Then I jabbed the end of this hanger into the canal. Do you know what it's like for this to be done? It's like taking the blunt end of a microphone and jamming it into a metal wall located inside the ear drum at full pitch. He can't *hear* you."

The boy facing away began to breathe frantically from the details of the mishap. "Look Herschel, tell me exactly what I need to do to secure your mind. I need to have this man transported to an ambulance quickly. I'm your friend Herschel. Why did you deafen this young man? Why torment his being?"

DEAD CENTER

"Why not? These pussies took everything of value from me twice and now I take from them, painfully. Why? Are you going to arrest me? These sons of bitches are the cause of disarray. I'll kill myself before they tackle me to the ground with such brutalities that await. I ain't going to prison for these committed crimes!"

Herschel continued his speech. Robert closed in on him.

"I'll fucking do it! I'll take out all in this room before I leave here to be caged!"

"Fine then." Robert locked his palm tight around the end of the steel structured weapon. He led the hollow barrels to the temple of the first male.

He began to fight for air after feeling the cold density of the gun pressing to his skull. "Do it Herschel. Kill him. What are you waiting for? Time will not slow." Herschel's face changed to confusion. "Do it Herschel. Do as you say you would." He stiffened his finger tips around the gun. "Don't look away from me. Pull the trigger Herschel."

"I can't."

"Don't be afraid. Do it damn it!"

"No. I..."

Robert jabbed the barrel into the man's head. "Look into my eyes you hateful bastard. Confirm what you claim you would do as your adrenaline pushes you. Pull the trigger Herschel. Do it now!"

"No."

"Pull the damn trigger Herschel!"

"No! I can't."

"Kill them. Cold blood. Get your feelings out in the open. Look at me!"

"This is not legal! You can't do this."

"Legal? Who owns justice in this room? You're going to jail for this anyway. Maybe I should shoot them and say you done it. Now. Is that justice? Answer me! The courts would believe me over you."

"No."

"Is it justice to torture these criminals and bind them? My time is passing. Do it Herschel." Robert shoved the gun causing the stalk to punch into Herschel's shoulder. "Do it Herschel. You useless excuse for life. Do it damn you!"

"No!"

"Do it. What are you waiting for?"

"No!"

"Do it."

"No!"

"Do it!"

Robert pulled the gun away into his own arms and retracted the shells which bumped the floor. He exhaled deeply. Herschel held his face with tears.

Robert moved the couch and replaced the glock into his shirt. "I told you Herschel that I was here to help. Stay put. Don't move." Robert walked to the door and placed his hand upon the latch of the deadbolt lock.

"Where are you going?" Herschel asked.

"To let the squad in." *Silence overwhelmed me when I turned about. My heart weighed heavy with a fainting lack of breath.* The twist of the lock's switch was the changing of aggravations of nature. The click was as though someone had flared the daytime signaling the moon to take position for an eclipse of light. *The mood of the man from which I deflated from chaos had changed from the certain sound of the door.*

Herschel's eyes enlarged. Robert opened the door wide and threw two fingers into the air toward the law officers. This signal was to show a relief cure of the situation. The SWAT soldiers swiftly jogged to the house and drew back with their weapons.

Herschel pulled a dagger from the mantle and charged Robert, tackling him from behind. Robert's chin smashed the porch. Herschel repeatedly stabbed him in the back with wide strokes of gained momentum.

The officers aimed their automatic guns and began to fire. "NO!" Robert Yelled, for in hopes that some thought was present that Herschel still could of been helped.

Chapter 3 *Don't See*
(Ten weeks later)

Police Major, Jermaine Wilson, held the door for Robert, welcoming him into his office. "How you feeling?"

"Better. Almost one hundred percent. The cartilage of my ribs have mended with strength."

"That's great. That's great, Copeland." Wilson leaned back into the swivel chair and held the pencil at each end. "Now, for the real reason I called you in here on your first day back since the accident. You're no longer to hold the position of negotiations any longer."

"You're firing me?"

"No. I cannot. Ever heard of the three strikes and you're out? You're down to your last strike, Copeland.

Sharp shooters are the one's who take out people in hostage deals. That means no room for failure. I hire negotiators to talk the opponents down so we can render them in cuffs. That means no failure, damn it! I can't afford to keep you on that level anymore. You're a liability. One that will sooner or later end in a lawsuit from the victim or you be the victim."

"Sir, I was not up to par as I laid awake all of the night before."

"Why? Thinking of what?"

"Of the bank robbery case. Of how something was not right with the guy with the explosives. I mean major, the tires of the get away vehicle were examined. They must have let the air out of each tire, about one third of the way. Then filled them with about twenty three pounds of flammable tire sealant which is used for leaks or flats. This added to the dramatic explosion of the car."

"I order you to take the new open position of employment with my company."

"Which is?"

"Don't smart off to me you regretful piece of trash! You will be in charge of the people's advocate for minors at the state juvenile shelter. A voice for the public. This way if you mess up it's harmless with no fall backs on me."

"You want me to be a case worker for children?"

"Also, I order you by the state to attend the Thompson stress help team, three days a week. If you do not you will be picked up and forced to do ninety days in the local psych hospital. I want to know what's going on in your fucking head, Robert! You caused me to get my ass chewed by every political socializer and his mother. Even the crooked governor is saying that my staff is incompetent."

Randall Ford Jr.

"A shrink?"

"Get some help. Relax a bit. Use this in your favor to catch up on some self time. Consider this a much needed vacation. After the evaluations come back from the therapist, then we'll talk. I think you've burned out and seen too much. Now go and take your black ass out of here."

Robert pondered and asked, "What?"

"Black ass, If I'd said your white ass, you could sue me for discrimination. If I had said simply your ass you'd have me on a verbal threat. So I'm black, I can say that. Here take this folder. This is your first case. Your first appointment for the crazy doctor is at 1:30 tomorrow. Now, get the fuck out of my office!"

The following day Robert entered the Thompson building. The receptionist relayed his route onto the second floor. There he matched the session room door to the card she wrote for him. He knocked onto the door. "Please, enter," he heard the female voice reply.

He walked in and saw the lady sitting in a plush chair facing away from him. She wore silk black stockings that completely faded her natural skin tone. Her shoes were formal and strapped around the leg just above the ankle. Her heels were sleek and thin. Sultry was the covering that hid her foot by stocking but only as to show the shape. *For the outline was curved and fainted my imagination with exhausting thoughts of wild sensuality.*

"Please, Mr. Copeland, want you have a seat directly behind me." He sat cautiously and reclined into the chair. *Her hair was blonde with platinum streaks as it was the only visible part of her I could now see from the back of the seat.*

Her voice was tender and soothing as therapy upon my conscience. Her left shoe was pried from her foot while she pushed it down for comfort.

"Why must I sit away from you?"

"All apart of the procedure, Mr. Copeland."

"You can call me Robert."

"Very well. Mr. Copeland, I have a very long drug out list of questions that I must by law, record for my own personal diagnosis, to ask. Please respond yes or no. Only give an explanation when asked a question for information. Are you comfortable?"

"Yes."

"Have you ever wanted to kill someone?"

"Kill as in frustration or as in cold murder? Like, oh I could kill that red light runner or kill from a deranged mind?"

"Mr. Copeland, I can see that this could be very difficult for the both of us. You are also highly trained in the psychology field and acquire much knowledge of education from this area of study. However, the longer you take, the longer it takes for you to be back on track. Am I clear?"

He rolled his eyes. "Yes."

"Murder?"

"No."

"Murder of yourself?"

"Never."

"Dreams of killing someone?"

"No."

"At the present, do you feel more love or hate for the world?"

"Considering the world is made up of hatred, I try to feel love."

"Have you ever had sex before?"

He chuckled. "At age 28, yes I have."

"Masturbate?"

"Yes."

"Constantly?"

"No."

"Constantly as in once or more daily?"

"No."

"Constantly as in once or more every other day?"

"No."

"Have you slept with more than twenty people?"

"Yes."

"Thirty or more?"

"Yes."

"She shifted her eyes and asked, "More than fifty?"

"No."

"Would you have sex with a married woman before her husbands eyes, if requested from both partners, as he was not visible in your sight?"

Robert stood. "Listen Miss Secret Identity, is this therapy or couch confessions?"

"Mr. Copeland, you know as part of an expert analysis is to uncover what stresses a person. Now as sex is common for that, either to build as a lack or relieve as fulfillment, I have a job to do. However, if you prefer, you may relocate for three months and be asked the same questions by another.

Only difference is here you leave in forty-five minutes. A psych ward will more than likely bind you twelve hours of the day then dope you to sleep the other twelve. I have steps to take to figure out the matter as to why you contain such built up agitations."

Robert looked away and removed his hands from the seam of his waist. He slightly scrunched his face to divert frustrations that aired. She continued as she heard the crinkle of the chair while he sat in compliance.

"No." He stated.

"Do you masturbate under or lying on top of blankets?"

"Under, but not as to subconsciously think to be caught as you inquire my personality flow."

"Have you ever paid for such services from the street?"

"No."

"One night stand?"

"Yes."

"Unprotected?"

"Yes."

"Complimented in bed?"

"Yes."

"Lied to in bed?"

"Yes."

"Watched someone having sex?"

"Yes and I masturbated," he said sarcastically.

"Have you ever had abnormal sex?"

"Abnormal? What is that?"

She exhaled wearily. "Have you ever performed bondage on another? Have you ever participated in an orgy?"

"No."

"Have you ever ejaculated onto any part of a females anatomy?"

"Yes."

"Into the face of another?"

"Yes."

"Torso?"

"Naturally."

"Breast?"

"Yes."

"Neck?"

"It runs don't it?"

"Okay, to save some time, is there any part that you haven't?"

"Yeah. Elbows," he joked. "Now I know why you had me sit where you couldn't see me."

"Which part of the females body do you desire most to look upon Mr. Copeland?"

"Which part? Let me guess at what you may have thought. You as a woman would probably guessed it to be the obvious. Breast or the butt. A woman's hair and legs are the early stages of checking a woman out. Having all these features are exquisite, but it's the hands and feet that make her sexy.

The experience in her touch. Every movement that bends her slender foot. Whether it be the way it looks while kneeling or the heel that push the toes flat and creases the bend of it. The veins that circuit. So that's it."

She lightly ran her thumb under the collar of her blouse. "Very well. How long has it been since you had sex, Mr. Copeland?"

"One year, seven months."

Robert watched the hands of the clock round the hour. The last of interrogations shut in from her chart. "Last question, Mr. Copeland. Do you feel like a failure?"

He paused for the longest of intervals. "I do."

"Good. Thank you. Please, see your way out. Set time to return on Wednesday. Goodbye, Robert."

He stood and tugged at his neck by the rubbing of tension. "I still don't get it." She checked her list and seemed preoccupied. "I don't understand this. I know all that you know. It's like we're discussing a psychology class from college."

He made his way to the door and glanced at her once more upon his exit. "So how come I can't get a question in?" He laughed.

"Sure," she replied, while writing onto her tablet. "What would you like to ask me, Mr. Copeland?"

"You're serious right?"

"Just to let you know I am a fair therapist, I will allow you to ask me one question."

"One question?"

"One question."

"So it can be anything?"

"Anything at all."

"When was the last time you had sex?"

"Thirty eight days ago. With an actual partner, three hundred ninety-eight days ago. Have a good day , Mr. Copeland."

The next morning Robert parked in front of the protected care complex just outside of the county line. He entered the building and was cheerfully greeted by the receptionist. "Hi. You must be Robert. I'm Gertrude, head of the facility."

DEAD CENTER

"Yes."

"We were expecting you per Jermaine Wilson's order."

"Yeah, thanks for the reminder." He gave her the document and tucked his hands into his pockets. Robert's structure was a trim medium build. His beard was stubbled and rough. His hair, mild and sandy in color.

"Oh. You're assigned to little Billy. He's a troubled eight year old boy. Here's his file. His poor mother's nerves are gone wired. She was apart of the bank robbery some months back."

Robert's face quickly turned with interest toward her. "Why is he here and what exactly is wrong with him?"

"His mom temporarily placed our custody over him as her head is a nervous wreck. The robbery damn near put her in shock. She's coping alone at home. She thought it was best to have him here under the state's care. Her insurance plan is exquisite, so we have no problem with it.

For as the little boy is concerned, he just wants to go home. He's in tears day after day. Crazy, to feel insane I guess. Just needs someone to talk to you. We don't provide that care here. That's what you're here for." He looked toward the papers.

He feels as though he's just tucked away inside of an institute. Rightfully so, I mean that's just about what this place is. When the time comes for court you will be his voice and will lean against the decision of the judge to choose the proper path for Billy. Good luck. Your court date will be in eleven days. You can visit him four of those days for three hours each visit."

"Where is the boy?"

"Down the hall, room 34. You'll need this swipe card to enter every gate which is approximately sixteen feet apart from one another. This entrance device will not access after the eleven days have expired."

Robert slid the black edge of the laminated card releasing the button allowing a full entrance. He cleared all of the gates that mazed as a labyrinth until he made his way to the room. Doors were prohibited and removed from every room. He rapped the metal molding of the doorway and saw the boy stretching with an attitude.

"Billy? Can I come in?"

Billy shrugged his shoulders. "Who are you?"

"My name is Robert Copeland. What are you playing?"

"Basketball."

"You're good."

"Should be, it's the only video game that I have. The television doesn't work right, so I have to repeatedly work at this dull game. Why are you here? Are you going to rescue me?"

"Rescue from what?"

"Are you here to take me home, back to my mom?"

"Billy, where is your mother?"

"I didn't think so. You're just another social worker in quest of why this, why that. What I need is a friend."

"Look Billy, I'm new at this."

"Why does my mother dislike me?"

"Billy, I'm sure that's not the case at hand."

"I'm stuck here until I'm eighteen aren't I?"

"I don't, look Billy, just relax."

"Relax? You think it's okay with me to be kept in this cage? Like some damn puppy awaiting your mercy to take me home."

"Watch your language. I mean, Billy I'm here as your advocate. I maybe able to get you into a relatives house as perhaps to be your guardian for now and until."

"Until what? Fuck you! Don't like it do you? Fuck fuck fuck!" Billy began to cry as Robert stood and glanced about the floor. "See, you should have taken this game away from me for cussing. I was bad. You should've disciplined me."

Billy cut the television off and pulled his knees to rest under his chin. "I'm sorry, sir."

"Call me sir again and you will be sorry ," he joked. Billy laughed and sniffed his nose.

The following day, Robert showed persistency while entering the stress management office with promise. "Please Mr. Copeland, want you come in?" Lisa said, while she arranged a bundle of fresh flowers over her desk.

"Do you need for me to turn my head or something?"

"Don't be silly, Robert. The meaning behind such dramatic affect was to bring out the frustration side in you. See, when pressured, we sometimes tend to answer questions with severe honesty."

"Please want you?" She waved her hand toward the recliner that was positioned in front of her.

Her appearance was beyond the burn that singed the urge to stare. Hard at first, as her face was the capturing of beauty to leave one speechless. Her eyes were honey. Her apparel was natural from her postured position from which she stood. Her skirt was formal. The black cloth stretched and snugged her hips. Professional indeed she remained as her eyes never left mine. Her smile was fantasy.

"Mr. Copeland, today we have only one question. That is, what is the underlying significance towards your past experience which has to do with your personal relations of your job versus who you are?"

"In other words you're asking me why I fucked up twice in a row?" She kept eyes on his as not to be startled. "Lately or when those things occurred, something just didn't sit right with both situations."

"Explain."

"I can't."

"Why not?"

"Cause I don't understand myself."

"Why not?"

"Why ask?"

"Why procrastinate an explanation?"

"Why trust me?"

"Why wouldn't I?"

"You didn't Monday?"

DEAD CENTER

"Don't change the subject and tell me."

"Forty-two more minutes of this?"

"Now Mr. Copeland, what's going on in your thoughts?" He smiled. "In which I refer to as the situation of the bank robbery and the Knowles incident."

He ran his hand through his hair and concentrated on the tile blocks of the ceiling. "Alright, it's simple ma'am."

"Lisa."

"It's simple ma'am," he joked. She placed her thumb against her lip to guard her laughter. He continued to look above and said, "When I had the robber in my grasp, I knew the end of the situation was at hand.

What went wrong was totally out of my range of general psychology or tradition with negotiations. Someone was on a cell phone with him. I didn't actually see the phone, but I did notice the mic wire that was pieced to his ear. The soft click of my flip cover phone seemed to completely toss the man into a different state. I can't stop thinking about this. The man knew my name or perhaps the man on the opposite end told him.

Same type scenario with Mr. Knowles. It seemed as though the odd snap of a doorlock switched him into an insanity fit. I know it's just me. That's just years of worry."

"Do you fear for your life?"

"No. I thought only one question was to be asked today."

"Well, we do have thirty-eight minutes to kill."

Randall Ford Jr.

"I like your name Lisa."

"Thank you Mr. Copeland. So, these two people were changed instantly. Out of every odd place of timing these last two cases were that weird?"

"I know I guess I'm just overdone with this profession."

"Vacation any?"

"Not in twelve years. I thought I was to see the head guy around here, Mr. Thompson."

"Mr. Copeland, you have to see me first before we turn you over to him. He's the best. I diagnose you and he takes over from there."

"Oh, I see. You ask all the low down questions, profile me, and he gets the credit."

"Robert?"

"Yes."

"I like your name."

Billy sat in a sluggish manner staring at the eerie blank tube of the television. He lifted his eyes to greet Robert as he stepped inside his room. "Why'd you come back?"

"Good afternoon to you to, Billy."

"I don't feel like discussing anything today. I just want to be left alone."

"Billy, my time with you is limited. If I leave now it counts as a full day."

"Even if you convince the judge to allow me to leave with a relative that will not support my mind from the loss of my mother's love."

"Billy, where does your mom live?"

"Twenty-nine eighty-two Brooksdale. Why, you want to go and fuck her?"

"Hey!" Robert yelled, as he neared him. "Very clever Billy. Nice try for me to lose my temper and get booted away from you. Push everyone away because you feel abandoned right? That's your treaty purposed unto me. Well, it's not going to work because I'm here as a friend."

"Sure you are." Robert reached into his overcoat and pulled the plastic casing from his inner pocket. Billy's eyes lit from the new video game in his sight. "I don't believe it, Baseball 4000!"

"Shh. Keep it between you and I. They consider this a bribe around here."

"Are you going to converse with my mom about me?"

"Yes."

"Tell her I miss her and I love her and all that she is. Will you remember that?"

"I will."

Chapter 4 *Don't Worry*
(Fourteen days later)

Robert lay onto the chair and burdened answers to Lisa's questions. "Have you ever been in love," she asked.

"Once."

"Do you often lie to protect others?"

"Yes, that's my job...or was."

She pretended to write and then stacked her folders onto the end table beside her. "Well, Mr. Copeland, this is all. We've completed our course."

"I'm sorry?"

"I've fully diagnosed you and will be passing you on to Mr. Thompson. He will provide further therapy for you."

"So this is it?"

"Actually, no. Mr. Thompson required a full three-week period for all patients to spend under my supervision with full sessions. No less time will he set for this. Very strict and by the law he holds his position. However, between you and I, I cut the corners of persistency and determine a followup thoroughly."

"What do we do with the remainder of our time?"

"Whatever. One more appointment and we will be through. Also, by the rule of your Major, you must agree to come to the next appointed scheduled visit."

"What is wrong with me?"

"Nothing is *wrong* with you, Robert. I set up these questions from the book and added my own line of questions. Years ago, I came up with a label I used to refer to people with cases such as yours. *Don't worry.* It's not a legit title, nor is it a correct term. It is just my personal way of applying it. I call it the White Cage Syndrome.

In other words, you feel bound as a person, caged by society. The flame of the bars are white which represent purity. As for your environment, you consider there to be a little bit of good in everyone. You also feel as though you are one of the good people of the world, but you are closed in as you wrestle with your own stability of doing the right thing."

"In some ways, I'm just like you, I guess," he stated.

"Maybe."

"Have you ever been in love, Lisa?"

"Once."

"Recently?"

"That's a subject I prefer to keep at a distance, Mr. Copeland."

"Well, maybe one day some lucky guy will free you from your cage."

"It's more like a prison."

"What crimes have you committed to be bound by this cell?"

"What permission was granted for you to lay blame?"

"No conviction, just asking."

"I live alone. I do all for myself. I am very capable of pleasing myself. I need a man for no reason, Mr. Copeland. From the first time you entered these doors, I could sense a preoccupied tone in your voice. You need a woman, and I'm not her."

That afternoon, Billy walked alongside Robert in passing of the courtyard.

"Billy, you know the trial is Friday. What do you want me to tell the court in your defense?"

"Do you have a cell phone?"

"Why?"

"I want to call my mom. Robert, we're out of the view of the main office window. No one will see. Please."

"Billy, you know I can't do that. This is the line of the playground. We can't walk past this spot."

"Robert, your shoe's untied."

"No it's not."

"Robert," he whispered, "yes it is." Robert knelt as to suffice the boy's need to become ear level with him. He pretended to lace the strings. Billy clamped his palms tightly to the sleeves of his coat. His eyes locked in a strain of desperation.

"Let go Billy."

"You've got to help me sir."

"I told you Billy, your mom..."

"The bad men came last night."

"Who are the bad men?"

"They creep the halls at night."

"Don't fairytale reality with me for attention."

"They walked past my room. I ran to the entrance to observe them. They wore all black. Their faces I saw not from the wrapped masks."

Robert's vision blurred from the intense pack of blood that filled his head as Billy described the same as the previous bank robbers. "What did they do?"

"They change people."

"How?"

"By the snap of their fingers. Save me Robert. Don't let them get me!" Vague belief twisted in Robert's pupils with shock. The nurse began to observe from the office window. "Your shoe is tied now."

They walked inside and then to Billy's quarters. "Billy, I know you're not lying to me as you told me a familiar image of the men." He removed his coat and hung it over the bedpost. "I forgot my coat." He exited the room. Billy scurried to it and confiscated the phone and hid it under his mattress.

Robert was halted between the bar-like structure of the doors and his card refused entrance upon his attempts to leave. "Mr. Copeland?" He heard the receptionist's voice protrude through the intercom speaker located in the ceiling. "Mr. Copeland, it appears that you entered wearing a long overcoat."

"Oh. I left it."

"Stay placed and it will be retrieved for you." She surpassed Robert and made her way to Billy's room. She took the jacket from the bed while he played the video game.

"Did Mr. Copeland leave anything else behind?"

"No, ma'am, I don't think so."

"Ma'am? Learning some manners from Copeland I see. About time, you little shit."

She walked from the hall. The doors opened and she handed Robert the article. "Thanks, I apologize for that." She lightly fondled his hand with the flat side of hers, while he continued. She moved her eyes downward to make obvious her lust for him.

"Don't mention it," she replied. Gertrude was short and overweight. Her hair was auburn and coupled with large spirals. The lipstick she wore was red and loud.

Robert jogged to his car and spun away. He rubbed his face to spark focus.

Chapter 5 *Don't Think*

"**C**ongratulations, Mr. Copeland, we've completed course with you after fifteen sessions," Lisa stated. He lay flush in the chairs lining. "I have your analysis ready for Mr. Thompson first thing in the morning. There's only a few more questions. I need to fill in the blanks. Do you prefer the night time or the day time?"

"Day."

"Are you depressed or happy?"

"Neither."

"Choose one closest to you."

"Happier."

"Explain that conclusion you just reached."

He looked her direction over and blinked constantly. "It would be unprofessional for me to submit that unto you as you know exactly the waking thoughts of my expressions. I'd be lying if I said I wasn't attracted to you."

"Please, Mr. Copeland I..."

"Why ask that if you thought I'd say anything different?"

"Courtesy with a professional level is how I desire your time."

"I have a few questions I'd like to ask you, Lisa."

"Robert, I'm not obligated or subject to this."

"Ask me to leave then. Do you not feel the chemistry between us?" She closed her eyes briefly and then looked away. "Tell me to leave, or answer my questions. When again was the last time you had sex, Ms. Davis?"

"Mr. Copeland, I will not be asked such ignorant things."

"Tell me to fuck off and report me. Do it, Lisa." She sealed her notebook and fidgeted her index finger along the metal spiral. "For three weeks, and fifteen sessions has passed. Five-hundred and nineteen minutes I spent in your company. Tell me you don't get anxious to see me coming through those doors as I do for you."

"Robert, you're a part of my job, that's all."

"Good, then you should not refrain in the questions I ask. Tell me Lisa, when was the last time a man massaged your scalp until you dozed off to sleep tingling from the touch?"

"That's none of your business."

"You know mine. You know all sexual about me." She pressed her lips tightly and then released them. "You know I spit on myself. Is that a sight that is equal unto your mind as compared to my sleeze of thoughts that I've been having of you?

When Ms. Davis, have you last felt the touch of a mans hands glide from your ankles to the center of your core? When was the last time you rubbed your inner thighs together in anticipation for someone to touch it as you try to capture the heat of it with your scrubbing legs?"

She placed her hand onto the end of her skirt and tugged it down as to keep a proper formality of lady-like ethics. He sat upright and stood. "When was the last time someone viced your breasts between the grip of masculine hands?" She closed her eyelids and allowed her lips to pry keeping her teeth clenched.

"When was the last time a man inlayed his fingers center of it and then dug lightly from there to the top of you?"

She panted stoutly and stood up. "Enough. Leave now, Robert!" She walked over to her desk and fumbled nervously through her paperwork.

"Say my name again," he said, while walking closer to her from behind.

"Make me," she whispered.

Her eyes melted and buried themselves with the heat from the virile touches of his rigid fingers that gripped her from shoulder to wrist. "When Ms. Davis, was the last time you felt a mans torso firmly brushing against the flesh of your nude backside?"

He lightly pressed her back. She responded and rested the side of her face against the desk. She pulled her skirt above her waist and returned her hands to flat submissively onto the surface of the wood. Her eyes remained closed.

He pressed the band of the stocking's hem at midthigh and began to delineate the lace design with his finger. Her bottom lip relaxed and fell loose from the tense urgency to withdraw from strain. He pushed his left hand inside of her panties. He began to grip her butt tight with a vigorous scour.

She pushed her angled position to force herself flush against his readiness. She then placed her hand against his hip and said, "We can't. Not here, my job. Tonight, my place. Be ready for me as the heat from your phallus is wild as though a cinder. Jumbled and ruined my emotions declare my mind untamed."

He exhaled deeply. She staggered to an upright stance and stiffened her skirt back into place. He put his forehead to the back of her neck. "Long the time of the day as to forgive the moment, but keep sensitive the stormy thoughts of a reckless night that awaits us," she said. "Rest these feelings of excitement as I will fare with you tonight. For this debility you instilled upon me has numbed my ability to reason.

Now, I am allowed only the path for a ravenous hunger to endure you inside of me." He embraced her with honesty. "Be ready for me. Anticipate me." She slid his hand from her stomach and lifted her skirt upward. She grazed the warmth of his hand against the wet lining of her panties. She then untucked his hand and said, "Want me severely, as though painful.

Find it hard to walk away from me. Need me as to kill for me. Be ready, for tonight will be brutal against patience as I welcome you into me. *Don't think* on this moment. Dwell on the oncoming night that will soon have dictatorship temporarily over the world until the sun awakes madly, but rises with cheer."

"Are you a father?" Billy asked.

"No," Robert replied.

"No children, huh?"

"No."

"Where is your father?"

"I don't know. Left mom when she told him she was pregnant. His name was John."

"My mom's name is Kristen Rebecca. My favorite color is neon blue. What's your's?"

"I don't know, never thought of it."

"Are you a detective?"

"No."

"Have you ever shot someone?"

"Yes, but not job related."

"What do you mean?"

"Nevermind that Billy."

"It's always best to talk about your problems. That's why you're here aren't ya, for me to share the stress in my life at the present. I'm your friend, I'm here for you."

"Billy, listen, just keep being a kid. Let not the times worry you. I'm going to persuade the jury to render you back to your home."

"Who'd you kill. Was it a bad guy in the line of fire or was it a robber that escaped the hands of justice and ran?"

"Actually Billy, I killed one of the good guys. When I was seven my uncle which was on the police force for thirteen years, was an avid gun collector. One day he left the cabinet cracked. I opened the weapon safe and took hold of one of the rifles that stood upright upon the brass hook that spiraled into a center rotation. I played army, aiming the fire arm at every creature I saw. I aimed it at the dog, my grandmother, everybody. I even tried pulling the trigger. It was jammed into the frame of the ring.

When Phil came home from work I hid and jumped out from the couch to surprise him. The gun went off. The smoke cleared as I saw him dead. Since then I use no means other than compromise to reach those in need."

"Don't let those things harden you or lay blame on your mind," Billy stated. "For whatever it is worth to you, I wish I had a father like you. Did you contact my mom?"

"I did."

"Does she miss me!"

"Billy, ever time I called, I stated my name and purpose. She just hung up."

"Rebecca sure is pretty, in case you were wondering. Wouldn't that be cool if you could be my new Daddy?"

He bent down to him and asked, "You know what your problem is Billy? It's that you're a good person trapped in a bad world, but you never give up on people. You never fail to see the good in people."

Chapter 6 *Don't Feel*

Later when the sun was to set with the time, Lisa stood in her closet as to decide the fashion of the night. She ran her hand over the black silk nightgown that buttoned the front side. Startled, she walked towards the direction of the ringing phone. "Hello?"

"Ms. Davis, this is Mr. Thompson. How are you?"

"Fine."

"Great. Now, Ms. Davis, I'm only calling to say that I look forward to picking up the last session with Mr. Copeland tomorrow."

"Oh?"

"I've given it thought and would like to begin my analysis upon him in comparison with the systematic literature that you've given me."

"Sure, I'll let him know."

"Just have him routed by the receptionist." He hung up and she placed the receiver on the wall base. She slipped into the lingerie wearing no underwear. She lit the blaze of the fireplace.

(Several hours later)

Robert knocked on the door. It loosened and opened from his touch. "Hello?" He pushed the door wide and shut it behind him.

"Come and sit directly behind me in the empty chair," Lisa said. She sat with the back side of the chair facing him as though the first of their meetings. He sat from behind facing the opposite direction of her.

"So are you going to ask me some questions?" he joked.

She breezed a slight laugh and pressed the back of her head to his. "Do you know what the hardest part of my job is? It's listening to your voice. Magnifying, rare, and murderous it is to the breaking of feeble error as to turn me violent from inflicting sorrow to touch the lips of the one who speaks. So long have I been without a dominating figure to wound me in fashions of honorable lovemaking."

"Let me see you," he said.

"Not yet. Let me entice you with a framed thought of dirtiness that will stain your mind. Close your eyes." She leaned back and draped her legs abroad each arm of the chair catching the balls of her feet to the edge of the computer desk.

"All of the hours past the sun that set, I've been sitting here in this leather chair, caressing my breast and grazing myself imagining that they were touches from you.

A fool I should be as to permit the craze of daydream to build with my physical wondering and explorations."

He grabbed the armrest of the seat and said, "I can smell you."

"Rightfully so, as my bareness is exposed and aching for your harsh touch. Expose yourself where you sit." He pulled himself through the opening of his pants.

"Pull me from this torching quicksand that claims to bury me in a funeral. Grant me the right to see your body in front of me."

"*Don't feel* me before you use your senses to imagine and picture me in your head. Dance with the thoughts of stretching me from prolonged abstinence. I'll probably flare with orgasm as soon as you enter me from the rigid circumference of your veins."

"This wait for me to feel you is abuse."

"Before you do, I have to ask you a question. Without to see me, how greatly do you desire me?"

"For the tunnels are endless with the blackness and disappointing to not reach the end for air or light."

"This is exactly how I live." He turned his head slightly with interest. "I live in darkness as your voice and soon to be touch is the light I need to see the feel of you. Reject me if you must. Hate me, I'd regret, but through my senses is how I feel."

"What do you mean?"

"I'm blind, Robert. Please don't hate me or feel trapped with me."

"How could you have made eye contact with me?"

"Where I position the patient recliner is directly the shine of the sun from the office window. When it has darkened the red tint over my eyes, I know it was due to the movement of your head. Therefore, I estimated where you'd be."

He turned his chair around and ran his arms from the sides and put them to hover over her shoulders. Her lips parted and her eyes tightened from the touch. "Hate you, I could never, for you are perfect to me. Love you, I could. In love with you I might." He ran his hands down her shirt and extracted each button from the threaded hole.

He realigned his hands to feel his way without the use of a visual map. "Make me feel what you see. Use your body's senses to discover me." He curved his palms to outline her breasts. Voluptuous and heavy they boldly sculptured about her chest. She squeezed the seat of the cushions by digging her nails to tear into the vinyl.

He streamed his fingers onto the flat of her nipples and dropped his hands inside of her shirt. Her sides were firm and rippled when she inhaled. She rested her neck to the top of the chair and pointed her toes downward in a reflexive action to respond to the closer movements of his roving hands.

More intense his passion grew. Her skin was soft. Her abdomen was level was not in athletic form. Curved and feminine. He removed his hands and teased her into a rage of instability by putting them onto her thighs. She began to exhale with an audible respiration. Consistent and deep was her rhythm.

He brought his hands in closer as her mouth slowly began to drive open. Her calves flexed by the contrac-

DEAD CENTER

tion of the sitting squat. Finally, forever had passed. He stationed his finger to meet her agony to be doused with such affection. He brushed the top of her with each fingertip of his right hand with a light claw-like fashion. The repeated soft running of each finger stole her breath and numbed her fantasy as compared of the reality. He continued this style.

He aligned his left index finger vertically into her crevice as to fill for space. With the sudden of insanity he swivelled her chair to face him. He put his forearms under the bends of her knees and led her to the end of the seat. He penetrated her brazenly and full. He stopped and throbbed from surpassed quickness.

"Don't move."

She contracted a soft flow of heat onto him. "Go ahead, it's okay."

He moved outward slowly from her and held her tight. "From the first that I heard your voice I felt my heart drift apart. From the time I saw your face, my mind deadened from a loss of thoughts." He slid into her again causing her to edge once more. "From the first time that I touched you was the waking of my senses." Slowly he began to capacitate her.

He picked her up into his arms and kicked the chair from his path. He laid her back onto the desk's surface. He began to ease into her with slow penetrations. Each time was the building of blood. "Forced you have made one to surrender and eject this aggressive withdrawal."

"Do it on me as I want to feel the love from our making. Allow me to feel for my sight will not let me see it."

Randall Ford Jr.

The fireplace reflected its light to shift shadows about the walls. Quiet was the room. She lay on top of his body. Deep the two slept for the creating of love was as the years spent loving hope. The night took its time and was slow to pass. *I dreamed not through the night as to wake and her be a dream that would have left my world in a trance and disfigured my mind.*

Chapter 7 *Don't Breathe*

Robert arrived at the office of the Thompson building for his final interview. He was led by the assistant receptionist into the elevator. "Finally get to see the big man?" she asked.

"So they say." Laura's hair was reddish brown and straight and was evenly bordered past her shoulders. Her nails were short and black. The sleeves of her sweater met the mid-section of her hands. Her boots glistened from the shine of the black vinyl. Her jeans sank low in the front becoming her erotic curves.

"Mr. Thompson is the best in the state and the most referred therapist of the east coast."

"Why is that so? Why do I hear this often?"

"Because he's the best in his field. Also he's actually the only hypnotist in town. Judges and captains from law enforcement agencies from states over send their employees to him."

Laura's escort ended at the fifth floor of the building. Robert stood at the open doorway. "Please, won't you come in Mr. Copeland?" Mr. Thompson asked. Mr. Thompson sat across from Robert.

"Mr. Copeland, this is your last visit here and I have to inform you of your last required appointment here. Ms. Davis has analyzed you and your case. However, I must by law do a specific observation on your subconscious state. This is only to be sure that your job mishaps were only stress related. Don't worry I'm not going to dig around in your head. I do a mere slight under hypnotic trance on you to be sure if your stress level is parallel with Ms. Davis' systematic documents."

"How is this to clear for a precise determination of logic?"

"I have to be sure of this. Besides, this was requested by your major in order for me to sign a release form before you can report back to duty. Unless, you enjoy being a child's advocate?"

"Do you need me to lay down and stare at a swinging pocket watch or something?"

"That's not necessary. Relax yourself and your mind." He stood and walked over to him. "Close your eyes. Think not, but only imagine. The meadows of crystal and orchids of silver. Fall into this field of bright glimmer. Picture this free space as the world, Robert. This is a place where hate does not belong. A field of muddy ponds and grassy banks.

The fall of the leaves embank your steps. Allow this evaluation to sweep your mind." Robert's head felt floaty while he grasped into this false state. "Elude not your feelings. Let this scenery that I have displayed unto you, soothe you."

"Mr. Thompson?" Lisa interrupted Robert's dream. He opened his eyes and sat upright.

"Ms. Davis, can't you see we were in the middle of a hypnosis here!"

"Sorry, sir, I should have asked Laura first of your client's presence." She lay the stack of folders onto the table by the door's entrance.

"That's okay, please send Laura in to walk Mr. Copeland out."

"Yes, sir."

"Do we need to do this over?" Robert asked.

"No need, Mr. Copeland. You began to slip into fantasy with no fight or struggle. Therefore, that gives me belief that you were just stressed as supposed. Here is the letter to send to your major. Might I suggest taking a couple of weeks off per year?"

"So the nutcase is free to leave the asylum?" Robert joked.

"More like the overworked returning to the job. Oh, and by the way, Mr. Copeland?" Robert turned to look at him. "Only when you can see the white of the cage is when your syndrome will be lifted." Robert continued to exit the door in which he considered the advice metaphoric as a good outlook on life.

Laura shouldered closely by Robert in the elevator. He stared straight ahead as though a statue. She tossed her head over towards his direction and grinned with a seductive pull. "So, how'd it go?"

"Great. No complaints."

She slung her hair over her right shoulder and ran her nails over her neck. "Would you like a blow job?"

"I'm sorry?"

"Did you not hear me, or are you just shocked? Would you like to pump my mouth or would you prefer me to do the work?"

She placed her free palm about his chest. He grabbed her wrist in attempts to subdue her intentions. "Why would you ask me that? You hardly know my name?"

"Why not? You act as if you've never had one before." She pressed herself to his body. "I'm hot and you're ready, I can tell."

"I have a girlfriend." He extended his bent arm to guard himself from her enticements.

"No one would know. I'll leave no evidence behind, know what I mean? I can get you off before we hit the bottom floor. I'm hot and you know you want me to whip my hair about and squat in front of you."

"Laura, please!" He grappled her arm and pushed it behind her. "Laura, stop!"

The elevator stopped roughly. The sharp alarm signifying the first floor was set. With the sudden of seasons, that seemed to be the case, Laura's mood was that of the changing.

"Have a great day, Mr. Copeland, and be careful."

"Look, Laura. Don't take it the wrong way. You're a very lovely lady, but I can't."

"Excuse me?"

"What I mean is that for whatever reason you offered yourself for my pleasure, I don't know, but I have a girlfriend."

"Are you coming on to me, Mr. Copeland?"

"No...nevermind."

Puzzled and dazed from the conversation, Robert fled from Laura's presence and walked out into the parking lot. He opened the car door and entered. He made his way to Rebecca's house to further his preparations of tomorrow's case.

Robert walked up to the screen porch and began to knock. The door cracked the length of the brass security chain. "Ms. Wells? My name is Robert Copeland. I'm from the Children's Protective Services." The door shut and then opened widely.

"Come in," Rebecca replied. "Sorry for the precautions, I guess, can't ever be too sure these days."

"Ms. Wells, thank you for permitting me into your home. It's urgent that we discuss the upcoming case. Can you fill me in about how you feel about the whole ordeal?"

"Nothing's been right since the robbery. I live in fear everyday at the bank. Do you know what it's like to have a gun dangling above your forehead?"

"I do."

"I can't deal with the destruction of my nerves and my emotions."

"Ms. Wells, I know some things in life are hard to face, such as in your son's case."

She rubbed her hands together furiously. "You don't understand what horror really is until it catches you in the open. Madness, I've become as to watch the memory over and over again in my head."

"Ms. Wells, your son's trial comes due in the morning at noon. I must get all of the information I can that will counter my factor of rightful persuasion unto the court."

The phone began to ring. "Excuse me, Robert." He turned his head towards her while she answered the phone. "Hello?"

"Mom! It's me," Billy stated hysterically. "I love you. I'm okay. Mom, can I come home tomorrow? I got Baseball 3000. I can't wait to show you how good I've gotten on it. Do you miss me?"

"Who is this?"

"Mom, it's me, Billy."

"I don't know any Billy." The walls shrunk as Robert overheard the words that projected from her. She appeared dizzy and euphoric. She began to pace the kitchen floor.

Chapter 8 *Don't Believe*

Robert stood. "Ms. Wells, I must be leaving now." She took the long carving knife from the wooden holder and charged him. She caught the side of his shoulder ripping his shirt and breaking the skin.

Robert tripped over the corner of the coffee table landing her weight on top of him. He held her forearm to block the blade that pointed towards the bridge of his nose. He locked her other hand after she rammed it into his chest and neck. The puncture of the blow stung by the force of her rings.

He quickly dodged her. She unraveled her fingers causing the knife to plummet to his face. The steel sliced a long but thin portion of the flesh of his cheek. He could hardly exhale. His diaphragm was locked from the adrenaline. The blood smeared about his face and neck while he endured the punches from her.

He twisted the knife from the wood of the floor and threw it from her reach. He bound her fists. She returned her attack by the butting of her head. "Ms. Wells! Cease this combative violence."

"Thief, robber, liar, murderer!" she yelled.

Without to inflict physical harm on her, Robert squeezed her and pulled her hair upward as a brace. The spare phone that he took from his belt began to go off. She forfeited her fight and relaxed her muscles. "Hold me," she said.

With a stunned heart, Robert felt her come down onto him. She held him with her knees separated and sprawled over his waist. The palms of her hands placed just underneath her shoulder blades. She raised her head and put her fingers over his cheek. "You're bleeding! What happened?"

She brought her lips to his and massaged them. He eased his way from her and left the house. He bent over near his car to catch his breath. He ran the directory of history calls of his cellphone. He dialed Lisa's number.

"Hello?" she asked.

"Hey, it's me."

"How come you didn't pick up just now?"

"Odd story."

"That's weird. You wouldn't believe the one I just heard."

"Listen, I need a favor. I know you're not supposed to do this, but I need you to run a name for me; Rebecca Wells."

"I counseled her."

"I was hoping that you would say that."

"But I can't. I can't disclose such confidential information by law."

"Lisa, please, I need your help."

"Why don't you just ask Laura? Apparently, you two hit it off."

"What are you talking about?"

"Did you enjoy her? Was she as good as they all say she to be? Did she make you cum before you hit the first floor?"

"Lisa, nothing happened."

"She said, that you said, she was a very lovely lady."

"I took no advantage of her, Lisa, I swear!"

"She told me you came on to her. Nonetheless, came on her as well."

"Damn this day!"

"I heard she doesn't even flinch."

"Look, I'll come by later. I didn't do it, I promise." She disconnected the line. The rain was abundant as he drove. The smog of the windshield distorted his view. He pulled into the police station and then ran into Major Wilson's office. He burst into the room and engaged the door. "Major Wilson!"

"Settle down Copeland. What's wrong?"

"Here." Jermaine took the release paper and looked it over. "I'm back now, sir. Listen. About the Billy Wells case, we need to make sure his mother doesn't retain custody of him."

"You're not *back*, Robert. You are not a detective. You are negotiations."

"Major, please, I plead your help here. Something's gone wild with this town. Strange things have been happening today."

"Did you not get help as I've requested, Robert? Your mental stability is rampant at this point. You should weasel out of here. Laura called and reported that you tried to rape her moments ago."

"What!"

"Robert, you know if you were not my son, I'd shackle you as we speak."

"Your son?"

"Your mother was a good woman before cancer took her from us."

"Major, it's me, Robert, the same cracker motherfucker you've been ragging on for the last twelve years, sir."

"I remember when you was a little boy Robert, asking me why mommy had to leave."

"What the fuck is going on major?"

He removed his coat. The nine millimeter hung in the balance from the strap of his shoulder holster. "I don't see you before me, Robert. Time for you to go."

Robert walked with haste through the station. All of the officers cast stare upon him until he reached the parking lot.

Robert sat at a local park. He watched the ducks of the lake feather themselves with the sprinkles of the rain. He flipped his phone from the vibrating tone and greeted the caller. "Yes?"

"Robert, it's Billy. You've got to help me!" Robert stood and looked about his surroundings. "They're going to ship me off out of state tomorrow, right after the trial. My mom doesn't know me. She hates me, I called her. The bad men came last night."

Billy's voice became quiet. "I gotta go. Gertrude's making rounds."

"Billy, wait!" The echo of a dead line was immense unto his ears. With distraught awareness he began to rekindle past words that flooded his mind. *The bad men came...Mr. Thompson is the best there is, and the only licensed hypnotist in town.*

The enlarging of the pupils of the bank robber.

He ran in a frenzy to his vehicle and drove to Lisa's home. He got out and beat on the door. "Lisa, open up. It's me."

She opened and said, "Oh, you just missed Laura. She blew about thirty guys waiting for you, but you never showed up."

"Yeah, that's funny." He locked the door and led her to the sofa by his hand. "Lisa, something weird is going on."

"Tell me about it. Why just today my boyfriend received some terrific hand to mouth treatment from the company receptionist tramp bitch."

"Lisa, stop it! I did not touch her, nor did she touch me."

"Well, explain the rumors that arise on the whole damn second floor."

"She tried to allure me, but I refused her display of her explicit greed. I told her I had a girlfriend. Did she tell you that? Something's wrong with this whole town, Lisa. Everyone I came into contact with as of late shows some sign of mind loss."

"The whole town, Robert? Be real. Are you feeling well?"

"Yes. Listen to me. I think Mr. Thompson is behind this."

"This what?"

"I don't know. We got to get away from here. It's not safe."

"And go where?"

"Anywhere. Away? I don't know."

"You're scaring me Robert."

"Don't be afraid."

"You're still under a lot of stress, I can tell."

"No! This is not related to my health damn it! I'm sorry, don't back away. I'm sorry, Lisa!"

"Hold me please. Love me close." She hugged him. "Have me like you did last night. Forget the world for an instant. To save the world, you try out of the good heart you have. Leave it in limbo for now, along with all worry of this. Make love to me. Forget the times that anguish your imagination."

She felt about his face and kissed his neck. "For me, loosen this hardship for one night. Clash with me please." He pulled her in close to flush his lips to hers. She kept still and said, "Make me do everything that you desire. Whatever to do to please you is what I would.

Teach me how to shed you of this stress. Execute your mildness and indulge with your fantasy. Drive me crazy. Order me to your demands. Dominate me as I wish." She dropped her skirt to fall to her bare feet. She unlaced the straps of her hips that were the support of her panties. She placed her knees to dig into the cushions. She faced ahead with her arms limp by her side.

He stretched his hand between her legs from behind. The spread of his palm placed center of her breasts. He slithered his feel to her stomach. He then creased his fingers to gently tease her.

Her breath was snatched away by the caress. She bent her neck back to even her mouth to the side of his face. She clamped her front teeth into his neck and killed the dull pain by the circling of her tongue. She pulled the sensitive skin layers by her mouth until bruised.

She brought herself to his ear and said, "Unleash this eagerness. Reject all gentleness from your fingertips." She dug her nails into the comforter. "Let the fury of my body throw you from this imprisoned solitude. Hold not my hands unless to press them to the bed. Lay not your weight onto me as to create sensation, but hold me in place and limit my movements. Make me a hostage of freewill with the choice to be conquered by you."

He latched onto her calves and dropped her legs out from under her. "Touch it," she whispered. He slid his hand fully to cover her.

"Why should I?"

"The placement of your hand is insane as you near it." He carefully wrapped the elbow bend of his free arm over her neck lightly.

"Tell me why I should hand your request over unto your most delicate of skin."

"Distinguish this heat that is contained between your fingers. Irritable it has become for you to rub against it."

He placed his thumb before the flesh that lie between both cavity openings and massaged it. "Do you want me to, desire me to or crave for my will to pleasure you by touch?"

"Neither. I need for the strong tingling sensation to burst. For this present point in nature to feel every sculptured tip of your fingers is the lioness that is restless."

He pried her with two fingers while she continued. Her heart beat quickly which offset her breathing. "Only to draw myself tight and relax is my attempt to control this feeling. However, this physical dilemma has only ignited my tender area."

Her back sank into the cushion of the springs. He plunged into her as to cool the fever that makes the mind illusive. He drove himself repeatedly into her. She spread her fingers about his hips on either side. He tugged her hair catching the roots. He began to lightly

DEAD CENTER

bite her nipple causing her to slip into the boundaries of orgasm.

She ran her hands about his toned back curving her body into a cramp. She forced her teeth to deepen into his trapezium. The movements that were rushed had stopped in delight. She smiled and ran her finger against her neck.

She pulled him by his shirt closer to her face. "If the entire world seems to be different and against you, maybe it's just you. For this grave depth of satisfaction you've brought to me has weakened me." She began to whisper, "I'm your prisoner now."

His heart raced. The excitement of fear from her words left him exhausted. He blinked rapidly. "Why would you say that? How did you know that I use that term in compromise? What is going on, Lisa?"

"Every woman wants to have sex with you, Robert. Black, white, brunette, they all wish for your lust."

"What is going on? Please tell me."

"This is the only light that can shed into your disarrayed mind."

"Have I lost my mind?"

"How could you lose something that doesn't belong to you?"

He pushed himself from the bed and walked back until he touched the door. "Who are you? Who am I? Why am I dizzy with confusion?"

She extended her legs wide and began to fondled herself. "Don't you want this? Come and desire this." He tucked his shirttail and struggled for air. "Robert, the only advice I can give you is, when you see the color of the cage, then will you be free."

She moaned lively as he left the room. He peeled from the yard of the house and pulled his cell phone from the dash. He dialed the number and placed it to his ear.

"Billy, listen carefully. Who are the bad men?"

"They come at night around midnight. They change those kids here into different people. These kids are as zombies. They're the ones whose parents go to trial the next day. Tomorrow is my trial. They will come for me tonight. You've got to rescue me." Robert closed the phone ending the call.

Chapter 9 *Don't Remember*

A police cruiser passed and slid into a semicircle into the opposing lane. The officer sparked his blue lights. The car's grill bumped into the rear of Robert's. He fought to maintain a steady control of the vehicle.

The squad car repeated its battering of the rear suspension by fully ramming into the trunk. The second strike gashed the fuel tank. Robert became frightened from the gas hand that dropped. He sped his car with peak velocity. He ran into the opposite lane and slammed the brakes. The tires screeched loudly. Smoke flooded and surrounded the car from the burn of rubber.

He depressed the accelerator catching up to the cop. The officer stomped the brake pedal. The air drafted from Robert's oncoming retaliation. The two vehicles were locked. The officer twisted the steering wheel to avoid the tree that towered the roadside.

The cruiser hydroplaned to the side. Robert's car jammed into the driver's side of the police automobile. Robert opened his eyes and found himself packed into the driver's section of the car. The door wedged from the dented hinges. The steering column shoved the steering wheel base into his stomach.

He made the door ajar. He stood as the intensity of the impact grew inside of his neck. He staggered to the police vehicle. He put his hands onto the door and looked inside of the window. The driver lay dead. His eyes remained open but glossed. He pushed his upper body and began to excursion on foot. His cheekbone darkened from the bruise and a slight impending limp developed from the accident.

Robert made his way to the child's advocate facility. He entered the front lobby. "Let me in, Gertrude."

She checked him over with the wonder of her eyes and stood. "Now, Mr. Copeland. You know you are not allowed to go back there after your time has expired."

Robert nonchalantly walked up to the metal desk in front of her. He wiped the surface with the back of his hand sending all of the papers and books onto the floor. Then he placed his shoe onto the edge and kicked it towards her.

Gertrude was pinned as he neared her. He grabbed each side of her face and kissed her. He ran his fingers through her hair aleaving her forted will. Content, she unclipped her computer tag. "Here you go."

She touched her hand over his. He backed away and carded the bar coded box of each door. His overcoat swayed right to left while he ran the hall. He entered

Billy's room and took him by the arm. "Mr. Copeland, what happened to you?"

"Nevermind that. Now Billy, I need for you to do me a favor. Stand very still and look forward. Don't blink. Be very still." He stood off to the side and held the flip phone into his palm. He slowly opened it and then shut it. The pitch sounded and echoed from the snap. Billy's eyes shifted not. "Look at me. Who am I?"

"You're my personal advocate, Robert Copeland. Why? Did you come to rescue me?"

"Yeah I did. Follow me. Don't lose step with me okay?"

"Where are we going?"

"I don't know."

The escape of air from Robert's body was in tune to outlive stress from the breakage of law. Devastation was a wait that would not bind his thoughts. His chest showed the hard intake of oxygen. He dug into the plead for help by the expressive show of manic confidence as he ran.

"When we reach the front office, don't look at Gertrude." They approached the glass doors that connected into a large square. He swiped the device and they entered the glass-like cage. He made the black slide shield of the card glide inside of the register. The door released not.

Robert jiggled the flat metal push knob. "Damn!" He retried the card, but was of no luck.

"Well, well, well." Gertrude smiled. She walked around the corner and then rested her shoulder to the plexiglass. "Mr. Copeland where are you going with little Billy?"

"Just outside to the courtyard for some air."

"Now you know the rules. No one is allowed out of the building after seven pm."

The glass was as a four sided cage cornered with an aluminum frame. The existing structure was designed to capture any violators that trespassed to prevent kidnaping.

"How does it feel, Mr. Copeland, to be caged up like a circus animal. Able to see out but unable to move about freely."

"By code 42 of the state, you are unlawfully withholding an estate of the law which is me. My licensed practice is the influence of the law. An agent and branch member of the county law enforcement by the force of restrain of government property by the branch of duty. Therefore, as advocate of this state and employee number 532 of the county under Major J. Wilson, I hereby declare you in violation of this law. Either you open the damn door or your days will be spent in a penitentiary."

Gertrude rolled her eyes and pressed the emergency release button. "Very well. You don't scare anyone, Mr. Copeland."

They walked past her and ran to her car. Robert pressed the electronic switch of the keychain. The tires screamed as they fled away.

"Is this your car?" Billy asked.

"No, it's Gertrude's."

"Gertrude's?"

"Mine is disabled. So I snatched her keys from her belt while I was kissing her."

"You kissed Gertrude? Yuck!"

"This car will disguise us for the time being."

"We can stay at my house."

"No."

"Why not?"

"Cause your mother is a loon." Billy's eyes sorrowed. "I'm sorry Billy, that was poor and tasteless for me to say."

Where do you go when an entire city is your adversary? Where to hide when you're the mouse trapped in a snake bed?

"Billy, how many bad men are there?"

"Four. They strove in a pack."

"What exactly do they do?"

"I don't know, they snap their fingers and the next day the kid they did that to is in some sort of spaced out zone."

"I think I know why."

"Where are we going?"

"To my apartment. I have to get my gun."

Robert's phone began to ring. He put it to his ear. "Yes."

"Who are you?" Lisa asked from the other end.

"You must have read my mind, because I was wondering the same thing about you."

"Oh I'm real that's what I am."

"Real? So real in fact that when we're together all you want to do is have sex, but when we're apart you come down with this freakish attitude."

Billy's face soured and asked, "Is that Gertrude?"

"Billy! Cover your ears!" He flattened them with his palms.

"That's why I'm calling," she stated. "Different in contact, but real over the phone."

"What warning are you trying to get across to me Lisa?"

"I tried to caution you when I first diagnosed you."

"Some fucking white cage bullshit!"

"You're the one trapped inside, but when you see the white of the cage from the outside of it, then will you understand."

The dial tone sounded. They arrived at Robert's living quarters. He pulled the handbrake up.

"Wait here. I'll be right back."

"You're joking right? With all you've seen through and all that I have been through as of late."

Billy kept close with his stride. Robert opened the door and searched each corner of the house. Billy stood in the doorway. He watched Robert entering the side room. He scanned his surroundings of the stairway balcony.

Robert paced from the room and pushed the clip into the handgun. He walked to Billy and stopped. He turned and faced the kitchen and stared intensely. "What is it Robert?"

"That trash bag laying on the floor next to the empty can. I took that bag out two days ago. I watched the pick up service haul it away that following morning. Billy?"

"Yes?"

"Cover your ears." Robert aimed the forty caliber and pulled the trigger destroying the contents of the bag. Confetti erupted and snowed the room. "They have been here already."

"Who?"

"The bad men."

They walked to Gertrude's car and began to enter. "What's your plan?"

"I don't have one."

"Why not?"

"What are you my conscience?"

"Every good guy has a plan."

"Yeah and every eight year old boy watches too much television."

"No blueprint?"

"Okay. look Billy, I think that somehow Mr. Thompson..."

"Who's he?"

Randall Ford Jr.

"He is the state hypnotist and therapist. He's in charge of all..."

"All of what?"

"All of the federal trial related clients. I think it's possible that he has put certain folks of power in the community under a hypnotic state. Your trial is tomorrow. Maybe he has something to do with the bank robbery case. That explains the robber's face when I clicked my cell phone cover. That also ties in with your mother as she is a witness and a victim. I've got to get to Thompson and stop him before its too late."

"That's your plan?"

He turned the key. "What?"

"That's not a very good one. All good guys need a good plan."

"Do you have a plan?"

"Had a plan."

"Had a plan?"

"I plan to become wealthy soon."

"How so?"

"I invented a word. Emplirical. Sort of like empirical only with an L."

"What does it mean?"

"I'm not sure yet. Maybe it could be a word for good plan. Or perhaps it could mean one who stands for justice with authority."

"What is your price for the word?"

"Thirty-thousand per letter."

"They got out of the car and walked up to the wooden doors of the Thompson office. "Stay close to me Billy. I'm sure Thompson is behind this nature." They entered the abandoned building. "Odd. Laura is not manning the front desk."

They reached the top floor and Robert kicked the office door in. "Ah yes," Major Wilson said as he began to spin around in a leather chair that sat behind the desk. Robert jerked Billy by the shoulder of his shirt and positioned him at the meet of the doorway before Wilson caught sight of him.

"We knew you'd show up here, Copeland."

"Good, now I know Thompson is behind this. Major, he's got you in sync to his ways. You're under his control, can't you see that?"

"Had a bad day Robert? Raping a lady in the elevator, murdering one of my officers and now kidnap. Where's the boy?" He beaded his forehead with the infrared beam accurately. "Don't resist. Hands behind your back."

"I didn't do those things, major!"

Robert sat in the old fashioned jail. The cell was eight feet by eight feet. The floors and walls were constructed of reinforced concrete. Time had passed. The night became the new face of the hour.

Major Wilson, walked to the bars and looked Robert in the eyes. "Time for your one phone call. How could you do this to me Malcolm? To worry your father like this?"

Jermaine slid the oversized bronze key into the slot. "Major, I'm not your son. Thompson has enhanced you into an off conscience state. Your former grievances has took past over your present life. Tell me what is going on?"

Lieutenant Jameson clicked the steel prongs of the cuffs. Major Wilson's smile raised to one side. He stood with his face to Robert's profile and yelled. "You tell me what's wrong! You are truly crazy."

"Everyone is not themselves!"

"No! Robert, you're the outcast here. You are the one on the ledge of insanity. I told you to get some help! "

"And I did!"

"No. You just got some from Ms. Davis. You did not receive the proper treatments."

"I am clear of these accusations that lurk! I did not rape Laura!"

"No! I don't believe you."

"Believe me damn you!"

"You're not sane anymore. The stress of your job caused you to become this way."

"I refuse to believe that. That is of your own made up mind." Lieutenant Jameson pushed him through the doors.

"You got three minutes. I'll be outside the door."

Robert dialed the cell phone. "Hello?" Billy answered.

"Billy, where are you?"

DEAD CENTER

"I'm still here in the Thompson building. It's creepy here. There are no lights but the glare of the street lamps."

"Billy go back into the room where Major Wilson was. Search all cabinets and drawers. Look for any papers on your mom's case."

"Are you in jail?"

"Yes. In fact I need you to help me. "

"How?"

"The detention area is about one half mile from you, at the heart of the square in town."

"I know where it is."

"Be careful. Here's my plan."

"You mean Emplirical, right?" Robert set up his intentions and ended the call. Mr. Wilson led him back to his cell.

The quiet of the night gave room for vigorous thoughts. "Copeland! You have a visitor," Lieutenant Jameson announced with authority.

Lisa walked in front of the cell and kept space with him. Her attire was formal and fashioned high with class. "Lisa! What are you doing here?"

She neared. "I love you, you got to help me. I don't have long before he comes for me."

"Who? Thompson?"

"Yes Robert. Listen to me like you were dying unto me. Thompson is the enemy of this all. You must by all means find him."

"Where is he, Lisa? Where?"

"All I can tell you is look for the cage. Save me from this dreaded plot, Robert."

"What cage? There is no cage. It's a metaphor."

"Look for the cage. When you see the color of the metal bars then will I be freed from it. Help me. Rescue me quickly it's the only way."

"I can't! There is no damn cage!"

She turned and sobbed. Her heels led the pitch that carried her from the room. Moments later Robert pressed his ear closest to the space of the bars. He breathed hard with the tip of his tongue resting between his front set of teeth. He exhaled deeply closing his lips. "Yes!" He said, as he heard Billy's voice.

Billy entered the front lobby and sported his way to Major Wilson. Jermaine stood in conversation with Jameson. Billy poked the small of his back. Wilson turned around and looked at him. He tilted his head slowly and squinted.

"Dad?" Billy asked. Dad, don't you recognize me? It's me, Malcom."

"Is that really you son?" His voice weakened from the astonishment of surprise.

"It's me Dad."

"So it is. You've come back for me!" He wrapped his arms around him.

"Wow. Is this where you work?"

He smiled profoundly. "Yeah, let me show you around."

They entered the cell pod area. Billy pointed at Robert. "Dad! I know him! That's my friend. Let him go Dad."

"Robert?"

"Yes. He's innocent." The booking officer positioned himself in line with the long hall. Billy glanced at Robert. He nodded the slightest of angels as to signal his move.

"Oh I don't know Malcom. He's a criminal amongst solitude. Beyond the bars, he's free to commit his wrong unto the world."

"Come on Dad. Let him go. Do it for me."

"That would make you happy, my son?" Billy shook his head and smiled. "Proud of me I want you to be. Happy you've always made me."

He unlocked the heavy door. Robert rushed him and pushed him and Jameson into the holding cell.

"Now that's a good plan." Billy stated.

"Don't you mean emplirical?"

Later that night after the sky had darkened and the world had became still from the rage of the day, Robert and Billy set themselves into exile.

"I'm hungry, are you?"

Robert parked the car in a crowdless lot in front of a convenience store. "Wait here." He entered the store and walked to the back where the dairy and frozen food was. He opened the cooler door and grabbed a half gallon container of milk and one cold prewrapped sandwich. The glass door shut on it's own allowing the rubber seal to recupp itself against the stainless molding.

He sat the items onto the counter. The clerk puffed heavily on the mild cigar. He was large in weight and out of shape. His attitude was obvious from the snarls he gave.

The cashier pushed the inside of the paper sack until it opened fully. He rudely starred Robert in the eye after placing the groceries into the bag. "$4.55."

Robert smiled and placed his hand center of the rolled up sack. He chuckled. "Look, I'll be back later to pay you. See I don't obtain any cash on me at the moment. I would let you run my credit card but you'd know who I was let alone the process information that would give away my whereabouts.

I've got a starving eight year old in the car. So, what do you say, pal? Let me ride and I'll double your money for the purchase later."

"How about, no."

Robert continued to smile. "With all honesty you should be paying customers to stand here and inhale the thick cancerous smoke in this place."

The man placed his hand on top of his and squeezed with pressure for he was burly and of size. He removed Robert's grip of the brown paper. He then brought his free hand from under the shelf of the counter, revealing the twenty-two caliber pistol. He laid it to the surface.

Robert scrunched his face and made a jet for the door. The hands of the watch must have stopped for time seemed no more in this slow motion of lifeless time. Everything had halted. Robert felt the vibrating thunder of the gun's release.

A police officer stood outside of the store with his weapon aimed to the sky. Robert exhaled the fear of the moment with a calm mind set. He looked down toward the bag he held. Tiny drops of blood thumped the thin sack. The trickle of wetness soaked through his shirt.

He extended the bag out and angled his head toward his stomach. The fleece of blood thickened. The hot led of the bullet was a fire that burrowed through the flesh ripping the side of his abdomen from tact.

The clerk stepped behind him. The barrel steamed from the shot. He put his arm around Robert's neck and stretched with a pull. The officer returned his gun to the hip holster and proceeded closer to them. "You're the one we've been looking for. I'm going to run you in, but first I'm going to give you a lesson in stealing."

The cop catapulted an infiltrating punch to his stomach within the region of his wound. The clerk drug him inside away from the view of the public. He bumped him through several tall rotating racks of condiments that stood middle isle.

The officer extended his sleeved baton and whelped the rear of his calf. Robert's equilibrium collapsed. The clerk began to attack his ribs while the officer supervised the brutality.

The two men lifted him to a stance. The cop ran with unloading jabs into his chest. The blow sent Robert through one of the freezer unit glass doors, shattering it.

Robert's world drifted into the hands of a blackout, but was quickly realigned with reality by their cruel fist. He tried to pull himself to his feet to better convey a defense. They threw him over the stacked cases of beer. He was lifted and then shoved into the previously busted door of the refrigerator.

His elbow slammed into the long fluorescent light that was just inside of the cooler. It broke in two pieces. Robert held onto the bottom piece. The cop charged him once more. Robert took hold of the back of his coat. He rammed the splintering end of the bulb into his gut.

With desperation the officer pulled at he glass to remove it. The fragile UV light chipped and gave way from the attempts until he became unable to dig the main piece from his body. He fell over from the lack of oxygen as his lung was punctured.

Robert fumbled his finger to reach the officer's duty belt. The cashier rushed the counter and secure the twenty-two. He towered over Robert's core and held the gun at him.

Robert strained with the snap of the handcuffs. The clerk locked his eyes with a lust to kill. Robert jerked the silver binders and pushed the one end open causing the metal to click.

The clerk's eyes blinked harshly. He rubbed his head and dropped the hand gun. Robert's body was sore and weak. He pushed the boxed cases until he was flat on his feet. The wounds of his ribs were that of the blade from Herschel's knife. The sporadic aches followed blood that drenched to the top rim of his pants. He stepped over the cop's leg and gasp with the pain that flooded his chest. He walked slowly to the exit only to discover a team of officers in a combative fort formed with their weapons drawn.

"What happened? What's going on?" the clerk asked.

Robert limped toward his direction and stooped down to get the gun. Billy slid behind the door panel of the car and sunk into the leather seat.

Robert turned to glance at the law army and then faced the clerk. He latched onto the small hairs of his neck and held the gun to his ear. "You're my prisoner now." He kicked the door wide and held the man as a visible hostage.

"Drop your weapon!" they yelled.

"I'll kill him!" Robert screamed. "Back off now!" The officers kept their target of him.

Billy leaped into the back seat. Robert opened and held the door for the clerk. Robert fell into the opposing seat and fired the engine. He held the gun to the clerk's temple for the enforcement officers threat still existed.

Robert drove in like manner along the highway roads. "What's going on here?" the clerk asked. The hard throb of pain from Robert's side angered him. He took the gun and placed it under the seat. "What is happening?"

"You and me have some unfinished business. Billy?"

"I know. I know. Cover my eyes."

"Brace yourself." Robert skid the tires until the car balanced to a leveled stop. He pulled the cuffs out and clicked them. The clerk turned rage upon him once again and he jousted for him.

Robert rammed his head repeatedly into the padded dash board. He pulled him with vigor from the car at the driver's side and left him on side of the road.

Robert drove for a distance and then pulled to the shoulder of the dirt road. He took his pocket knife and cut the seat belt from each end. He wrapped it around his stomach to seal off the bleeding from the bullet. He buckled the strap. Billy hopped into the front seat.

They parked the car in a forest of trees beside an acre of residential land. They began to walk and converse. "Where are we going?" Billy asked.

"There is a barn garage about six blocks east of here. We'll be safe there for the night until we can adopt a more cautious means of escape."

"Escape?"

"That's correct. We've got to get out of this town, Billy. With the bordering roads ordered closed and our vehicle under a bolo alert, I'm not sure how we're going to do that."

The leaves crumbled loudly from their venture through the woods. They entered the lot and stood behind the face of the street light that was mounted beside the barn. "Great, the doors are locked."

"How are we going to get in there?"

Robert shook the large doors. It's structure was weak and partially decayed from the years of weather abuse. He positioned his foot onto the right door and slid both hands inside the crease of the left door below the latch.

DEAD CENTER

He pulled with his palms and pushed with his foot. The door angled and gave way.

"Quick Billy you're small enough to squeeze into the space. Unlock the front entrance door once you enter."

Billy did as directed. The shed was old and musky. The floor was of dirt and the sun shown not upon it. The tools that aligned the walls were worn and mostly rusted. Billy walked around the large covering and ran his hand about the cloth of the object. Robert scavenged through the shelves that tacked the walls. Billy took the corner of the light brown cloth canvas. He tugged it until it peeled from the car which it disguised.

Immaculate and mint was it's condition. Classic it was modeled without a trace of touch. Glossed in black it mirrored his reflection. The enamel of the paint was as silk.

"Hey! Maybe we can use this old car to mask ourselves."

Robert walked over to the car. "Only one problem. There is no tag. This is a sure way to be captured by the eyes of the law." He went back to the shelves and dug through the drawers of the storage units located along the walls.

Robert located a solid flex hose used for dryer machines. He took the hose and slid it over the rubber mount made onto the single exhaust pipe of the car. He folded the hose to fit snug over the rubber and overlapped it sturdily with the metal tape. He led the other end through the center of the medium sized hole that was decayed on the wall.

He sealed the space with large strips of duct tape as well as each crack of the walls to prevent any back draft of the exhaust contents.

"What are you doing?"

"I'm going to hot wire it so that you can operate the heater. These temperatures are below freezing. This will keep you warm while I stand guard by the door. The people who live in the house off by the hill should not hear the roar of the engine." He lifted the hood and began to observe the train of the motor.

Billy sat at the drivers seat with the door open. "Will I ever see my mother again?"

"I've been working on that."

"What's wrong with her? How come she got so crazy when I called?"

"I don't know."

"Do you have a plan?"

"Matter of surprise I do."

"What is it?"

He jabbed the raw end of the pliers into the solenoid. "We'll call that plan two." The starter sparked and the motor stalled. "Pat the gas and turn the key Billy." Billy pressed the pedal constantly. The engine turned over smoothly, but idled with roughness due to the cold.

Robert removed the prop and laid the hood down gently. He peeled the tape back periodically and looked out from the cracks of the planks to observe the house. No lights came on signifying that their commotions were not known.

DEAD CENTER

Hours later, Robert removed the cap from the tank and filled it with the gasoline that sat in the corner while Billy slept inside the car. Robert leaned into the doorway of the shop and dozed into a brief sleep.

He was awakened bluntly by the hard pounding of the metal roof. He saw soldiers fashioned in full gear landing from their parachutes. He ran to the driver's side of the car. Billy sat up and threw himself into the passengers seat with panic.

Robert slammed the door and then depressed the accelerator. The car hurled through the front doors tearing them down. The wide tires gripped the dirt trails and hugged the curves of the path. The men of war dove to the side embankment from the wrath of his speed.

"What's happening?"

"Time for plan two."

As they passed, a county highway patrol vehicle began to flash it's blue light. Robert ducked his head to look from the rearview mirror. The patrol vehicle neared with torrent speed. Billy turned about and raised his head above the panel. "Great what are we going to do now?"

Robert floored the high performance vehicle. The road seemed to have vacuumed under the car. It began to vibrate and sway as it was set into peak motion. The police car continued to chase them. "I can't believe that this officer has become our militia of injustice," Robert stated.

Robert turned into a shopping center that centered a large mall. The cop tailed them and turned sharply into the lot. Robert circled the parked cars. His vehicle was flat to the surface, but cut steep in the grill. This design increased the pressure of air that pushed the chassis to flow about the pavement.

"Gun it!" Billy yelled.

Robert pivoted every free lane that hid in-between the line up of automobiles. The crossing of the road ended at the fire lane. The cruiser buckled it's right fender to the black quarter panel of the sports car.

Robert rotated the wheel into the opposite direction of the spinning vehicle. He kept the accelerator shoved into the floorboard. The groveling officer tempered his seize of Robert's life by boring into the bumper of the car. The brake light lense crumbled into scattered pieces. The fiberglass spoiler hung from one side and drug the ground.

Robert took control of the vehicle and stopped before the edge of the lot. The officer wedged himself directly in front of their car by it's side. The car was now between the concrete wall barrier and the patrol unit. The officers eyes were dulled and his face sat in a stupor.

Robert grabbed Billy by the neckline of his collar and ducked him below the dash console. The officer displayed the end of a twelve gauge shot gun and pulled the trigger. The shell disintegrated the windshield leaving debris of splintered glass in every direction of the car's interior.

Robert smote the pedal with his foot. The tires parched and created a cloud of smoke. The loud shrill reverberated into the air. The officer dropped the weapon and veered the car away from them to avoid demolition into the close by cars.

DEAD CENTER

"Hang on Billy!" Robert dodged the cruiser and circled the parking lot once again. He stationed the vehicle middle of the cars and stopped as though to dare the officer. The policeman revved the engine and then bolted into a stream of speed.

Robert pulled his gun from the shoulder holster. "Billy?"

"I know, I know. Cover my ears." he put his palms snug against each ear protecting the drum canal.

Robert pointed the gun discretely towards a mid-size industrial transformer that was attached to a distant telephone pole.

The sunlight flashed the reflective sticker of the cruiser. It neared with a furious violence. Robert remained calm from the reckless disorder that aspired for death unto them.

Billy pressed his ears harder and squinted his eyes. The police car peeled it's tires after each change of the gears. Within yards of contact, Robert fired the handgun clearing the electronic machine from the wooden pole.

The power lines tore and guided with the transformer. Robert fled. The metal structure smashed into the windshield of the cruiser.

The officer swiftly opened the door for escape. His gloves melted onto the steering wheel. The incandescent raise of the burning unit were welding degrees of electric shock.

Chapter 10 *Don't Forget*

The dew glistened from the rays of the sun that awoke the sky. "Where can we land a safe zone?" Robert asked while he pulled up to the local bank.

"The school bus!"

"Excuse me?"

"The bus comes by here every morning after the driver drops off the kids on her route. I know this because mom and I saw her every morning eating breakfast at the Ridgemont Café next to the bank."

"Perfect. What time does she come?"

"In about five minutes. Do you still think Mr. Thompson is behind all this? If so, why would someone want to hypnotize so many folks?"

"Whatever to gain from this I perceive not. I suggest it may be an attempt to control the ones who robbed the bank and get the money for his own use. Therefore, he's woolen the eyes of the law that would have prevented any notice of his accessory. Sort of like a good counselor turned bad."

DEAD CENTER

This is great Billy. No one would ever consider pulling over a school bus. Hold tight here and when you see me exit the bank, run with us. Alright?"

"Yes, sir."

Robert walked up to the glass doors of the establishment. He pulled the ski mask to veil his face. He walked into the bank. He aimed his gun to the head of the unsuspecting security guard. "Your gun now!"

The officer unsnapped the velcro of his holster. Robert took it by the wood grain handle and commanded him to the floor. "Everyone on the ground!" He pulled both triggers firing the pistols into the air.

Dust floated from the ceiling tile. The tellers and customers scattered to the ground. "No one move!" He ran to the end of the teller line. He grabbed Rebecca's shoulder and pulled her over the counter.

"Please don't kill me!" Her nerves vibrated in her veins and left her heart to palpitate with great animosity. The tingle of her neck was the surge of death unto her.

Robert ducked her head and ran through the double doors. The bus had parked and the driver made her way next door. Billy left the car and followed them onto the bus. The keys were stationary inside of the ignition.

Robert sat Rebecca into the first seat. "Please don't kill me! Please! I have a son! Please!"

"Mom! You remember me!" They hugged. Robert started the bus and backed it out into the highway.

"Get away Billy, this man just robbed the bank!" Robert removed the mask and tossed it to the side steps.

"Ms. Wells, listen to me! My name is Robert Copeland, former head of negotiations with the FBI and the local law enforcement committee. Do you recognize Billy?"

"My son? Of course I do. Where have you been?"

"Just as I have predicted," Robert stated. He pulled over onto the shoulder of the road and sat in the seats across from them. She gripped Billy closer to her.

"Mom, you didn't forget me!"

"How could I?"

"Ma'am, who did you see for counseling after the bank robbery months ago?"

"Mr. Thompson."

"Damn it! Rebecca you've been under an induced living hypnotism. I brought you out of it by reenacting it just now. This whole damn town is under his own euphoric narcotic control."

"Why?" Billy asked.

"I don't know Billy. Rebecca, do you not remember me from the other day? You attacked me with a knife."

"I never seen you before, ever."

Robert returned to the drivers seat. "For whatever outlandish reasons is behind this I do not know this or his motives."

"What's the plan?"

"No plan Billy. There isn't any plan! I am oblivious to everything. There's an entire population of deranged people after us. Everyone is under some sort of trance. There is no damn plan."

Billy glanced towards the rear of the bus and said, "Well, you better come up with one fast. Here they come."

Robert turned to see the threat coming from behind. Three police cruisers raced up the oncoming street. Robert stomped the gas and evened the vehicle onto the straight lane of the highway.

"Billy I'm sorry for lashing out at you. I was out of place."

"Just get us out of here and my mom into safety."

The bus reached it's top speed and the squad patrols circled the automobile. They began to batter the sides of it. The bus became unstable as the steering wheel pulled with the hits. The three cars slowed to capture momentum. They aligned themselves inches of each other from the profile of the bus with precise measures. They charged the bus with a catapulting method as trained.

The rear suspension collapsed from the impact of the brutal strikes. The bus became weightless as the force of air drove up under it. The inner differential dropped and scrubbed the pavement. Robert struggled to turn the wheel to prevent sliding.

The police cars suddenly stopped with a scream of brakes. The bus bumped the curb and broke the chain link fence. The grill collided with the hollowed metal foundation poles of the local water tower. The top bin of the water container began to loosen and echo as it gave way.

Robert quickly pulled his head together. He threw the seat belt from his lap. The warp of the bus' frame disabled the manual entrance. He made his way to the side window opposite from Rebecca.

Robert kicked the window from its pane. He helped Rebecca and Billy from the glass. He pulled his weapon from his pants and ran for safety. The tip of the water tower containment unit lost its stability and arched towards the ground below.

The thunder of the metal explosion was as a bomb targeting from warfare. The water flooded the surroundings. The earth now became a sea. The large wave swept the ground and rode onto the extension of dry dirt. The tides clashed harshly against Robert's body.

Robert was separated from the two. He caught the side mirror and held it before the waves forced over it. He watched as Billy and Rebecca were pulled from the danger but apprehended by the awaiting officers.

He allowed the running water to carry him to the opposite end of the disaster. The patrol units were immobile to aid his arrest from the created pond.

Chapter 11 *Who Am I?*

What *madness is this that has come over the world?* Robert panted from the run. The wet clothing gave chills to his skin. The cool air was brisk against the damp polyester of his suit. He rested on the dirt of the earth in the field.

The trees pined with an immense spread as to cover the day light. The ground was hard from the previous frost and lack of sun light. The trees bordered the freeway but stretched for miles before end.

Robert tucked himself inside of a ditch along a soiled embankment. The night arrived. The tint of the woods shadowed deeper than the clear of the sky. Only the moon was visible from a distance.

Who am I? I ask of myself. Had Herschel stabbed me to death and do I now reside in a grave? Perhaps my body lies cold but my senses continue to transfer. Could it be that this circus hour of events has been brought on by my paranoid thoughts or by a thoughtless space of imagination?

Randall Ford Jr.

As ice my hands feel. With no feeling of circulation, my feet numb. Should I wish for someone to cover me with dirt and bury me as I lay? I cannot create a fire for the helicopters that lurk overhead seek the very heat of my flesh. Be it of the dead of winter is that which is responsible for my invisible camouflage unto their infra tracking.

Is this illness in which I have been handed really a regression of a delirious head? Why has my mind became as the victim under my own negotiations? This can't be myself. This can't be the powerful reality at hand. Thompson holds these mysteries and answers to my wonder.

Who's eyes are these that rest in my skull? They see so much but confuse my brain as they are the misconception of true verity. Without to rest my eyes from days past has left my face to hurt.

This invading darkness of skies that taunt me is the never ending attack that seeks my never ending vesture for fight. A long battle drawn the fist of an invisible enemy. Oh the world has become a blanket of a vast plain of withered life. Only the glare of the moon's light to rest over my eyes is the proof that reminds me that the heart of my body still has a pulse.

The very tides that beset me are the struggle to flood above my head and steal the air of my lungs. Courage I hope will walk beside me.

My conscience is an imagination. My reality a dream. My breath like iron. My thoughts spin like vertigo. The warmth of my hands is hiding from me. The times as I stood under the hot rays of a sun's cry are the presence of my thoughts.

I'm not crazy. Everyone else around is dully insane. Therefore to talk to myself would be an honor of an intellect without reprimand. My ownself to trust is all that I can do. Let it fall I must not. The morsel of bravery to stand against an entire town.

The cold temperatures caused Robert to drift into a brief dream while he slept. He sat across from Lisa as they were in a session. "You know Ms. Davis, they say that color does not exist unless it reflects light upon it's shape. That's kind of like a person who is happy and content also honors a secret. Hidden inside are things that keep him or her emotions lively.

Some would envy such and suggest them to have a secret as said person is joyous in life with the things that make up his world. Some consider him to hide the secret with such an exuberating love for life. When indeed the person's joy is from God, family, and the love of life.

When the sun gives us light, that same light shines on us with a million shades of hue, only for our pleasure to view. As you sit before me in the warmth of this room all I can feel is the heat of the sun.

It's no secret within myself that you bring out these feelings of endless nerves which I am thankful for to be so blessed.

The burning of the sun that lights upon your beauty is as a halo's glow. The biggest threat to a man is his own self as to fall into a society which loves only himself. However, the most beautiful dream of a man is the one he knows to beware of such existing feelings.

I don't want to keep any secrets from you. I love the crippled sway of your loose strands that fall out of place. I love your skinny fingers that have mesmerized every touch to cause lustful hurt. Your smile has struck me with a hard addiction. For this is the creation of weakness and the death of my own ability to restrain.

Marveled at your sight, I am stabbed with a cruel anguish. The pain of having never had to known how it's like to hold you or kiss your skin or cause your forehead to condense through the touching of your arousal would be my loss.

I guess this is the beautiful dream of a man, but reality is to make the dream more vivid with physical eyes and touch only. For we can see clearly who we are loved by through the way we show our compassion from our bodies. Our eyes are the dream and the hands are the definitions of love."

Robert rested his hand onto her back and pushed her into a slump. The tips of his fingers were like silk that screened from her lower back and massaged their way to her neck. "When it rains people sit under shelter or behind walls and witness the pour of the clouds. For an instant to thought how would it shock you to close your eyes and walk into the storm? Your clothes drenched and your skin shriveled.

The running coldness of the water upon the drought day of the summer puddles and streams over your feet. Knowing others are watching as you stand free. To smile in the evanescence of nature is the perfection they see as they stare. The hearts of the earth and the rain shower I become one with."

Robert awoke and became alarmed from the squeal of the canines that hunted after his scent from afar. *Their growls turned into an unwanted onslaught of an-*

ger. Their vicious drool was before me with no understanding for my appeal.

I grasped my adrenaline and climbed as though a mountain. To my heels I fiercely stood. Under their attack I was waged. The degrees of an arctic temperature was that of becoming a part of the woods. The environment calloused from the climax of burning weather. The red of my face was the blistering thirst to set a kindling warmth.

The dreadful jab of claws that thorned me was the mark from one of the predators that sought me. I stumbled but kept my bold stance in balance. The large shepherd mongrel seemed rabid. He hated me even without to know my heart. Only the voiced command of it's master officer could separate his fangs from my wrist.

I could not feel the sting of his gnaw for the cold deadened the sensation. The weight of the dog was a burden. Robert picked him up from the drape of fur behind his neck. He fell to his knee and felt about the ground underneath his shin.

The beast's eyes were ravenous with an evinced show of rule through his bite. Robert laid onto his side and extended his arm. He took the huge rock that sat under the sediment. He secured it between his thumb muscle and forearm.

With fatality he crushed the face of the dog relaxing the snout tendon. The sight of the blood embedded a strong hold against the defiance that lay blame over him from the puzzled actions of the town.

He back tracked his steps and angled his direction to exit the woods. He came out just behind the vacant squad vehicles. He opened the door of one of the cars and pressed the yellow trunk release button.

He walked to the open metal hood and fumbled through the contents therein. He took the long crowbar tool and laid it over the brass loop that clipped onto the latch of the boot. He slammed it repeatedly with might until the metal bracket bent upward. He hopped inside and pulled the lid closed holding it by the broken lever as it was incapable of functioning in a locked position.

After some time had passed, two officers had entered the vehicle and cranked the engine. The ride from the back was harsh. Every rugged form of the road was felt. Finally, the car stopped and the two doors shut. Robert let the hydraulics of the trunk pick the lid up slowly. He saw the two men place heavy masks over their faces as they were now parked inside of the juvenile center.

He stayed low from their range and entered the door from which they left to swing. The two men crept down the still hall and entered a room where two children slept. They stood above them and woke them. They waved their index fingers from side to side approximately two inches from their eyes. With immediate timing they snapped their fingers rendering the kids under a hypnosis.

Robert held his gun high and entered the room slowly. "Turn around," he demanded. The men rose fearlessly and faced him. Light headed he became from the rush of blood that surged his body. He held a tight grip with his right hand and placed the bottom side of his palm to wrap around the under side of the handle.

Robert's eyes sagged from the endless insomnia. His arm bruised and swollen from the dog bite. The cuff of his shirt was ripped to the shoulder. The dirt which he rested upon caused his appearance to dinge.

"Where is the cage? Answer me!" The men flinched not. "Remove your masks now. Don't mess with me! Game time is over. Now I'm only going to ask this twice. Where is the cage?"

"Why only twice?" the man asked.

Robert cocked the grid hammer of the revolver and said, "Because that was your warning."

"You're scared. You couldn't shoot anyone. Remember your uncle?"

"Tell me damn it!"

"Where do you think the cage is? No clue right? Perhaps its in your head? You wonder about what's going on don't you?"

"Don't play with me!"

"Your skills are weak. The psychological achievements of your time means nothing anymore. For you cannot use calmness to persuade me, you show force."

"Guess what?" Robert pulled the curved trigger and fired one bullet in to each leg right above the knee caps.

The man blurred a scream that woke the building. Robert returned the barrel to the first man. The gun oozed smoke and the metal of the revolver became hot. He eased the prints of his thumb to push the lever down and up. "Now that was your warning. Remove your mask."

The man complied quickly. "The cage is located on top of the old courthouse. It is a state monument. There you will find Thompson and Lisa."

"Tell me what has gone wrong with this town."

"I will not." Robert trimmed the smooth shear of the trigger against the middle of his index finger. "I suggest your presence be vanished at once, Mr. Copeland."

Robert looked about the hallway. Every child from the corridors stood before them. Their eyes all enlarged. Sleepwalking they seemed, but awake they were. The approximation of the crowd was about one hundred and ninety.

"With a single snap of my hand I can send death to greet you, Mr. Copeland. For these children are all under my personal hypnotic illusion. Dare me to sound the alarm to march them to attack you."

Robert's breath became audible through the exhaling of his nose. "So that makes me your prisoner now."

The man smirked and sighed. "Mr. Copeland does this mean that you give up and surrender?"

"Through twelve years I've been phrasing those words unto venomous scum like yourself. However, something just occurred to me. I've never made anyone my own prisoner." Robert grabbed a nearby boy and placed the gun to his head.

He began to walk in a circle around the man with the child in his clutch. The man squinted in slight at him. "So is this how it feels to hold an innocent life hostage? Is this how it feels to be in control of things? I'm willing to predict that if I took this young one's life it would bring all of these children out of their fear in which you have placed on them.

I assume that their eyes would react to the situation and overthrow you instead. Is that the case?" The man's face drew from the bitter excitement. "Odd how I'm now the physical administer of a criminal suit with the convicted mind of a good person. But, with all honesty I'm not that way. Good at heart I live. However, my mind is a little confused by my environment.

All of a sudden folks around here think that I am a different person. Most people I've known for years know me not. Cops surround the state and county line as I can not escape. My girlfriend is whacked out of her head. My boss thinks I'm his son. The police are heavy on my ass. Frostbite has infected part of my legs. My temple pounds from this throbbing flee that has left me no room for sleep.

My girlfriend, by the way, who is whacked out of her fucking head, tells me to look for some cage. A group a zombies surround me and you of all of these people tell me the exact whereabouts of Mr. Thompson."

Robert closed in on the man and left the boy to stand alone. He bent his arm under his chin and put the gun to his head. "See, it don't work that way. To take or control the one's who are not applicable of gaining such power of treason is not an option. But, to take the one out who does is the strong point of my psychological advantages."

Robert walked him backwards in-between the group of children until they were outside. "Get in the car."

"Why?" the man asked.

"You're going to drive me to Thompson."

"No, I will not!"

Robert pulled the trigger shooting him in the top of the foot. The man yelled deeply. "How does it feel?"

"Fuck you!"

Robert shot him in the back of the shoulder as he sat. "How does it feel?" He grasped to stay conscious.

"Like the excursion of vessels, muscle, the bone," the man replied.

"Good. You lived to tell about it. Now I got one piece of lead left in the chamber and I'm not going to waste it on this torture. The final shot will be the end for you." Robert pressed the gun hard against the crown of his skull.

"Alright! Alright! You fuck!"

Robert clutched his arm over his back and lifted him to his feet. He opened the driver's door of the cruiser and sat him inside. Robert took position of the seat beside him. He stuck the keys inside of the ignition switch and started the vehicle. While they journeyed, the man began to smile.

"What's so damn funny?"

"I should have simply agreed to take you to Thompson. Escorting you to your own death will be a very pleasing attribute for me." The man started to chuckle and then laughed aloud.

Robert cracked a smile and looked over at him. His face was red from the strain. Robert swiftly placed his hand over the man's knee causing the car to soar through the wind. After the car reached full speed he took the gear shifter and threw it into the park position.

The man's face bounced against the steel reinforced steering wheel. It spun in an angle leaving a cloud of smoke. The man's face puffed from the blows of the wheel. "That was to let you know, I didn't find that humorous."

Chapter 12 *The Diagnosis*

Minutes had passed. The man glanced towards the open end of the hand cuff binders in which Robert had secured one end onto his wrist. "It's impossible."

"What?" Robert asked.

"To escape your mind."

"No talking, just drive."

"That is unless someone pulls you out of it themselves."

"Quiet!"

"I know what questions replay in your mind as you sit."

"So tell me."

"You wonder that if you lit the earth on fire, how long would it take for the flames to consume a path back to where you started the fire. Am I right? Or is it the ponder of what would happen if the world began to rotate backwards instead of the course of it's present axis?"

"Stop talking now!" Robert threw his arm to his collar, but was blocked by the man's elbow. He locked the opposite end of the chrome cuffs over his wrist which connected under the wheel grip. The two were now bound to one another.

The man gained speed rapidly. "Slow down," Robert said.

"What's the choice you've reached for now? You have one piece of ammo left. Are you going to use it to shoot me, then take the wheel or shoot the chain of the cuffs for your escape? What's it going to be?"

Robert shot the gun but missed the links due to the pot holes of the road. He braced the bottoms of his feet to the dash pad. The man yelled with the tone of live anger and plowed the vehicle into the foundation of the old courthouse.

The steam from the busted radiator filled the car. Robert sat straight into the seat. The driver slumped lifelessly over the wheel. The windshield was a film of shattered specs. The stiff tension wired through Robert's neck. The smell of gas from the broken injectors leaked wildly about the motor.

Robert pulled the wheel until the bolt plate gave way. He made his way to the front of the courthouse which was unoccupied and used as a museum. He drug the man that was entwined by the cuffs and the wheel along with his steps. He pulled him up the flight of metal steps until he reached the top floor.

The air thinned and Robert's energy depleted from exhaustion. "Robert, is that you?"

"Lisa! Lisa where are you?"

"Above."

Robert became nervous when he looked overhead and saw her pinned in a large cage elevated inches from the ceiling. "Lisa, hang on. I'm coming!"

"Very well done, Mr. Copeland," Mr. Thompson said. He came around the corner and smiled.

"Thompson!"

"No use in trying to free her, Mr. Copeland."

"Let her down now!"

"I must say you've come a long way. You've cornered me and found your girl. However, I must leave you for now. But as I fade, you will be able to hear me as I convey the explanation of what's going on."

"No!" Robert screamed, as Mr. Thompson disappeared before him.

Mr. Thompson awoke sharply beside Robert's body as they both lay inside of his office. Thompson stood and walked over to Robert's body. "I know you can hear me Robert."

Robert scanned the courthouse floor over. "Where are you coward!"

Mr. Thompson laughed while he eyed Robert's lying body. "Mr. Copeland, my name is not Thompson, but I'll get to that momentarily. Congratulations, you've found the cage. Therefore, all of the insane events of your crazed world deserves to be thoroughly explained.

Two days ago, in your mind, you came to me and I attempted to hypnotize you but I was interrupted by Lisa's intrusion. However unaware of reality, you did slip into my trance that I placed over you. Actually from the time I hypnotized you until now, you have only been lying in this chair for about twelve minutes.

Through the power of the mind I've been directing these police chases, the courthouse scene and your run from the law, all through the power of hypnosis.

Deep isn't it? Weird how in fantasy land you can crash cars, survive bullet wounds and have every woman throw themselves onto you.

Nevertheless, let me start from the beginning. See Robert I work for a government related company called Zear and Ginn. I am the company's psychiatrist and head of therapy care. Here we create certain ideas and experiments for private officials.

These experiments or empiricals as we like to refer to them as are secret and above the judicial system that label everything legal. We look for top notch people to perform these experiments on. We transform them into a human machine. Only one exception there are no mechanical parts added but one.

A silver antenna like rod is surgically placed into the center of the victim's brain. This is used to control and track our experiments. Also this particular needle allows the individual to empower himself by releasing a monstrosity of adrenaline, speed and strength. Bred protection so to say, as these men's job functions are to serve as personal bodyguard protection for the prime ministers and other U.N. associates.

Mr. Copeland, we had our eye on you for a long time. Your psychology skills are unique. Your courage is great. I decided to use you as to progress into one of our experiments as you acquired high degrees of leadership and psychological wealth. This was a task that pinned me down with time and mind racking phases.

Then it hit me, Copeland. The things in your dreams aren't much diverse from the reality that you live in. Robert, I did hypnotize your boss and Billy's mom. They helped me in placing you into my hands. In your hypnotic state they are abnormal. Even in reality they still are. I will release Mr. Wilson back into his world. However, Rebecca will remain seduced with mind control. Your surgery will render you with memory loss.

You proved exceptional unto our further study of experiments. You became a fear unto our team. You uncovered many clues to many intense situations. We did not want you to discover our doings.

I apologize by such means of getting you here. First, you had the odd bank robbery case. That was real, but under my enhanced controlled hypnotism. I had some clients that were regulars of mine convinced through the mind to rob the bank. I was the one who was on the cell phone with the lunatic aboard the building's top.

DEAD CENTER

That plan failed. Next, I hypnotized two teens to break into Herschel's home. This was yet one of my controlled freaks. I set his mind to kill you. Fallacy found me once again, as Herschel was shot down by your men.

However, through these missed attempts, I finally nailed you when I used psychological force versus physical force. In other words, I played your own game of negotiations by using Lisa to persuade you to be hypnotized by me. And here we are.

Ms. Davis works for us, but the poor hearted lady must have fell in love with you. She is what we call a spread. A highly paid prostitute, I guess you could say. She tried to interfere with your hypnosis by interrupting us, but I was successful.

I hypnotized you to gain your conscience and discard your previous life. Notice when you left my office, every woman wanted you. Laura in the elevator, Lisa even more, Gertrude and Rebecca. That was the shock of an erotic fantasy play in your subconscious thinking.

In your dream, Lisa seemed different in person, but crazy apart from you. Reasons why is because she tried to sneak in here a few times and undo the hypnotism, but it did not work. For I give everyone a way out of their hypnotic state.

Herschel's for instance was when he heard the snap of a door closing he'd be freed. Whenever a door closed, he turned to fight the world. Even the unfortunate young man who's ear Herschel sliced off and then deafened. Forever in this state, the boy will remain because, he also was to hear the door shut to come out of his fantasy. Now he will be declared mental and sent away.

As for you Robert, you finally conquered your goal of finding the cage. In just minutes away you will be brought out of your coma-like stage only to be placed in another state of mind to become an empirical.

You will undergo severe injections of steroid uptakes with mass magnifiers. The surgery of your head will be quick. We have new technical ways of instilling the needle into your brain. This rod will be portioned center of your brain which will puncture the limbic matter wiping out all memory of your mind. Leaving it dead.

There is really no sense in me discussing these matters with you because you will not recollect any of it after the next hour or so of the surgery. Don't worry. Lisa will be kept in a safe place for a while. She's a traitor to have turned on us for your sake and the sake of love.

Lisa is one of a handful of women whose job is to entice he empiricals and work the right side of their brains that respond through sexual stimulation. She enticed you in the office and eventually had you.

We had an order to detain her requested by Mr. Zear himself, as he has learned of her impregnation. That's right, Robert. Congratulations. Too bad you'll never know your son. Mr. Zear has some empirical plans in mind for him. Until you're fully empirical material, I'll quickly run through the next few months of your life for time is winding.

The first needle will be a ninety day evaluation process. If you succeed our limitations we will give you a more advanced needle. This will leave your memory cleared again.

Billy is a mere boy caught up in all of this. I have counseled his mother after the bank robbery. This was all done on purpose of course. Although you are in a trance, she is still in a trance and will be until the day she is passed. I will convince the courts to release Billy into her custody.

You will need a family to disguise you. I will leave Rebecca in this hypnotized state and make her believe that you have been her husband for years and Billy the same as your son.

As this experiment is to continue properly, you will need a new address, social security number, and a new name. I will leave you with one of my numerous identifications that Zear and Ginn has issued me. Every employee has a few phony names to fall back on. This is to protect the likeness of our company. Lisa's was in fact Linda.

I liked the hunt of this whole thing. So I'm going to give you the things that once belonged to me personally. My old house at 916 East Dale Rd. My old social security number is your new number which is 243-889-2014.

Now I have to pick out a new name for my ownself since Thompson can not be used anymore. I always liked the name Barrett, Kenneth Barrett. That suits me.

Rebecca's name will be changed to Clary and Billy's new name will be Alex. As for you Robert, my birth name, which is my old name, will be registered to you as your new name, which will be, Braylen Adger."

Author's note:

Dead Center, is the fist novel that I have had published. Originally, set to be a comedy, after the first chapter, I transformed this story into a suspenseful romance.

Another novel, which I currently hold under construction, **Jill, Malorie, Katie,** is a hardcore comedy. Dan wakes up one evening laying on his livingroom floor. Unaware of anything, he is hit with a sudden strike of amnesia, similar to Braylen's state.

Dan and his best friend, Jonas, both work at the Zeir & Ginn Network. Through a string of comedic events, Dan is faced with a decision to make; Jill, Malorie or Katie.

Some names of that novel were changed as not to mix the two.

The very first novel that I wrote was called, **One Step Higher,** which was followed by a second part entitled, **No more Games.** I eventually took every romance/action scene from them and placed it into the, **Thin Bird** novel, with the storyline centered to be the sequel to Dead Center. Also I titled chapter ten of Thin Bird after my first novel.

The **White Cage Syndrome**, was not at first to be the prequel. This was a story idea that I had about a hypnotist who places people in a trance to rob banks and so forth. With time, this novel fit perfect as the prequel to Dead Center. Although this be the case, White Cage Syndrome, was going to be the sequel. Alex Adger was to be in place of Barret's doings.

I hope you've enjoyed reading this book as much as I had writing it for you. If you like this novel, then you're sure to love my next aligned projects coming soon, **Beautiful are Thy Feet** and **To Feel the Sun.**

www.randallfordjr.com